AS WILD AS IT GETS

THE CAPER'S COOL
THE HORSE IS HOT
THE GAME'S ON TRACK
THE WIN IS NOT

KENN LORD

LUMINOSITY PUBLISHING LLP

AS WILD AS IT GETS
THE CAPER'S COOL. THE HORSE IS HOT.
THE GAME'S ON TRACK. THE WIN IS NOT.
Copyright © May 2020 KENN LORD

Paperback ISBN: 978-1-9993066-8-7

Cover Art by Poppy Designs

DEDICATION

To the thrills of the Thoroughbred Racing World, and the stalwarts who keep them happening.

PROLOGUE

ON A SATURDAY AFTERNOON in March, not long after the 20th Century ended, there was a nasty incident at Kings Park Racecourse in Brisbane, the capital city of Queensland, Australia.

Race Five had just been run, and there were disturbing murmurs in the crowd when the three placed horses trotted back to the winner's circle.

The murmurs suddenly became a roar that shot waves of confusion over the racetrack. A stunned crowd watched in silence as the upset, driven by a torrent of verbal abuse, threatened to turn violent.

At the main gate, one of the security guards answered a call on his handset. After a few seconds, he ended it, telling his companion that the racket had made it hard to understand what was happening.

"Some kind of trouble with a horse called The Stinger," he said.

His mate's ears pricked. "The Stinger? Mate, that's Cooper McCoy's horse."

"Is it? I'm not sure."

"Cooper McCoy; his granddad was Charlie McCoy."

"Charlie McCoy, the big-time trainer?"

"The legend, mate"

"Strewth! Whatever that trouble is, it's getting worse."

"We better look into it!"

"Gung-ho, mate—Let's go!"

One of the most baffling upsets in racing history was raging in Kings Park. The most improbable thing is that it is still steeped in mystery. There have been stabs at the truth, but they were mostly wild guesses. The facts were blurred then, and still are.

The true story has never been told; and if it ever is, it's doubtful if anyone would believe what really happened.

1

**THE McCOY STUD:
SOUTH WESTERN QUEENSLAND
NINE MONTHS EARLIER**

*S*OMEONE ONCE WROTE THAT *life is little more than a series of episodes following on from one to another, blending so perfectly they can rarely be singularly identified or correctly remembered. For Kitty McCoy, the episode of The Stinger began when she believed she'd had her quota of episodes; that at her late age, life had done with them. And so, this ordinary day dawned for her like every other ordinary day. Yet unexpectedly, another episode of her life began that day, and as time went by, she was able to identify the exact moment of its beginning.*

A RISING WINTER SUN eased its soft light over the outback landscape, twenty-five kilometres west of the comfortable country town of Roma, several road hours west of Brisbane. A rowdy flock of pink and white Mitchell cockatoos greeted the dawn, squawking and flapping in the gum trees.

The painted white guard rail circling the McCoy Stud training track gleamed in the dawn light, and an early morning mist hung over the green grass of the infield.

Propped with her forearms on the guard rail, rugged up against the winter chill, Kitty McCoy stood with one foot resting on the rail's lower beam. She wore a brown duffle coat, denim jeans, brown leather boots, an angora beanie and leather gloves.

Standing beside her, with his hands deep in his pockets was her grandson, Cooper McCoy. At twenty-seven he had deserted the city to live with her in the west, and when he made that decision, he rekindled Kitty's fondest memories of the world that had once been hers. She stood there in the dawn light reflecting on the miracle that had brought Cooper back into her life.

The McCoy Stud had been famous in its day; alive with the hoofbeats of Charlie McCoy's Thoroughbreds, tails dancing and manes clipped; eager for the spoils of the nation's racetracks.

Charlie McCoy was a blueblood star-maker; a man of champions; he knew his horses, knew them and loved them. He had the touch; within him, he carried the secrets of man-horse bonding. He was born with the gift, but he was lost to the world too soon. He was in his early sixties when the horse he was riding, spooked by a lightning flash and a crack of thunder, stumbled and crashed in a wild storm. Charlie's head hit hard against a gum tree and he was dead in an instant.

Robbed of the man she adored; Kitty could not bring herself to stay in the racing game. She auctioned Charlie's horses, closed the stables and talked of putting the McCoy Stud on the market. At the eleventh-hour, Cooper stalled her plans when he arrived on her doorstep after tossing in a career in real estate in Melbourne, where he lived with his parents, Kitty's only son Jack, and his wife.

Cooper didn't look like big-city Melbourne. He was country GQ; tall and lean with a strong face and cool blue eyes. He was a confident package with no hint of an overblown ego. Women looked and looked again.

But Cooper was restless; possessed by an urge for the kind of life he felt he wanted, and his urge finally saw the light.

"The city and city people are off my radar," he told Kitty. "Charlie McCoy is my blood and I want to be close to him."

Kitty had doubts and called her son Jack in Melbourne.

"He's made up his mind," Cooper's father told her. "He's socked away a decent pile from his commissions; he won't be a financial strain on you, so he may as well get Charlie and horses out of his system."

Cooper got nothing out of his system.

He haunted country racetracks, spurred on by the excitement of watching Thoroughbreds run. He knew country racing was minor league. He didn't care. Charlie McCoy was his blood.

Aided by the rented muscle of casual roustabouts, Cooper brought Charlie's Stud back to life. The stables were cleaned every day; the training track was made hard and fast; its infield grass mowed and neat. Bore water kept it green.

The McCoy Stud was playing a waiting game, and Kitty had a misty feeling that Cooper had tapped into Charlie's spirit.

The weeks passed, and Cooper's dad called Kitty: "He seems to be where he belongs and if it's okay to have him up there with you it's okay with us." Cooper McCoy had discovered where his heart lived, and his heart was eager to find horses to fill his grandfather's restored stables.

A few weeks later, he was standing near the horse stalls at the Dalby Picnic Races, a pleasant social event on Queensland's Darling Downs, when one horse caught his eye. It was a definitive moment, and Cooper's mind held it. He wasn't sure why, but of all the horses he'd seen, this one was different somehow.

He was no champion; he had finished mid-field in the race he'd contested that day, but there was something about him; a look of belonging to the game without knowing how to play it. The horse was alert and bright-eyed, a bit too eager, like a kid kicking at a football and missing the connection. Cooper checked the stall for the horse's name and turned to one of his friends.

"Do you know anything about a horse called The Stinger?"

His friend smiled. "A real good looker, but a bit of a brumby, very ordinary run today. Why?"

"He's got something, I think."

"He's got his owner in trouble. Costs a fortune to keep and train and refuses to come good."

Cooper brightened. "You mean he could be for sale?"

"I reckon the bloke who owns him would give him away."

Cooper said no more; as soon as he got the chance, he tracked down The Stinger's owner and made him an offer.

The man cocked his head. "Are you yanking my chain?"

"I'm not yanking your chain."

"You really want to buy my horse?"

Cooper nodded. "Is he for sale?"

"Mate, if you give me the money it cost to feed and train him for the last six months, he's yours—and I'll throw in the float."

Cooper picked up The Stinger the next morning.

Two-and-a-half hours later the stallion was prancing around the oval at the McCoy Stud while Kitty and Cooper looked on.

"Nice looking animal," said Kitty. "What are you going to do with him?"

Cooper stated the obvious. "Train him up."

"Train him up?"

"That's Charlie's game, isn't it?"

Kitty took a closer look at the gelding and thought he seemed a bit awkward. "You'll need heart."

Cooper put his arm around her shoulder. "I've got all the heart I need, right here with you, Kit."

"Wishing doesn't make champions, love."

Cooper threw her a look. "Who told you that? Not Charlie."

KITTY LAY IN BED that night, deep in thought.

Cooper as a horse trainer? How could an ex-real estate whiz from the big smoke cross boundaries to unravel the secrets of the racetrack? Cooper had spunk and a wagon load of determination, but would that be enough?

The boy was an amateur. What did he know? How could she stop him from taking on a challenge that was sure to end in heartbreak?

She made up her mind to talk him out of it and turned over to snuggle into the welcoming softness of her pillow—but as she drifted into the unconsciousness of sleep, her mind resisted.

The moon was shining through the lace curtains and it was throwing pretty patterns across the patchwork quilt. For one other-worldly moment, Kitty felt that Charlie was with her in the moonlight. She closed her eyes tighter to keep the feeling from going away. Then suddenly everything was clear, and she heard herself say—

"You sent that horse to him, Charlie. It came from you, didn't it? It's why he's here, isn't it? To learn from you."

Charlie stayed a moment longer then drifted away into the moonlight, and Kitty fell asleep.

COMING OUT OF HER reverie in that chill winter dawn, Kitty watched The Stinger gallop around the track one-hundred and fifty metres away. He straightened up for the run down the short straight with the rider standing tall in the saddle.

Cooper hit the button on his stopwatch as the horse and rider passed him.

Kitty glanced at the watch. "Well?

"Not bad; not good; we'll keep trying."

She gave him a pat on the butt and dropped the old cliché. "Rome wasn't built in a day, love."

Cooper looked at her. "He is improving."

"So, he should, with all the attention he's getting."

"I love that horse, Kit."

"I know."

"I want him to be the horse he was born to be, and I think he knows it; does that make sense?"

Kitty smiled in agreement. "It does to me."

"Should I change his name?"

"What for? When I was a girl, a Stinger was the name of a cocktail made from fine brandy and crème de menthe and it was *the* drink to drink if you wanted to be with it."

Cooper flashed a smile. "Okay, Kit, the name stays."

THE EPISODE OF THE STINGER had made its first move, but far away in the bustling South China Sea city of Hong Kong, it was soon to be crossed by its first dark shadow.

2

VICTORIA PEAK, HONG KONG:
TWO MONTHS LATER

IN THE ANNALS OF horse racing history, Michael J Flynn's name is likely to be well remembered. Once met, he was a man not easily forgotten. He was seated at his desk in the study of his elegant residence high above Hong Kong's Victoria Harbour. Opposite him on a gold brocade-covered couch sat a small Asian man of indeterminate age. He wore a white suit, a pale cream shirt, a silk tie of the same colour and cream leather shoes. His white panama hat sat on the couch beside him.

The Asian man's name was Adrian Messenger; at least that was the name he went by. He sat perfectly still with his eyes on his impressive host, who sat opposite him. A gleaming marble desk separated them.

The mysterious Michael J Flynn did not look like a nobody. He had once; not anymore. At forty-four, he was a man of the world; his own world. In it, he lived alone, operated alone and existed only for himself. He had no friends, he had acquaintances he treated like friends, but only if he wanted something from them.

His lovers stayed around until they no longer excited him, then he told them to go, and promptly erased them from his memory. He looked like a god and behaved like a demon.

He deserved to be left alone to wallow in his ego-driven vacuum, but he was never left alone because, despite everything, he was too fascinating to be ignored.

Michael J Flynn looked across at Adrian Messenger, smiled and said, "The wager is as follows: Kings Park Racecourse, Brisbane, Australia, this coming Saturday; Race Four, horse number Three, The Mating Game."

"Win or place?"

"On the nose."

"Risk?"

"None."

Adrian Messenger reached into his pocket, took out a small leather-covered notepad, wrote the information down and said, "On a one-to-ten scale, what is the amount of the investment?"

"Ten," said Michael J.

"Are you sure? I need to be certain."

"I said ten, and I mean ten. The Mating Game's odds will be six to one."

"Mr Flynn, this is a most important transaction. All our other agents in Singapore, Sydney and Melbourne, will be alerted."

Michael J replied, "I realise that. I will be in Brisbane for the race."

Without changing his expression, Adrian Messenger asked, "Is that wise?"

"Public relations. Brisbane is a hospitable city."

Adrian Messenger waited a second or two, then said, "We're in business."

"Always a pleasure," said Michael J.

"When do you leave for Australia?"

"Midnight tonight."

"Hotel?"

"The Brisbane Marriott."

Adrian Messenger studied his notepad, and read out loud:

*"Kings Park Racecourse
Brisbane, Australia.
Race Four; Horse Three -
The Mating Game."*

He looked up. "Is that correct?"

"Correct," said Michael J Flynn.

"I wish you a safe trip," said Adrian Messenger, who returned the notepad to his pocket, picked up his white panama, stood and left the study without another word.

Michael J Flynn watched him leave and ceremoniously gave him the finger.

3

THE WONDERFUL WORLD OF MICKEY FLYNN

WHEN HE WAS GROWING up in the urban jungles of Sydney's inner west, Mickey Flynn was a rangy, cheeky-faced kid who was everyone's bet to turn into the loser of the century. But deep inside the complex machinery of his street-smart mind, Mickey believed he was never born to lose. He came on like a low-life bogan who used his foul mouth like a nuclear weapon, and he let it loose on everyone who crossed him. But at the age of sixteen going on seventeen, he exhibited the first traces of an emerging larrikin charm that separated him from the sappy kids he hung around with.

His father was a brainless boozer. His once-pretty mother, Dotti Flynn, took in washing and ironing to help pay the rent. A reluctant Mickey was her delivery boy. One of Dotti's gentlemen clients was a Mr Davis, a divorced man who lived in a big respectable flat, a dozen tram stops closer to the city. Mr Davis was a penciller for one of Sydney's well-known bookies. He was a well-heeled, dapper man of forty-seven, and Mickey's larrikin charm was not lost on him.

As it happened, one lucky day when Mickey was delivering Mr Davis's starched shirts, Mr Davis answered the door dressed only in a singlet with a towel wrapped around his waist. Mickey entered the flat, and as Mr Davis closed the door, Mickey walked into the bedroom to hang the shirts in the wardrobe like he always did. Having done so, he turned to look at the screen of the television set facing the bed. On it, three naked studs were having the time of their lives. Mickey was immediately riveted. This was nothing like the raunchy R–Rated stuff he and his mates hired from the Blockbuster video for their 'choke-the-chicken' games. This was steamy enough, and downright kinky enough, to be watched in awe.

Mickey was no angel, he knew about stuff like that, he'd even messed around a bit with a few of his more adventurous roller-blading mates, who hadn't? But this was taking things further. The studs were studs, they sure weren't hung like his skinny mates, and what they were doing with each other was amazing to behold. Noting his interest, Mr Davis made his move.

"You like what you're seeing on the screen, Mickey?"

"Yeah, sure do, Mr Davis."

With that, Mr Davis let the towel drop away and Mickey's eyes did the Lambada. Wow! Mr Davis wasn't hung like his skinny mates either. About four seconds later, Mickey felt his interest rising. The cosy bedroom suddenly seemed warmer; then seemed ever warmer when Mr Davis closed the gap between them, took Mickey's hand, and guided it to what he referred to as his 'John Thomas.' Things got even warmer when Mr Davis undid the fastening clip on Mickey's faded denim jeans, lowered the zipper, pushed the jeans down and slid his hand down the front of Mickey's boxer briefs, to man-handle Mickey's 'John Thomas.' Mickey caught his breath and closed his eyes. A few minutes later when he opened them, he was on the bed and a naked Mr Davis was demonstrating his oral skills on Mickey's eager teenage equipment. Wow, again! How good can it get? It got better when Mr Davis teased Mickey into returning the favour.

Not long after, when it was all over and Mickey had climbed back into his jeans, Mr Davis paid for the laundry in cash and added a fifty-dollar bill.

"That's for you, son, it's all yours. If you don't tell anyone where it came from, maybe we can have some more fun when you arrive with next week's starched shirts."

Mickey smiled a broad smile and picked up the bag of soiled laundry.

"Sure thing, Mr Davis, only next time, how about a different tape?"

"Done deal," said Mr Davis. "Are you any good at numbers?"

"What kind of numbers, Mr Davis?"

"Next time, we should investigate the wonders of number sixty-nine."

Mickey knew not to look a gift horse in the mouth. Awakened to the possibility of earning fifty-dollars every starched-shirt day, he jumped at the chance.

As time went by, Mickey's talents grew to include 'John Thomas' sessions with Mr Davis's bookie boss, Matt Moses, and at the same time with Matt's wife, Allison Moses, who referred to Mickey as 'an even better stayer than the winner of The Melbourne Cup.'

It was Allison who introduced Mickey to some of the finer things in life, like French bubbles, chicken liver pate, lobster thermidor, and the thriller movies of Alfred Hitchcock. Mickey's favourite was – *To Catch a Thief.* He fell in adoration for Cary Grant. Even more so when Allison told him it was rumoured that Cary 'batted for both teams,' and that one of Cary's playmates was the super-butch actor, Randolph Scott. Wow! If Cary batted for both teams, he was Mickey's chosen role model!

He studied Cary's cool, substituting charm for wild ranting. Carefully cloning Cary's suave behaviour, he took on board one of the great clichés of social networking— 'Bullshit baffles brains.'

With Allison's help, he studied the investment business. While other young men his age were hitting the booze, and screwing anything and everything, Mickey was keeping Mr Davis and Matt and Allison Moses happy in the bedroom, in the swimming pool, in the spa, on the barbecue deck, and sometimes in the kitchen when Allison was frosting his 'John Thomas' with strawberry-flavoured whipped cream.

Through it all, Mickey's sharp mind was unravelling the mysteries of the money maze. He made mistakes, but he treated failure as his teacher and never gave up. By the time he was thirty, Mickey Flynn no longer existed.

In his place, smoothly inhabiting the same body was Michael J Flynn, all-wise investment councillor, a man about town and a well-heeled bachelor of the decade. Two years later, Michael J discovered the wonders and thrills of the turf when he accompanied Matt and Allison Moses on a visit to the prestigious Hong Kong Jockey Club. His world turned around again. Not only could he have the mind-stirring excitement of the Sport of Kings, but he also found he could manipulate the game if he played smart, a few bucks here, a few 'John Thomas' encounters there, plus heavy doses of Cary Grant smooth, and bingo! Michael J Flynn, complete with silvery-grey Cary Grant streaks in his hair, was Mister Racing!

With the money he earned, made, conned, or won, he bought himself a restored mansion on Hong Kong's heritage-rich Victoria Peak and flitted between that illustrious address and his rented Sydney apartment at Point Piper. Lively social occasions on Victoria Peak were merely his way of 'getting in' with the big-time racing fraternity, and it wasn't long before he was one of the prime players in a discreet international betting syndicate that was in business for one reason only—Big Money!

But Michael J also fell in love with prestige and power. He loved being singled out as an A-List citizen of the world and as a sports connoisseur par excellence! True to his new-found form, he cut Mr Davis, Matt and Allison Moses out of his life because he didn't need them anymore.

Michael J Flynn had arrived!

But in the lonely caves of his existence, his alter-ego, Mickey Flynn, King of the Sydney West, was still the puppet master who pulled the strings. And nobody but an idiot crossed Mickey Flynn!

4

**KINGS PARK RACECOURSE:
THE FOLLOWING SATURDAY**

LORRIE EDWARDS LOOKED LIKE someone from one of those over-hyped television shows, 'How to be Made Over in Ten Easy Steps.' Lorrie didn't need to be made over. She looked fine the way she was.

She wore her clothes like she'd had her tongue in her cheek when she put them on. She dressed on a budget and still looked great—one of the lucky ones; her flair was priceless.

Her favourite shade was mushroom-pink and that was the colour of the short-skirted low-cut body sheath she wore. Her hosiery was the same shade; so were her strappy stilt-heeled shoes. She set off the uni-colour look with ropes of deep pink beads, pink bangles, a big beige shoulder bag with a bold brass clip, and a pink-banded beige hat that hid most of her honey blonde hair. Sassy; very sassy.

Lorrie drove her smart white Subaru to the gate of the VIP carpark, flirted with the security guy when she flashed her badge and drove to her reserved car space. She was out of her car in a second, smoothing her skirt, checking the angle of her hat, and grabbing her bag from the passenger seat. In another second she was off, strutting like a catwalk model in the direction of the entry gate at the eastern end of the racetrack. The two security guards at the gate stood aside to let her through when she flashed her badge again.

She smiled at them. "Have a good day, boys," she said and strutted on towards the trackside lawns.

The youngest guard gave a low whistle. "I could have a good day just walking behind her for two minutes. Who is she?"

"Lorrie Edwards; Her father is Eddie Edwards, owner-trainer; Not in the big league but no dummy."

The young guard shook his head. "No dummy in the daughter department either."

His mate said, "Her dad has a runner today. Race Four."

The young guard looked interested. "Yeah?"

"Saturday Night Fever, back from a spell."

"No chance; not in Race Four; that's The Mating Game's race. Word is that Michael J Flynn, that wanky hotshot from Hong Kong, is here to see him win."

"I've heard that."

The young guard sighed. "The only Saturday Night Fever I'd be on for is the one I'd be having with that horny chick."

Lorrie hit the paved terrace between the lawns and the main grandstand and picked her way through the tables at the front of the lower level grandstand bar. She collected whistles and raunchy comments from studs made bold on a few beers and took no notice.

"Ice princess," said one of the studs, "but that arse is a boner magnet!"

As Lorrie passed from the shade of the bar and neared the sunny steps leading down from the main public grandstand, Rex Powell, anchored beside the stand's lower row of seats caught her eye and started down the steps.

Rex was an ordinary-looking punter. He wore a felt hat and cheap dark shades. He smiled at Lorrie when he almost bumped into her.

With one smooth swift movement, she extracted an envelope from her bag and gave it to him. He immediately pocketed it.

"Saturday Night Fever," she said, "race after next. Invest it all; fifteen thousand at twenty-fives if you can."

Rex walked back up the steps into the grandstand.

The exchange was lost in the general movement of the crowd and Lorrie strutted on to be joined on her right by Betty Coe, who seemed to come from nowhere. Nondescript Betty had a nondescript handbag dangling from her forearm. She held a Race Book. The same swift envelope exchange took place and Lorrie repeated her instructions.

"Saturday Night Fever, race after next, twenty-fives if you can."

Betty nodded and vanished into the crowd.

Lorrie approached the next set of steps near the western end of the stand where Edna Austin was studying a form guide. The envelope exchange and the same instructions were repeated. Edna continued studying the form guide.

James Bond couldn't have done it better.

One man and two women who looked like regulars at a beer and prawn night at the local pub had just been briefed on a forty-five thousand-dollar betting plunge in cold hard cash, and nobody noticed a thing. Not that it was big time.

It was play money in the big league, but it was a heavy bet on a horse with an outside chance, and for good reasons, Lorrie didn't want it known that Saturday Night Fever was running with heavy stable money on its back.

At the eastern end of the grandstand terrace, Jewel Blanch saw Lorrie coming and waited to connect. Jewel, twenty-something, was a standout picture of designer flash in navy and white with red shoes and a saucy red hat trimmed with navy and white ribbons. She'd been put together with great care. As organiser and compere of Kings Park's popular 'Fashions on the Field,' she liaised with all the important racetrack people. Jewel was a filly who played the field. Her ex-husband, a snooty well-heeled legal eagle, had dumped her for someone more 'politically correct' and it had cost him plenty.

"Sensational ensemble, darling," said Jewel when Lorrie stopped in front of her. "If you weren't one of my judges today, I'd insist on entering you."

Lorrie frowned. "I'm a judge?"

"You did promise, remember?"

"I'm a bit distracted. Sorry, my dad has a runner today."

"I noticed," said Jewel, "he's up against Michael J Flynn's big hope."

"The Mating Game, yes."

"Michael is super confident."

"My dad's optimistic."

"He wouldn't be a trainer if he wasn't."

"Have a saving bet on Saturday Night Fever just in case," said Lorrie.

She leaned closer to Jewel and lowered her voice. "For your ears only, honey."

Jewel blinked into the sunshine. She was doubtful, and it showed. Lorrie knew about Michael J Flynn. He was one of the biggest names in the industry. He had no horses of his own but sponsored and supported several top trainers and jockeys with backroom funding. His payback was insider information on form and track trials. If Mr Flynn had his cash on a runner's back, it meant a sure thing was on the cards!

"What price is your father's horse?" Jewel asked, not really caring.

"Take twenty-fives, honey," said Lorrie. "You can buy me a new LV handbag if you win."

Jewel laughed. "If your father's horse gets up, I'll buy you the entire LV collection."

"A promise is a promise," said Lorrie; "I'm off to the race stalls to keep my dad company before the race.'

Jewel watched her sashay away. "If I had a butt like that," she said to herself, "I'd be doing more than keeping my loser father company."

AT THE HORSE STALLS, the group of Saturday Night Fever minders included Eddie Edwards, and his two permanent stable hands; Cassie Morgan, a young apprentice rider, twenty-two, ambitious and in training; Jeff Dysart, Eddie's right hand; twenty-eight, country-born; in love with the racing game; fiercely loyal to the boss.

The other minder was Frank Davenport; early thirties; polished, confident; trendy with a cock-of-the-walk air and keen bright eyes. Frank was a cunning racetrack professional, open to opportunity, and primed to pounce. An old friend of the Edwards' family, he was Eddie's conduit to the ins-and-outs of the big-money world of racing via valuable contacts in Hong Kong. He'd lived there for five years before returning to Australia not more than five months ago. Eddie had been first on Frank's visit list, for what was soon to turn out to be an obvious reason.

Standing quietly in his stall, Saturday Night Fever was groomed for his shot at the winner's circle. Eddie appeared calm and collected; the only evidence of inner tension being the staccato flickering of his eyes. Frank looked at his watch and spoke quietly to Jeff Dysart, who was all alert.

"It's time," said Frank.

Jeff opened the bag he was carrying and extracted a small round tin. He removed the lid to reveal six or eight green cubes that could easily have been coloured sugar. He tipped them into his cupped hand and offered them to Saturday Night Fever. The horse nibbled while Jeff gently patted his head.

Frank reassured Eddie. "Undetectable, swab proof, prime offshore merchandise, tested and tried, safe as a stick of guarana chewing gum; no side effects." Frank checked his watch again. "Fifty minutes from now, Saturday Night Fever will be a speed machine, and nobody will detect a thing."

Eddie was nervous but impressed. "You should market the formula."

A negative from Frank; "Blow the secret and end up out of the game? No way! No risks. No problem! That formula was a cheeky experiment, too dangerous to use more than once."

The horse finished nibbling the green cubes, and Jeff put the tin away.

"All done," said Jeff, "and no questions asked."

"Stay close to him," said Eddie, "don't let him get lonely."

Jeff winked. "Right on, Boss."

At that moment Lorrie reached the stall.

Frank took one look at her. "Enter the class-act of the day. How do you do it?"

Lorrie looked back. "Come off it, Frank. It's just a game."

Eddie's question was more to the point, "Done the deed, honey?"

Lorrie nodded. "The Rex-Betty-Edna team in the stands have the cash and they know what to do with it."

Eddie clapped his hands once. "That's forty-five big ones in the ring here, plus another twenty on the TAB at different windows. We're sitting pretty; all we need is for our horse to win."

"Apple sweet," said Frank.

"Anyone for a nerve-tonic in the Members Bar?" quipped Lorrie.

"Let's go," said Frank.

Lorrie put a hand on Eddie's shoulder. "We'll be back before Fever's run, Dad; Race Three is due to start in about ten minutes; that's plenty of time to get set for Fever's Race Four boil-over."

Eddie flicked her quizzical look. "Boil-over?"

Lorrie lowered her voice; "You know there'll be one if Fever wins, Dad."

"Longshots have won before."

"Not with Frank's kind of gas in the tank."

"It's all under control, kid.

"Fever's not running against any old opposition, Dad."

Eddie got her point. "I didn't know The Mating Game was one of Mike Flynn's pets when I entered Fever in the same race."

"Forget it. What's done is done."

Lorrie left the stall with her arm casually linked in Frank's.

Cassie eyed their departure and grinned at Eddie. "Does Flash Frankie know he hasn't got a chance with Lorrie?"

Eddie grinned at her. "How do you know he hasn't?"

"She's too smart and he's too smooth—bad chemistry."

"Could be."

"Okay, try this, he's Hong Kong, she's not."

"What does that mean?"

"I spent a year in Hong Kong nosing around the tracks after my dad took me there when I was fifteen. I saw heaps of operators like our boy Frankie. A lot of them were too smooth for their own good; all they thought about was the money."

"Meaning?"

"They had no real interest in the horses."

"You think Frank's like that?"

"Hong Kong was where he learned the game. He's a money man."

"What's wrong with money, Cassie?"

"Nothing, but if Fever wins today how do you know he couldn't have done it without those little green cubes?"

"You think I'm not playing fair?"

"Let's just say that our boy Frank talked you into a little insurance."

"Who said he had to talk me into anything?"

"Look," said Cassie. "I've seen a lot of the tricks of this game and I'm on your side. I'd just hate anything to go wrong."

"There's no evidence of any of us making big bets. The bookies' bags will be full of Mating Game money. Do you think they're going to ask questions if they're paying out small stuff on our long-priced outsider?

"I guess not, Eddie."

MICHAEL J FLYNN SAT with Jewel Blanch at a quiet table in the Kings Park Members Bar. His suave was in full network mode. He wore a charcoal Prada suit with a grey striped shirt and a grey silk tie. His shoes were black Ferragamo, his watch was top of the range Piaget, his fingernails were buffed to a shine, and his hair had a fake tint of Cary Grant grey for an extra serve of distinction.

He ordered a bottle of Dom Perignon, 1966, a great year.

When the waiter brought it to the table, he made the mistake of bringing two chilled flutes, which Michael J waved away.

"Not in chilled flutes, old sport, the frosting on the glass inhibits the bubbles."

Jewel was impressed, not only by Michael J's cultured voice but by his fine manners. How could she know they were all invented for cause and effect?

He'd read about the no-no of frosted flutes in some ritzy wine manual. He wore Prada because George Clooney wore it, and the 'old sport' handle was lifted from the dialogue F. Scott Fitzgerald wrote for Jay Gatsby.

How the hell would Jewel know about that? All bets were on that she'd never heard of F. Scott Fitzgerald or Jay Gatsby either.

With his charm running amok, Michael J continued, "It's rather pleasant being in Brisbane again, it's a diamond-bright city."

"One of the reasons I love it," Jewel said.

"You'll love it even more when my horse wins."

Michael J glanced over at the bar's entrance as Lorrie and Frank entered the room. His eye held them for a few seconds.

"Who's the lovely vision in pink?" he asked.

Jewel told him.

Michael J flicked an eyebrow up. "Eddie Edwards has a daughter?"

"Do you know Eddie?"

"I've met him, never met her. Perhaps I've met the wrong Edwards."

Jewel took a sip of the Dom 66, purred, and said, "Eddie has a horse in Mating Game's race, and Lorrie thinks he's a chance."

"Then the pretty lady's confidence is admirable but misplaced."

He nosed the delicate aroma of the fine Dom bubbles. "Wonderful," he said.

"Bottoms up," said Jewel, touching his flute with hers.

Michael J Flynn looked her right in the eye. "One of my very favourite positions."

FRANK ORDERED A SCOTCH and soda, and sparkling Perrier water for Lorrie, who gave Jewel a little wave.

"You know who's sitting with her, don't you?" Frank asked.

"Everyone in the room knows, and they're trying hard not to stare."

"Mr Flynn is Mr Flynn, after all."

"Michael J to you Frank, and to everyone else who's impressed."

"Who says I'm impressed?"

"You're not?"

"I'm not."

"Do tell."

"I rubbed shoulders with him in Hong Kong. He's got a big head and a big ego to go with it. He's got a reputation as a big syndicate punter and a dirty player."

"As in?"

"Not into losing."

"Is anybody?"

Frank took a pull on his Scotch. "I guess not."

"It's going to be an interesting afternoon," said Lorrie.

A third person approached the table occupied by Michael J Flynn and Jewel Blanch. Lorrie recognized him as Flasher Doyle, one of the more interesting of the ring bookies. Flasher was fifty-something and into all kinds of deals. His nickname on the track was 'Anything for a Buck,' and like *Dances with Wolves*, the name meant what it said. Flasher wore Boss suits, ties and shirts, none of which did a thing for him—his personality and speech patterns did.

He was more Aussie-brash than Paul Hogan.

AT THE TABLE, JEWEL realised Flasher and Michael J wanted to be alone with each other and prepared to leave.

"No need to, darlin'," said Flasher. "Stick around if you're into shop talk."

"I've got shop talk of my own," said Jewel, "and I've got things to attend to."

When she left, Flasher took her seat. "What's the plan with the race?"

Michael J took a sip of the Dom. "Two speedsters, Amaroo and Debt Collector will lead the field to the first turn. The Mating Game will settle behind them and hold his position. The two leaders will drift out at the turn into the straight. The Mating Game will break through for a dream run on the rails, and it will all be over."

Flasher was impressed. "How much is all that costing you?"

"Peanuts when you think of how much we'll collect from down south and offshore."

"I love it when you talk dirty," said Flasher.

TWENTY MINUTES LATER AT the horse stalls, Jeff was preparing to lead Saturday Night Fever to the saddling paddock in front of the Members Stand. Cassie stood by to accompany him. Pre-race stress had Eddie in its grip.

His throat was dry, and he took another pull on the water bottle in his right hand.

Cassie gave him a pat on the back. "Are you okay, Boss?"

Eddie nodded. "I'm okay."

"Then make sure you look like it's just another race on just another sunny Saturday arvo. Let's keep it all Joe-Cool."

Eddie took a breath. "The suspense is killing me."

AT PRECISELY EIGHTEEN MINUTES before the race, Lorrie's three-person team of Rex Powell, Betty Coe and Edna Austin, each with big money in hard cash, moved into the betting ring, and the minor plunge on Saturday Night Fever hit a green light. At the same time, Michael J Flynn fronted the bookie beside Flasher Doyle's stand and placed a healthy bet at six to one.

That triggered a flurry of Mating Game betting. Rank and file punters, sensing a plunge, moved in before the odds dropped out of sight. The flurry worked in favour of Lorrie's team. While the money ran hot for The Mating Game, forty-five K at twenty-five-to-one was invested on Saturday Night Fever, and nobody could have cared less.

MEANWHILE, LORRIE AND FRANK were investing a further twenty big ones at the betting windows of the TAB, where Fever's price was still reading twenty-fives. Frank had one of his connections investing a further forty-five thousand in Sydney.

IN THE SADDLING PADDOCK, Eddie, making a decent display of his necessary cool, talked quietly to Bronco Stevens, the jockey booked to ride Saturday Night Fever. "He's fresh but he's in top condition for this. Apart from that, I can't tell you anything more. You've ridden him before; you know how he runs, and if he's well placed at the turn he could take off."

"He's a bit frisky," said Bronco.

"He's just happy to be back."

WITH THE HORSES MOVING round to the starting barrier, Eddie joined Lorrie and Frank in the fourth row of the Members Stand. A few minutes later Michael J Flynn arrived with Jewel to take their seats in the second row.

In the race caller's box, Bart Anderson's powerful binoculars were focused on the action at the starting barrier on the other side of the track. His pre-race comments were loud and clear.

Eddie's hands were trembling as he held his binoculars to his eyes with a firm grip. He could feel the beads of unwanted sweat breaking out on his forehead. His heart was pounding, and he could barely hold himself together.

One second later, he caught his breath when he heard the clang of the starting bell and saw the horses jump. His trembling grip on his binoculars firmed. Somewhere in the middle of the big field, he caught the flash of Bronco's gold cap.

Bart Anderson called the action at the first turn:

"Amaroo jumped like a tiger to take the lead; a head away second is Debt Collector who raced up on his outside. Behind them, The Mating Game is nicely tucked away on the rails."

Michael J Flynn, with binoculars focused on the field, smiled. So far, so good. The plan was working.

In the main grandstand, Betty Coe nudged Rex Powell. "Where's our horse?"

"Middle of the field," said Rex, "holding his own on the outside."

Watching from the rails in the saddling paddock, Cassie reached for Jeff's hand as Bart's call continued:

"Amaroo has a lock on the lead as the runners approach the turn. Debt Collector is keeping pace. The two leaders are looking good, a length and a half in front. The rest of the field is packing up as they run to the home turn. Third on the rails in the box seat, The Mating Game is poised to make a grab at the leaders, and he's winding up."

Eddie swept the field with his binoculars. His horse was still eight lengths away. He felt Lorrie squeeze his arm.

The field hit the turn and bunched up. The crowd was on its feet. Bart's call hit a startled note. *"Amaroo took the turn badly, he's shifted out taking Debt Collector with him, opening up a golden run for The Mating Game on the rails."*

"Yes!" said Michael J Flynn, lowering his binoculars. Jewel grabbed his arm in excitement.

Bart was pumping out his call: *"The Mating Game lunged forward to take the dream run on the rails, Amaroo and Debt Collector can't hold him as the field ribbons out."*

Frank Davenport was not watching The Mating Game. When Saturday Night Fever took the home turn and straightened for the run to the post, Frank's keen eyes watched for the tell-tale sign. It came as he knew it would.

The horse's stride lengthened, his head stretched forward, and Bronco rose in the saddle to pilot his mount home.

Bart's race call became frantic.

"The Mating Game shot to the lead but look at Saturday Night Fever! He's unwinding a blistering run on the outside of the field. Yes! Look at this horse go!

Bronco Stevens is riding him away from the pack and he's taking on The Mating Game twenty metres from the post."

The crowd went wild.

Frank was statue-still but his head was a mess. The crowd was frantic.

Eddie's vision sharpened, and he caught his breath again. Then he saw the golden flash of Bronco's cap as Saturday Night Fever rocketed up to catch The Mating Game and take him down by a long head in the last couple of strides.

Michael J Flynn's jaw dropped.

It was all over.

In the bookies' ring, Flasher Doyle was thunderstruck.

"Jesus Christ," he said, "how in hell did that happen?"

In the saddling paddock, Cassie tightened her grip on Jeff's hand. "Don't look now," she said, "but that win is going to piss off a lot of major players."

In the main stand Rex Powell, in company with Betty Coe and Edna Austin, was all smiles as he scanned his betting tickets. "Not a bad afternoon's punt. We've cleared seven grand a piece in commissions."

There was no delay in the call of correct weight. Bart Anderson announced that the placings were official: Saturday Night Fever was in. Lorrie, standing close to her father, caught the look he gave her—a mixture of relief, excitement and sheer joy. She leaned in and kissed him on the cheek.

"It's okay, Daddy," she said, "we're home free."

IN THE MEMBERS STAND at the Roma Racetrack, Cooper McCoy handed his grandmother the pile of folding money she'd won on Saturday Night Fever, and said, "Why did you back that horse, Kit? No one fancied it."

"I saw the movie. Everyone said the swearing was terrible, but I loved that Bee Gees music, and I thought the story was wonderful."

Cooper gave her a look; "No kidding."

"It was about this boy who everyone said was nothing much," said Kitty, "and then he came good in the end."

She wanted to add: *That's what I want for The Stinger, and that's why I backed Saturday Night Fever.* She counted the money she'd won, put it in her handbag and said, "Intuition should never be down-played."

5

LORRIE'S DEVOTION: AS DEEP AT IT GETS

L ORRIE EDWARDS HAD AGREED to Frank's sugar-cube cheat because she cared about Eddie. To everyone else her father was just another trier with just another dream, but not to her.

She'd seen how his dream drove him; how he loved the game, how he loved his horses, and like every other trainer who fell in love with Thoroughbreds, he wanted the ultimate thrill. Eddie wanted the Big One; he wanted the Melbourne Cup, and Lorrie wanted him to get it. Someday, she told herself, it would come. When he'd started out, Eddie did it tough; he took the knocks like everyone else but with his mind on the job he eventually starting kicking butt. He was moving along nicely until the day his wife Pat came home with the news that she had breast cancer.

Pat was a fighter and she took on the cancer with a positive attitude that gave everybody hope. But it was an attitude tinged with unconscious deceit, and despite Pat's courage, this was one battle she was not fated to win.

She was game all right; she put up a fight that was valiant to behold—she kept punching with so much spunk that Lorrie believed she'd recover. But Pat was taking on a killer that had been programmed to win from the start. As the weeks turned into months, it was clear she was headed for heaven.

The day before she died, in the painless zone of morphine calm, she held Lorrie's hand and whispered words that Lorrie could never forget:

"Look after Eddie, he's a lost boy, darlin', and when I'm gone, he'll need you. There's just you and him now, so be there for him, honey, and don't let him lose his way."

That was six years ago. Lorrie was eighteen, Pat was thirty-nine, Eddie was forty-two, and throughout the following twelve months, he damn near fell to bits. Eddie was losing it; his drive was running on dying batteries, sleepless nights and too many empty bottles. He let most of his stable hands and horses go. Opportunities were drying up, he was looking old and tired, and he was talking about giving up.

At the same time, Lorrie had her heart set on being a hairdresser with a glittery salon, and a swish clientele of A-list egomaniacs. She was the apprentice with a future. But when she saw Eddie falter, she knew the situation was crucial. She put her ambition on the back burner and did what Pat had asked her to do. It helped that she shared her father's love of horses; as a kid, she'd sat with him time after time watching *National Velvet* on television while Eddie raved on about the wonders and glories of the racing game. Her memories of those sweeter times made it easier to bring him back to life.

It took over three years, but she was there with him every day. She made his meals, put the brakes on his bottle time, talked horses to him and found herself learning the tricks of his trade. The more she learned, the more interested she became, and a few months later when she sat in a chair at the local hairdressing salon, she was surprised to discover she was no longer interested in being the hairdressing apprentice with a future.

Eddie started getting better training gigs. His scores were modest, but he was back on track and his reputation was out of the loser league. He was paying his bills and making money. Lorrie's savvy was up a notch; she was soon regarding herself as the trainer with a future. As her skills grew, so did her confidence, and Eddie began taking her input seriously.

She talked him into keeping his operation small, but as things improved, the need to stay modest left him. His dreams for the Melbourne Cup came back and he started looking for big money to make them come true.

At that point, Frank Davenport re-entered his life.

Frank's father had been a trainer friend of Eddie's in the good old days, and Frank and Lorrie hung out together when they were kids. Frank's mother came into a pile of money when her father died, and she was able to grant her son's wish to explore the racing scene in Hong Kong. When Frank left for the Orient, Lorrie was a butch teenager who hung around Eddie's stables in jeans and boots, check shirts and a ponytail.

But the Frank Davenport who went to Hong Kong on his mum's cash was not the smooth operator who came back five years later, and Lorrie was no longer the butch kid he'd left behind. Frank had grown up in Hong Kong. He'd been around, he'd majored in bedroom sports, and he was ready to play the game of a man-about-town. Lorrie had grown up too. Her flair was in full flight.

The butch teenager had morphed into a streamlined chick with honey blonde hair, a taste for classy clothes, and an idling engine that hinted at the presence of fiery spark plugs. It occurred to Frank that she was the kind of companion he needed to gild his new-found image. Give him his due. He tried. But he had to get his randy rocks off with someone else.

Lorrie had boyfriends by the score knocking on her door. Naturally, she test-trialled a few studs for permanent positions on her roster, but none managed to tone down her interest in horse training, or her devotion to Eddie for too long. She became what's known as 'unavailable.' The studs who doubted the validity of that label went home with their condoms still neatly packaged in their hip pockets.

Lorrie was not on the wham-bam-thank-you-ma'am menu, but because she looked as though she should have been, she was giving the testosterone industry pause. At the same time, she was nobody's handbag, and Frank got the message.

He was good-natured enough to be patient, and while he was biding his time, he was given the chance to test-try the wonder drug that one of his acquaintances in the Orient had made available. Saturday Night Fever's win was the payout, and Lorrie was cautiously grateful:

"You've made my dad's day, Frank, he means a lot to me; so much that I don't mind the cheating, but I won't go into that now, it's enough to see him so happy."

Frank was pleased. Lorrie hadn't exactly encouraged him, but things were looking up. After Saturday Night Fever, so was his bank account, and Frank was suddenly hungry for more; as much more as he could get.

6

THE BRISBANE MARRIOTT: MICHAEL J'S AFTER-RACE FURY

MICHAEL J FLYNN SAT perfectly still in his top-floor suite.

On the coffee table in front of him, an open bottle of Dom rested in an ice bucket. Beside it was an empty champagne glass.

Standing looking vacantly out of the suite's wide windows, Flasher Doyle sipped from a bottle of Carlton Crown Lager. The mood in the room was distinctly dark.

"I've spoken to Hong Kong," said Michael in a peeved voice. "My contacts there are not happy! They've done a bundle on what I said was a sure thing—a guarantee. The same in Sydney and Melbourne. Eddie Edwards has cost us all a bloody fortune, to say nothing of what he's done to my reputation."

Flasher shook his head. "What can I say?"

"Could Edwards have pulled a swift one?

"The rumour mill says no."

"A pile of cash for Saturday Night Fever hit the ring in Sydney, and you took a big bet or two up here."

"There was no money from the Edwards stable, MJ."

"They could have had touts. It's all feels dodgy to me."

"I haven't heard anything, MJ, not a whisper."

"That horse was eight lengths away at the top of the straight and came home like a runaway train."

"There was no evidence of anything."

"Edwards is a crony of Frank Davenport, and I strongly suspect Davenport had a hand in that win. He's a Hong Kong tout. I wouldn't trust him as far as I could kick him, and I don't want the pair of them thinking they can pull their tricks on me! They've caught me off guard and I don't like that!"

Flasher shrugged. "What can we do? The stewards were happy."

Michael J took the bottle of Dom out of the ice bucket, refuelled his glass and dropped a bomb. "I want Davenport and Edwards out of the way!"

Flasher frowned. "Out of the way?"

Michael raved on. "I want them out of the game, permanently."

"How do you mean?

"I don't care what the stewards say; that race was a setup, and I've got egg on my face. There's got to be suspicious talk, and I want you to find out what it is. As from tomorrow, I'm spending time at the beach. I need to think, but you can get me on my mobile. Contact me if you've got anything to report, anything at all."

Flasher got the message. "I'll be all ears."

"I'm dining with Jewel Blanch tonight. She hangs with Lorrie Edwards and she may know something. If she does, I may be able to charm it out of her, one way or another. I'm good when I'm pissed off."

Flasher dropped a wink. "One way or another. Way to go, MJ."

"Leave her to me. Either way, Edwards and Davenport are going down. Those two small-time hicks have stymied a major syndicate kill! I staked my reputation on that race. It was a no-risk investment. Got it?"

"I'm on the job."

Michael J took a fresh mouthful of Dom. "I've never been a good loser; it wasn't born in me and it's too late to change, so get to work, old sport; I won't be ungrateful."

"Go get 'em, Boss."

Mickey Flynn grinned back. *Fuck yeah! I'll get 'em. Whatever it takes, I'll get the bastards. Nobody treats me like a dropkick and gets away with it. Those two bastards are going down, and I'm not talking cock-sucking!*

7

NORTH POINT TRAINING RACK, BRISBANE
TEN DAYS LATER: SEEDING THE DREAM

THE EDWARDS STABLE WAS in the northern Brisbane suburb of Boondall, a nicely appointed property of modest size not more than five or six road minutes away from the pretty North Point Training Track, which hadn't accommodated a race day since the early years of the Pacific War. It was still well-maintained and perfect for light work. Saturday Night Fever's upset had dumped a cartload of cash into Eddie's bank account, and it had been good for everyone; all in all, a successful coup.

Ten days had passed since his win, and Eddie was in high spirits at the North Point track. The Fever victory had granted one of his dearest wishes: He'd had his eye on a well-bred gelding called Thunderdome, owned by a friend of his with a stable near the Hunter Valley in New South Wales.

The handsome four-year-old was lightly raced but had shown potential at two starts at Randwick in Sydney but his owner, convinced by racing experts that he had more promising horses in his stable, listed Thunderdome for sale.

After the Saturday Night Fever windfall, Eddie was on the hotline to his friend in New South Wales. Five days later Thunderdome arrived at his new home in North Boondall. The chestnut gelding's bloodline could be traced back to a Melbourne Cup winner, and Eddie was full of ambitious fuel. Cassie and Jeff, Eddie's two horse-mad stable hands were thrilled.

Early on the first Tuesday morning after Thunderdome's arrival, Eddie had him working out at the North Point track. Cassie was in the saddle; Jeff was standing with Eddie; both watching the horse's easy gallop.

NOT LONG AFTERWARDS, SOMETHING happened that seemed unimportant at the time, but it was to set a bizarre bid in motion—one of the most daring and dangerous money moves ever attempted on an Australian racetrack.

While the morning sun was still hanging low over the middle-distance seascape of Moreton Bay, Frank drove Lorrie up in his shiny new dark blue BMW and together they joined Eddie and Jeff to watch Thunderdome's workout.

After a few minutes, Frank said, "I've seen that horse before."

Eddie reacted with pride. "He could well be my bid for the big time."

"How's that, Eddie?" asked Frank.

"He's true blue, and I'm talking blood. He's all class."

"Not the last time I saw him."

Eddie stopped watching the trial. "Where was that?"

"The Dalby Picnic Races not all that long ago."

"I don't think so," said Eddie.

"I'm sure of it," said Frank. "After all this time around horses, I've developed a keen eye."

Eddie frowned. "Keen eye or not, that gelding has never raced at Dalby, Frank. I've got his history; he's never been there."

Frank watched closely as Cassie reined her mount in and trotted him to the running rail.

"Damn it, Eddie," said Frank, eyes on Thunderdome, "I know I'm not mistaken. That's the horse I saw race at Dalby, I remember his name. It's The Stinger, right?"

Eddie frowned. "The Stinger?"

"Isn't that his name?"

Eddie shook his head. "Not according to his papers. You're looking at Thunderdome, he's the horse I bought with some of Fever's winnings and there's no way he's the dud you saw at Dalby."

Frank blinked and said, "Well, I'll be damned."

He remained silent through the exchanges that followed: Cassie gushing over Thunderdome's obvious abilities, Eddie's elation, Jeff's enthusiasm, and Lorrie's admiration. Frank's mind was churning.

Could the two geldings be related: same bloodlines; same sire; same dam? Maybe he'd been mistaken. No. He was sure of it. He knew horses. He had a sharp eye. He knew! He'd met The Stinger's previous owner in Dalby. He knew the horse was changing hands and assumed Eddie to be the buyer. But Eddie claimed he wasn't, and he had no reason to lie.

Frank was spaced. Had he inadvertently discovered something amazing?

As he stood distracted by such thoughts, he heard Lorrie's voice:

"Frank, you're not answering. Eddie has invited us to dinner tonight; it's a sort of delayed celebration."

Jolted out of his thoughts, Frank replied, "Sure, that would be great, just great."

FRANK DAVENPORT DIDN'T REMEMBER too much about that day. Although he concealed his ambitious fantasies beneath a veneer of street smart, Frank was a dreamer and a hunch player. He'd never had a regular job; the racing game was his world. He knew the ropes and he'd learned the hard way. He'd had tough times, who hadn't? But he'd found out that the game was always better if you played every hunch without thinking twice.

Cashed up for some time, thanks to Saturday Night Fever, Frank had intended to persuade Lorrie to return with him to Hong Kong, but that idea was being second-guessed by another idea that was much more exciting and challenging, a plan that could relegate the Saturday Night Fever caper to the lower rungs of the windfall ladder.

After Frank showered and shaved for dinner, his mind was on fire. With a towel around his hips, he stood on the balcony of his rented fourteenth-floor apartment overlooking the South Brisbane reach of the river and gazed out at the view without really seeing it. He was thinking of something else:

Thunderdome and The Stinger; Two horses; two geldings; two chestnuts so physically alike they could be twins; equine Corsican Brothers! One a potential champion, the other an awkward hack. How had it happened? He kept asking himself the same questions and getting the same answer!

He was a betting man; a risk-taker. Was this a signal for a player like him to make a move? Suppose, like The Prince and The Pauper, the two horses could somehow be made to change places; not for always but for one magic con that could set him up for life! Suppose—Suppose.

DINNER WAS AT A colourful out-of-town restaurant called The Court of the Seven Lamps, a neat diner that specialised in Creole cuisine. The chef's star course was Prawn Jambalaya, and it was everything it should have been; thickened with okra and delicately spiced with Jalapeno chillies. The dessert was pecan pie with clotted pomegranate cream. The wine was Perrier-Jouët Rosé and it was sensational. Frank drank it to excess and remained totally sober.

After dinner, he moved with Eddie and Lorrie to the restaurant's landscaped courtyard for brewed coffee and toffee biscuits. They were surrounded by clipped lilly pilly trees woven with twinkling star-lights; in the background, a muted audio track played the velvet hits of Nat King Cole. The atmosphere was perfect for the pitch Frank was eager to deliver.

The coffee came, and Frank put his fantasyland-thinking into words:

Twin Bluebloods; a gift from somewhere in outer space.

What if Thunderdome, way above The Stinger in class, could take his place in one race, appropriately weighted against a field of lower-class horses; none of which would have the slightest chance of beating him?

The Stinger's lack of form would ensure fantastic odds; and as there was no risk of failure, this would be the very surest of sure things.

Thunderdome masquerading as The Stinger; a champion running as a hack!

What would the odds be? How would anyone ever guess the twist?

If the planning was right with every base covered, a fortune was there for the taking. Are we game to take it? Could we? Is there a chance?

The courtyard table was silent for interminable minutes.

Eddie looked lost. Lorrie looked shocked. Words fell from open mouths; Frank talked fortunes. Lorrie talked impossible. Eddie talked strategies.

Nobody made sense. Lorrie asked how. In the end, Frank's fortune-talk ruled.

"How much money are we talking?" asked Eddie.

"Megamillions if we're careful, and we'll be careful."

Eddie frowned. "It's a risk, Frank, a big one."

"As wild as it gets, Eddie."

"It's left-field stuff, Frank; I've got a few questions."

Silence for more long minutes.

"First up," said Eddie, "how do we get The Stinger?"

"He's a no-hoper, mate—we'll buy him. Budget price."

"How do we know we can get him?"

Frank was on a roll. "I made enquiries. He's running in a novice race on the day of the Roma Cup meeting in two weeks. If we go to Roma on the day, we can make an offer."

Lorrie piped up: "If we're going to play this game, we can't do anything without Cassie and Jeff. For obvious reasons, we'd need them both."

Eddie was coming around. "Naturally. Who asks them?"

"I do," she answered, "and if they refuse, there's no game."

Frank countered instantly, "Is there a game if they're in?"

Lorrie looked at her father. "Dad?"

Eddie's reply was a positive, "I'm a yes!"

Lorrie was adamant. "All right, Dad, but I'll need to know how, and it had better be know-how."

Frank was all smiles. "Step One taken."

"Not quite," said Lorrie, "what about integrity?"

Frank gave her a knowing look. "Where was our integrity when Fever won?"

"That was a different ballgame, Frank."

"Was it? Jeff plugged into stable gossip. The riders of Amaroo and Debt Collector were paid to set the pace before giving The Mating Game a break on the rails at the top of the straight. Michael J Flynn rigged the run for big money. The connections of the two horses couldn't blow any whistles without incriminating themselves so they shut their traps. We upset a bought race, baby."

Lorrie shook her head. "Then I have no argument."

Frank was jubilant. "Step One taken?"

Eddie sealed the set-up. "Step One taken!"

"Not quite," said Lorrie. "This is not a matter of a few green sugar-cubes. It's full-blown spitting in the face of the code; it's dangerous and I'm nervous."

"Relax," said Frank. "Everything will be worked out; fine-tooth comb."

Lorrie was still hesitant. "If the wheels fall off, who takes the hit?"

"The team leader!" said Frank. "Yours Truly. That's how sure I am."

"Fine for now," said Lorrie, "my father is one of my reasons for living. That said, I want to be in on every step of the exercise, and if at any time I consider it too much of a risk I'll insist on pulling the plug, no question."

"No sweat," said Frank.

Lorrie reached over and took her father's hand. "You're my world, Dad, and if I'm in, I'm doing it for you."

8

THE McCOY STUD IN ROMA: COOPER'S WISHFUL THINKING

KITTY McCOY STOOD ON the wide veranda of her well-kept homestead. Behind her, the painted white timber walls, shaded by the veranda's corrugated iron roof, gleamed softly in the sun. The walls had to be washed every week to keep them dust-free in the harsh seasons of the west, but they were worth the trouble.

"Paint 'em white," Charlie McCoy had said, "they'll reflect the heat in the deep summer, and we'll have less chance of roasting inside the house."

He was right. For extra cool, the homestead had dozens of casement windows and double doors to allow the air to flow through the big rooms. Rainwater was trapped in six enormous tanks for drinking and cooking, and bore water took care of everything else. Kitty's country kitchen was a work of old-fashioned art, and in it, she created home-cooked miracles from recipes passed down from her mother and grandmother. Her loyal helper, resident housekeeper and self-styled friend-in-need was Alice Adams, a fifty-eight-year-old widow who'd lived her life in Roma.

Alice was a capable no-nonsense woman of the west. She called a spade a spade, a shovel a shovel, and small-talk a pain in the neck. She'd brought up four sons, all married with responsible jobs. She was a grandmother six times over; proud as any woman could be; devoted to Kitty and the upkeep of the McCoy homestead.

Wearing a floral dress and a plain white apron, Alice walked out from the kitchen and along the veranda to where Kitty was standing with her eyes focused on the training track. It sat a short space away in the dappled shade of red gums. Alice followed Kitty's gaze and saw Cooper standing by the rails watching The Stinger's mid-morning workout.

"That boy has guts," said Alice, "he'll turn that nag into something by the sheer force of his will."

"That's my prayer, Alice."

"He's running his horse at the Roma Cup meeting tomorrow, isn't he?"

"He is," said Kitty. "It's his third start since Cooper bought him and so far, he's been pretty so-so."

"Lost your faith?"

Kitty turned to her friend. "Never, Alice, but horses can be real funny and this one doesn't seem interested in being a racehorse."

"What's the problem?"

Kitty shook her head. "He's a bit on the lazy side; his trial times are getting there, but when he's on a racetrack it doesn't happen."

"Don't give it another thought," said Alice. "Cooper's going to keep trying, and if that horse doesn't want to be a racehorse, he'd better get it into his head that one day he will be."

"Exactly what I keep telling myself."

"Then keep on telling, Kit. Wonders never cease."

"You know, Alice, I've got this funny feeling that Cooper's luck is about to change. There's something in the air—you know what I mean?"

"It's called hope, love."

"It's more positive than that. That boy didn't come here by accident and he didn't find that horse by accident."

Alice lowered her voice. "What are you saying?"

"Things happen for a reason. If you leave them alone, they'll work themselves out."

Alice let out a little knowing sigh. "I know exactly where you're coming from, Kit. I'm a crystal ball girl from way back."

9

THE SAME WEEK IN BRISBANE:
THE BALL STARTS ROLLING

AFTER DAYS OF QUESTIONING her motives and sometimes doubting her sanity, Lorrie made up her mind that she was for the caper. She was uneasy but committed; committed for Eddie. She was in it now; the wheels were turning; that was it.

EDDIE WAS PRIMED FOR his biggest-ever grab for the sweet smell of success. As the jigsaw came together, he was feeling like a new man. Frank was powering on positives. What were the odds of getting caught? Didn't matter! Frank was convinced he'd been given fate's green light, and he was not one to trash the fickle finger of fate.

LORRIE PUT THE PROPOSAL to Jeff and Cassie and caught a trouble-free win. No thinking it over. No doubts. We can do it! They were young. Reckless. High on excitement! Yes! Cassie would be in the saddle as the caper jockey, Jeff was caper caretaker, all too good to resist, 007 on galloping hoofs! With the major players on board, the caper was a go! Almost.

There was one player missing.

The Stinger!

10

SUNSHINE BEACH, NOOSA, STH/EAST QUEENSLAND: MICHAEL J HITS HIS STRIDE

WHEN MICHAEL J FLYNN played in the sun, he chose the best places.

Noosa was one of his favourites, an elite boutique resort on the shores of Laguna Bay at the northern tip of the sprawling Sunshine Coast, several kilometres north of Brisbane. Michael J drove there alone in his rented Lexus and installed himself in a luxury apartment overlooking the sea at exclusive Little Cove, high on the hill on Noosa's eastern rim. For five days he had kept to himself; surfing before breakfast and mid-afternoon, eating fine-food and lightening up his assaults on Dom Perignon.

Such was Michael J's regime, every time he needed to give his 'little grey cells' a Hercule Poirot workout—not that he'd ever read Agatha Christie, but he'd seen Peter Ustinov play the fussy Belgian sleuth in movies, and as Ustinov was intellectually high-end, he was fine and dandy in Michael J's book. In broad terms, Michael J's 'little grey cells' were cooking up skulduggery; ways to get even with the racetrack cowboys who'd demeaned his international reputation and plundered his bid to gallop into the syndicate's permanent good books on the flying flanks of The Mating Game.

The more Michael J thought about that, the more it triggered Mickey Flynn's same-old feverish raging: *"Bastards! They're gonna pay! They're gonna get*

Saturday Night Fever rammed up their chutes and I'm not talking the Bee Gees!" Mickey Flynn was not kidding!

One of the sideline talents Michael J prided himself on was his ability in the kitchen. He was so serious about cooking that he took lessons from a well-regarded matron of the gourmet world and delighted her by developing superior skills. He then took to heaping scorn on every one of the scores of cooking shows on television:

"Smoke and mirrors. Easy to fake it when you've got a camera and a television studio, hours of pre-prep time and tricky lighting. Those show-offs teach you nothing. Try making their recipes! Cooking shows are cheap reality television for the gullible—and with budget-priced celebrities!"

Michael J meant every word of his damnation, even though it came from the cowboy mind of Mickey Flynn, who grew up sinking three litres of Coca Cola a day, gobbling down Big Maccas, fries, thick-shakes, KFC, and cheap pizza every time he hit the food courts of dreary shopping centres. But that was Mickey Flynn and times had changed.

A well-studied copy of *Le Cordon Bleu at Home* had converted Mickey's low-life palate and helped rip off the flab that had started to gather around his gut. Michael J's spoken appraisal of junk food gluttons was as follows:

"Those mugs are into everything and anything. Fries coated with sugar syrup to make them turn golden in the deep fryer. Cheese topping on cheap pizza is second cousin to sump oil, and every bite you take of that junk robs you of energy and coats your brain cells with shit!"

And as 'shit' was almost the only four-letter word Michael J retained from Mickey's old-time vocabulary, it came across with such a resounding wallop that people had been known to wince when it passed his lips, but who could argue with such a well-informed citizen of the brave new healthy world?

After days of chilling and deep-thinking, Michael J was hatching a plan. His first move was to invite Jewel Blanch to experience a few days of his well-heeled hospitality at Little Cove. She'd been a very relaxing companion the night of The Mating Game defeat, and it occurred to him that if he played her more carefully, she could be used as an unconscious pawn in his move to bring down the Edwards stable.

When he called her with his invitation, he hit the jackpot right away.

She accepted, and with no prompting at all, she blurted out that she'd been invited to be the head judge at 'Fashions on the Field' at the coming Roma Cup. That announcement had negligible impact on Michael J until Jewel added that she'd arranged for Lorrie Edwards to be her assistant.

It got better.

Lorrie was making the trip in company with Eddie and mystery man Frank Davenport, the suspected heavy in The Mating Game boilover. Michael J was on full alert! He had to know what had motivated that odious little trio to attend what he regarded as a hillbilly race meeting for bumpkins in the country.

"Never leave a stone unturned," said Michael J, quoting one of his favourite clichés, "one never knows what could be hiding underneath."

He was talking to himself in the mirror of the bathroom while he shaved and showered in preparation for his social assignation with the alluring Jewel Blanch. Twenty minutes later, discreetly drenched in Pierre Cardin EDT, and togged in his imported Dolce & Gabbana casual gear, he was on his way to the Sunshine Coast Airport in his rented silver Lexus to meet her.

Two hours later, she was doused in candlelight sitting opposite him at his dinner table, raving about the excellence of his deceptively simple cuisine: Beluga caviar followed by Moreton Bay lobster and Burnett River scallops pan-fried with clarified butter, shaved fresh ginger root and white wine.

Dom Perignon sparkled in their crystal glasses. He geared the conversation to Jewel's fashion excursion to Roma, and casually angled the Edwards stable trio into the topic. With nary a hint of the aggravation he felt, his sentences hit the air with a ring of truth:

"I have enormous respect for Eddie. Saturday Night Fever ran a great race, and the win was a credit to him. In my opinion, he has a great future."

Jewel was mildly surprised. "You're not upset about that win?"

"On the contrary. In fact, you are in a position to grant him, and Yours Truly, a great favour."

"Do tell, Michael."

"I know he's a small player, so keep an eye on what he's doing. I'd like to help if there's anything I can do. I'm a man of influence and I feel it's my duty to keep Eddie kicking goals on the track for the ongoing good of the sport. I would appreciate it if you could follow through and let me know if there's anything he needs."

Jewel finished her mouthful of divine lobster and put her fork down.

"Do you mean that?"

He answered her in his most sincere Cary Grant purr. "I most certainly do."

Jewel was bowled over. "Michael, that's so sweet, I've never seen this side of you."

He looked across the table at her. "This place brings out the best in me. I'll have to start spending more time in this part of the world."

Jewel was beginning to register the tingle of the champagne. The enchantment of the candlelight was getting to her and she was feeling warm and vulnerable.

Michael's dessert was a magnificent Crème Brulee, a creation of his own talented hand. Jewel savoured every spoonful. She was in raptures. "I've never tasted Crème Brulee quite like this," she said. "What's your secret?"

Michael purred on, "Total devotion to the cause—and fresh duck eggs."

"Duck eggs?"

"Duck eggs."

"Where do you find duck eggs in Noosa?"

"You don't. I got them from a duck farmer, just up the road in Eumundi. They were laid this morning."

"Laid this morning?"

"The duck eggs, yes." He hit a pregnant pause. "I haven't been laid for days."

"That's hard to believe."

He sat back in his chair. "Would you excuse me for a moment?"

"Of course."

He rose; walked into the bedroom and reappeared seconds later minus his Dolce & Gabbana casual wear, his Ferragamo shoes and his silk socks.

His newly acquired tan accentuated the blazing white of his revealing French underwear.

"May I now repeat that I haven't been laid for days?"

Jewel looked at him and smiled. "What can I say?"

"I have a better question. What can you do?"

She didn't hesitate. She started undressing in the chair, but Michael stopped her. "Not quite yet.

"No?"

"Be patient, dear lady."

He moved to the kitchen, removed a crystal bowl of pink whipped cream from the refrigerator, snapped out the kitchen lights, snuffed out the candles, and carrying the bowl of cream, he signalled Jewel's rise from her chair.

Completely mesmerised, she stood; a puzzled smile lit her face.

He gestured like a doorman at The Ritz. "The bedroom is this way."

He followed her into the room, which was dimly illuminated by soft pink wall lights. He set the bowl on a bedside table, swept the filmy window curtains aside to reveal the moonlit panorama of bewitching Laguna Bay, shining at them though tall green pine trees. Below the bedroom in the unit's manicured fern-cluttered garden, grew three pink frangipani trees, all in full bloom. The scent of their blossoms floated through the windows on the gentle breeze. Further away, the seaside strip of the Noosa Surfing Beach, edged by chic low-rise apartment buildings, was faintly visible. Michael crossed to a neat audio system built into the wall, hit a button, and seconds later the low-decibel murmur of Errol Garner's "Misty," whispered into the room.

Held still by the magic, Jewel waited. He approached, teased her body with barely touching fingers, removed the rest of her clothes, then leaned down, scooped up serves of pink whipped cream and applied them to each breast. She shivered in delight.

"Oh, Michael."

"There's more."

Holding her still with one arm wrapped around her, he lowered his head to flutter his tongue over her hard nipples; lapping at the cream like a thirsty kitten, moving from one breast to the other until all the cream had disappeared. Still shivering in delight, Jewel watched him push his Italian briefs down to step out of them. The curve of his rampant rapier, bathed in pink light, signalled his excitement. He coaxed her to sit on the side of the bed and when she was in position, he whispered his instructions.

"Cover me with cream down there, baby. Turn me into an icy pole."

She touched him. "Down here?"

"Down there, all you can see, everything."

She diligently obeyed.

When she'd finished, he murmured, "Now eat it off."

"All of it?"

"All of it. I want to watch."

Errol Garner's "Misty" finished its third replay, and the Johnny Mathis version took over.

Jewel went to work, holding him close; her hands caressing his firm buttocks and steely thighs. She looked up. "Strawberries."

"The berries of desire, agree?"

"I love them."

"So do I."

The bed's cover had been turned down and when the first serve of cream had been devoured, he asked her to stretch out with her arms and legs delicately spread.

"Like an angel in the snow."

He sat on the bed and ladled more cream over the bullseye between her thighs and repeated his thirsty lip works. By now she was drifting around somewhere in the moonlight over Laguna Bay, breathlessly ready for what she knew was going to happen.

He ladled even more cream on her breasts, her chest, her abdomen and added another generous serve to the prize he was eager to claim. Then gently hovering over her like a bird of prey, he moved his throbbing rapier in creamy passes up and down her body, then smothered her open lips with fiery open-mouthed kisses. When he sensed she was so lost in ecstasy that she was completely helpless, he positioned himself above her again, lowered his steely body to cover her, then dropped his hand to guide his love wand toward the prize he'd worked so creatively to get.

Jewel was no amateur, but she'd never experienced a carnal showman like MJ Flynn, whose over-the-top approach was in full flight.

He took her in his arms. "I've been waiting five days for this pleasure cruise, and once around the Noosa seaside will not be enough."

He barely heard her whisper, "Is that a promise?"

It was Mickey Flynn who answered, *"Is the Pope a fucken Catholic?"*

And it was Mickey who made the flight memorable. Holding her close, his buttocks became the skilled human jackhammer he'd tested and perfected long ago on Allison Moses and Co and scores of willing joy riders.

When he broke the rhythm for a moment to catch his breath, Jewel murmured, "I'm no stranger to outer-space flights, but this is Apollo 10."

"Ya reckon?" Mickey blurted. *"You've had the all-day sucker and the Good Ship Lollipop. Stay aboard for the big one; I'm talkin' bottoms-up, chick—so turn on over and let's get it on the roster."*

Outside, the moon continued to shine softly on the rippling waters of Laguna Bay, and the aroma of the pink frangipani blossoms grew heavier. Michael J, finally in splash-down on his return to Earth, kissed Jewel sweetly on the cheek and said,

"We're all out of strawberry cream but if you fancy kiwi fruit cream, say the word and I'll rustle some up."

Johnny Mathis, on his umpteenth repeat of "Misty" warbled on.

11

THE ROMA CUP:
THE STINGER SHOWS HIS TRICKS

THE RUNNING OF THE Roma Cup presents Queensland's South West with one its zippiest sporting days of the year. The balloon rises at an official dinner on Friday night. By midday on Saturday, it's high in the sky, and there it bobs through a full afternoon's racing, and a trackside rock concert that begins when the races end to power on until Sunday's early light.

Roma Cup Day is no lazy country meeting with picnic baskets and laid-back social lollygagging. It's a big-time sporting gig and the town dresses up.

'Fashions on the Field' is a well-contested accessory with big prizes, and it's no joke for the fashion groupies of Roma; male and female.

Cup Day was all set to dish out the thrills once again, and its fashion contest chief judge was Miss Jewel Blanch, all crisp and crunchy in her favourite fashion combo of navy, red and white.

Sassily understated but giving her a run for her money in pale daffodil was chief assistant judge, Lorrie Edwards, whose look-but-don't-touch demeanour was having its effect on Roma boys, who didn't always get to see such luscious wet dreams in the flesh. Rounding out Judge Jewel's panel of associates were a prominent Roma community worker, a loquacious local councillor, and Mrs Kitty McCoy, widow of the town's most famous racing identity, the late great Charlie McCoy. Kitty had never met Eddie Edwards, but she was familiar with his reputation as the winning trainer of Saturday Night Fever. She and Lorrie bonded on the spot—birds of a feather.

Close to one-hundred-and-twenty entrants in the fashion contest were narrowed down to twenty finalists; fourteen ladies and six gents, who waited on the veranda of the roomy Committee Room, where light eats were being served in an atmosphere of social cackling and liquid refreshments.

In the trackside grandstand, vital observations were being made.

Race three was due to start in fifteen minutes. The horses were in the saddling paddock and the bearer of number nine saddlecloth was The Stinger.

Eddie took a close look at him and said, "You're right, Frank, he's Thunderdome's double for sure. It's uncanny!"

"Money in the bank, Eddie."

There were only ten starters in the race, and The Stinger looked fit and well.

Leading him around the enclosure was a trim, sharp-looking young man wearing jeans with a wide leather belt, tan boots, a blue and white checked shirt, and a fawn Akubra hat. Eddie assumed it was the horse's owner, Cooper McCoy, hardly the outback cowboy Eddie had been expecting.

Cooper looked like a city dude who'd gone bush for a sea change and some fresh air. Eddie felt a jolt. It was clear he wouldn't be discussing a horse sale with a lazy-talking country bloke.

Frank drew Eddie's attention to another surprise. "There's something about The Stinger I missed when I saw him at the Dalby picnics."

Eddie shot him a questioning look.

"Check out his front fetlocks—see the distinctive white patches, like little powder puffs? They're the only difference between him and Thunderdome."

"No problem," said Eddie. "Horses often race with bandaged fetlocks, a perfect cover-up."

In the saddling enclosure, the jockeys arrived with their saddles to get last-minute riding instructions. The Stinger's jockey, the well-regarded Splinter Hanson, a spiffy young Brisbane rider flown in by Cooper McCoy especially for the ride, listened intently to Cooper's brief:

"He's in good nick, he's pretty well-drawn, and he'll pack on early speed if you let him go. If there's a hiccup, you'll hit it at the turn into the straight. He's inclined to drop his bundle a bit, so ride him hard."

"He sure looks a picture," said Splinter, "I'll be giving him the works and that's a promise. If looks were a guide to form, he'd crap this race in!"

In the Committee Room, Kitty McCoy stole a quick look at her wristwatch. "Oh my," she said to Lorrie, rising from her seat as she spoke. "Race three is about to start, and my grandson has a horse running."

"I'll keep you company," said Lorrie, anxious to see the horse in question.

"We'll be judging as soon as the race is over," warned Jewel.

Lorrie followed Kitty out of the Committee Room and up the stairs to the main grandstand. When she saw The Stinger, the possibility of a successful caper shot up a point. Kitty, waiting for the race to start crossed her fingers and said a prayer, hoping like mad for a good result. It didn't happen.

The Stinger pulled his familiar trick. He jumped well, turned on some early speed and died on his run to finish second last. Lorrie noted Kitty's disappointment and didn't know what to say.

But the disappointment went quickly undercover, and they both returned to the Committee Room to choose the winners in the five categories of 'Fashions on the Field.' The choices weren't hard, but at the host podium, Jewel milked the winning announcements for all the drama she could drum up in a bid to give everything the glitter of a red-carpet ride in Hollywood.

Kitty was amused. "It's only a country race day," she said to Lorrie, "it's really not Royal Ascot."

"Tell everyone bigger is better and they'll believe it," said Lorrie.

After the race, there was jubilation in the Members Stand for Frank and Eddie, who said, "Cooper McCoy would be crazy not to unload his horse after that dud run. It was only a short sprint and he packed up at the turn. He's got no stamina at all. If we make a half-decent offer, he's got to take it."

"Let's go find him," said Frank.

Splinter Hanson had no explanations for The Stinger's bad run. "I had him well-placed at the turn," he told Cooper, 'but it was just like you said. He wouldn't run on. Bloody funny too, mate. It was like he deliberately put the brakes on. One minute he's running like a beauty, next minute he's throwing out the anchors; never had a horse do that before. Sorry, Cooper, I did my best, honest."

"I didn't expect you to get off and carry him, but I'd like to ask a favour."

"Let's have it."

"I'd prefer to keep details of my horse's form from becoming public property."

Splinter spoke up, "I don't discuss my rides with anyone. I never have. I never will. Have I made my point?"

"Perfectly."

End of conversation.

FRANK AND EDDIE FOUND Cooper at the horse stalls preparing The Stinger for the trip back to the McCoy Stud. Frank stated his case. Cooper was not interested to the point of mild hostility.

"The Stinger is my mate, and a bloke does not sell his mate. Not in Roma."

Frank was not put off; he knew he couldn't afford to be. The horse was the key player in the caper, and it could not go ahead without him.

Cooper's question was blunt. "Why do you want him?'

Frank was on the spot. "I think he could have potential."

"How come?" asked Cooper. "He didn't show any today."

Frank was on it. "He showed plenty until he hit the turn."

Cooper was caught off guard. "Yes, well, he's inclined to do that."

Frank grabbed the advantage. "If you say the horse is your mate, why wouldn't you want him to realise any potential he might have?"

Cooper hesitated. "Look, I can't make a decision like this off the top of my head. If you two guys are still here tomorrow, come out to the Stud. We're having a bit of a get-together with some of the racing people, and maybe we can talk it over."

Frank held his ground. "We'd love to be there."

"Do you have transport?"

"We drove up from Brisbane."

"Okay, it's an easy drive."

Cooper gave instructions on how to get to the McCoy Stud and wrote the phone number down. "Call on your mobile if you get lost but you won't. See you about twelve-thirty."

"We'll be there," said Frank, "so think the offer over."

"Goes without saying." Cooper led his horse away.

Frank faced Eddie. "We could have a problem."

"What do we do?"

Frank bit his lip. "Shit! If we don't have the horse, we don't have a caper, and if we don't have a caper, we've booted the best damn con I've ever seen, right in the rear end."

Eddie looked glum.

While Cooper was handing out a homestead invitation to Frank and Eddie, Kitty was handing one to Lorrie and Jewel.

Jewel looked bright. "You're entertaining racing people?"

"Fun ones; friends of my grandson, mostly. I think you'll like them, and you can't go back to Brisbane without sampling some country hospitality, to say nothing of our country food."

"We'll be there with bells on," said Jewel.

Lorrie gave Kitty a look. "You know I'm not in Roma alone,"

"I've noted that," said Kitty. "Your father and his friend are included."

One of the committee ladies diverted Kitty's attention, and Jewel turned to Lorrie. "Have you met the lady's grandson?"

"I have not."

"Fasten your seat belt. If his stud friends look anything like Cooper McCoy, I'm putting Roma on the must-visit list!"

Lorrie was not out of her mind with interest.

Jewel gave her thigh a friendly pat. "I wonder what a spunk bucket like Cooper does for kicks out here?"

Lorrie wasn't listening.

Uninvited dark clouds not unnoticed by club officials crept over the racetrack during the afternoon and a hasty decision was made to reschedule the Roma Cup forty minutes earlier so it wouldn't have to be run in the rain. It simply meant switching one of the earlier races, but the punters didn't care.

No more than four minutes after the Cup had been run and won, a downpour descended on the track, sending punters scooting for bars in the marquees, and the under-cover licensed enclosure where the rock bands were tuning up for their concert.

The last race was washed out, a fate that would have overtaken the Roma Cup, but there was no general exodus. The rain was ignored. Wet or dry, this was Roma's big day!

IN THE DINING ROOM of the town's historical School of Arts Hotel that evening, the conversation at the Edwards table was focused on Cooper McCoy's negative attitude to the sale of his racehorse mate.

"If he won't sell, maybe he'll accept a leasing proposal," said Frank.

"Maybe worth a try," said Eddie, grabbing at straws.

Frank's mind was on the job. "We could offer to take over the training expenses."

"Why would we want to do that?" asked Lorrie.

"Means to an end," said Frank.

"Big deal," said Lorrie. "How are you going to explain to Cooper McCoy that we want to invest money in a horse that has nothing going for it? If Cooper doesn't figure that out, his grandmother will."

"We can't just give up," said Frank.

Lorrie wasn't happy. "Then we'd better come up with something with stronger legs than a flimsy offer that sounds like sending good money after bad. Only a dummy would buy that."

"Too true," said Eddie.

Silence—until Frank said, "Okay, then what do we do?"

Out of the blue, Eddie slipped into a reverie. "Charlie McCoy was one of the heroes of the sport, a dead set gentleman. He knew what he was about and knew how to operate, clean as a whistle and that's how he's remembered."

Frank was perplexed. "So how is that relevant?"

"We should give it some thought."

"Not tonight, Dad," said Lorrie. "Let's go out to the McCoy's tomorrow. Maybe Cooper will have changed his mind."

The dinner dessert was homemade apple pie with grated nutmeg on top, served with proper egg custard made in a double saucepan, and it was almost too good to be true.

AFTER DINNER, EDDIE SAT in his room thinking. If he'd been a smoker, he would have puffed his way through half a packet of cigarettes. The afternoon storm had left a clean fresh smell in the air and the far away revelry of the racetrack rock concert came in faint bursts on the night breeze. Otherwise, there was nothing to intrude on his thinking. His mind was clear, and he was alone with his thoughts. He had been stoked by the sneaky Saturday Night Fever win, and he wanted the thrill of a rigged bet like that again. He challenged his mind to tell him how he could get it. When he woke up the next morning he was presented with the answer. Unwarranted discussion had killed many a great idea, so he kept his answer to himself.

LORRIE HAD TO HAND it to Jewel Blanch.

When the femme fatale flounced into the foyer of the School of Arts Hotel that Sunday morning, all dressed and ready to be driven to the McCoy soiree, she was something to behold. Struggling to get a handle on Jewel's look, Lorrie decided it was best described as big city Ellie-Mae Clampett—sassy short-skirted gingham, a cheeky off the shoulder cotton blouse and a pretty ponytail tied up with ribbons. Jewel looked so un-Jewel that Lorrie, who had settled for jeans and powder blue singlet top, remarked on it.

"Darling," gushed Jewel, "I didn't want to frighten the boys by appearing too-too Rodeo Drive. I'm sort of meeting them on their home territory, all fresh and innocent and appetising."

Lorrie gave her a second look. "Innocent and appetising?"

"As close as I can get, honey. How was I to know we'd be meeting the local race-going fraternity at a homestead barbecue?"

Frank, waiting in the driver's seat of the rented white Falcon appeared a tad detached; Eddie, seated beside him was relaxed and chirpy. The drive into the Roma countryside was short and interesting. After turning off the main road into a private driveway flanked by big black grass trees, the white veranda walls of the McCoy Stud appeared through the tall gums and green underbrush. The big homestead looked comfortable and welcoming; low gable roofs, wide verandas, generous windows and French lights.

To the right of the homestead sat the handsome training track with its white railings and green-green inner field skirted by tall red gum trees.

Closer to the house, shaded by a nest of tall waving pepperina trees was a barbecue court set with outdoor tables and chairs. At them, and around them were twenty or thirty people in separate groups.

Frank parked the Falcon beside the other cars lined up close to the barbecue court and opened the door for Jewel, who joined him. They walked together in the direction of the groups of people.

Eddie alighted, closed his door, opened Lorrie's door, and leaned toward her. In a quiet voice, he said, "I want you to agree with everything I say today. Understand? Everything I say." He was insistent.

Lorrie, slightly bewildered, said, "Okay, Dad, if that's what you want."

The guests were a friendly gathering of older couples, vivacious girls and young men there to enjoy the McCoy hospitality. Kitty and Alice had prepared bowls of fresh salads, cheeses, home-baked bread rolls, slabs of fresh pineapple and watermelon, cherries and peaches, sponge cakes and apple pies. Pork chops, rump steak, and sausages sizzled on the barbecue. One of the men was dispensing beer and wine at an outdoor bar.

Mitchell cockatoos hopped about in the gum trees and pecked at the berries in the pepperina trees. A country musician plucked his guitar; warbling country hits like "Wolverton Mountain" and "Gentle on My Mind."

Kitty claimed Lorrie and introduced her to Alice, then to Cooper, who had greeted Frank and Eddie. Cooper flashed a smile and shook Lorrie's hand. Realising the caper now hinged on his decision, Lorrie unconsciously held his hand a little longer.

He registered the lingering hand and responded, keeping contact with a firmer hold. He was inches taller than she was, and when she looked up, she caught the interested expression in his deep blue eyes. She thought how wise they looked. His light brown hair was short and straight, and his face, without being overly handsome, was arresting and masculine. Without thinking too much about it, Lorrie instantly felt that Cooper knew his way around a bedroom.

Holding his eyes, she said, "Kitty's told me about you."

"What has she told you?"

"That you love your horse."

"I'd miss him if he went anywhere."

Lorrie caught his meaning. "I'm sure you would." She felt awkward for a second, knowing she was there primarily to take his horse away.

Cooper released her hand and said, "Do you know about horses?"

"I've been helping my father train them for six years."

His gaze sharpened. "I didn't know that."

"So, the answer is yes, I know about horses."

Kitty excused herself. "Cooper, be a love and give Alice a hand at the barbecue. We're ready to eat."

Elsewhere, Jewel was in her element upstaging the pretty girls and flirting with the local lads. People began helping themselves to the buffet; carrying plates to tables under the trees, and drinking. The talk was laced with racetrack anecdotes, but it was all good-natured and charming, so much so that the hours melted.

By four-thirty, the food was history and the party had mellowed.

Frank approached Cooper and made his move. "Did you get a chance to think about our proposition?"

Cooper nodded. "I've discussed it with my grandmother."

"Is there somewhere we can talk?"

"Let's go inside. I'll get Kitty."

They sat at a round table near one of the big windows.

Cooper spoke first. "My grandmother and I don't understand why you'd be interested in buying The Stinger. He has no form, and he has not responded to training, so why would anyone want to bother with him?"

Frank went for optimism. "He wouldn't be the first apparent no-hoper to come good."

Kitty wasn't exactly buying. "My grandson has developed an attachment to his horse. He really doesn't want to sell."

Finally, Eddie spoke up. "He doesn't have to sell, Mrs McCoy."

Kitty's reply was dubious. "I thought that was what you wanted."

"Initially, yes," said Eddie, "but there could be an alternative."

Everyone was silent, and Eddie launched his bid. "I knew Charlie McCoy, I had tremendous respect for him. My training methods are based on his. I had conversations with him on racetracks, I took his advice and I was one of the sorriest people when he died. I was saddened when the McCoy Stud closed down and even sadder when Charlie's horses went to auction."

Frank and Lorrie exchanged glances.

Kitty explained, "At the time there was no alternative, Mr Edwards."

Eddie went on, "That I realise, but when I heard that Charlie's grandson had a horse that wasn't training well, I decided to put my hand up to do what I could to help."

Eddie looked directly at Kitty. "I'm putting my hand up for old time's sake, Mrs McCoy. I want to repay my debt to your husband. That may sound like a little thing, but it's not little to me."

The mood changed dramatically and there was a moment of silence.

Cooper broke it. "Mr Edwards, if you don't want to buy The Stinger, then what do you want?"

Eddie made his run to the post. "I'd like to see what my daughter can do with him. She's been my assistant for over six years. She knows her game, and I'd like to make my stable jockey Cassie Morgan available as well. I'll pick up all the expenses in return for a percentage of any money your horse wins in races. I'll also pay the girls' accommodation and expenses in Roma."

More silence. Nobody said a thing for fully twenty seconds.

Eddie didn't look at Frank or Lorrie, but he knew they were winded.

Correct. Frank was convinced he'd been watching a performance of the courtroom scene in a hoary old Perry Mason TV show.

Kitty was overwhelmed. "I don't know what to say, Mr Edwards."

She looked at Cooper. "Well?"

Cooper was staring at Eddie. "That's a very generous offer, Mr Edwards."

Eddie closed in fast. "Are you accepting it?"

"It depends. How long would all this take?"

Eddie was ready. "Let's say three or four months. That should give Lorrie enough time to get your horse ready for a race."

Cooper looked at Kitty, who said, "I'm all for it."

Another omen, thought Kitty. *The Stinger was getting his chance to come good, and she couldn't be happier.*

No argument. Eddie had turned the tricky situation around. Lorrie listened to his pitch as though she were hearing someone she'd never met. It all sounded as though he'd rehearsed it for hours, but the McCoys weren't thinking that.

Lorrie now knew what Eddie meant when he'd spoken to her as she was getting out of the car. In the discussion that followed, there were minor changes. Kitty wouldn't hear of Lorrie and Cassie renting digs in Roma when there was plenty of space at the homestead. They'd not only be accommodated in comfort, they'd be fed on Alice's 'proper' home-cooked food; their washing and ironing would be taken care of, and they'd have the run of the place—a genuine five-star offer. All Kitty wanted was to know when it was all going to start happening.

Eddie announced that it would take a week to get everything in place and to organise Cassie's roster. There was one final cautious word from him.

"I think it would be wise to keep our little exercise as low-key as possible. We don't want the sporting media latching on to the McCoy name and blowing anything up. We're not ready for that; we don't want media hype getting in the way, not until we're sure we've got a star in the making."

A star in the making? Frank's eyes were saucers, but Eddie had nailed it. The deal was done—a gentleman's agreement? Not likely.

Cooper insisted on a legal partnership and had a contact lawyer who could take care of same, and pronto! The conference ended, and everyone was happy.

JEWEL KNOCKED ON THE window and beckoned Lorrie to the door.

"I won't need a lift back to the hotel," she said, "I'm having too much fun and I can organise it later."

"Have a great time, honey."

"I'm out on an early flight in the morning. Will Frank be able to take me to the airport?"

"Of course, we're not planning to start the drive to Brisbane until mid-morning."

"Fantastic. See you at breakfast."

Kitty and Cooper walked their guests to the Falcon. Goodbyes, handshakes and smiles did the rounds.

Frank started the motor and headed for the main road. With the McCoy Stud retreating into the distance he turned to Eddie. "Where in hell did your spiel come from? Why didn't you say you knew Charlie McCoy?"

"I didn't know him."

"You made all that stuff up?" asked Frank.

"Last night."

"You old dog," said Frank, full of admiration.

"Okay for both of you," chimed Lorrie, "I'm the patsy in Roma."

That's what she said, but she doubted she meant it. She liked Kitty McCoy, and she liked the thought of living for four months in a big comfortable homestead in the west as a play-trainer.

Frank drove in silence to the School of Arts Hotel. By the time he parked the Falcon, he had the bare bones of a plan sketched out in his mind.

It was November now. Training could be underway by the end of the month. It could run through December, with time off for Christmas and New Year. Back on the job in January. Training would continue through February. The Stinger would need a run or two on out-of-town tracks, and the caper would be in the bag!

Best time to nail it? March, in the lead-up to the Brisbane Winter Racing Carnival. The industry would be racehorse happy. Southern trainers and owners would be showing off in the northern sunshine. Sportswriters, racetrack bullshit, predictions and in-depth articles about winning form. The perfect smokescreen! Who would notice a long-priced outsider galloping away with a minor event on a ho-hum race day? Nobody but us chickens! Made-to-order!

All's well that's planned well, with apologies to The Bard. Dinner in the School of Arts Hotel that evening was celebration-station. With the last piece of the jigsaw puzzle in place, Operation Stinger was Go! Finally!

12

THE SUN GOES DOWN IN ROMA, AND BILL HARRIS'S SPA GETS A WORKOUT

As THE SHORT SUMMER twilight began to fall over the McCoy Homestead, Cooper sat with two friends, Bill Harris and Sophie-Rose Hadley, all three tuned in to Jewel Blanch, who was sitting with them, riveting everyone's attention. Bill, a bright-eyed young eager beaver of twenty-six, owned and ran the New Millennium Sound Shop in Roma's Main Street. Sophie-Rose, twenty-three, was the daughter of one of the town's A-List families.

Lincoln Hadley and his wife, Georgina, an ex-big-city photographic model, lived in one of Roma's grand houses and played in the jet-setter lane. Sophie-Rose had studied something meaningful at Toowoomba's University of Southern Queensland. Currently, she was more interested in studying Cooper McCoy, who'd sent Roma's feminine temperatures soaring as soon as he took residence in the McCoy homestead.

It had been a typical November afternoon in the west—warm and humid. Bill Harris, with his eyes continually flitting over Jewel's form, made this deliberately casual suggestion:

"Folks. I've just installed a fancy spa on the deck of my cosy cottage. It's open for inspection if anyone's interested."

Jewel led the positive response, and the spa inspection was on.

Bill's cosy cottage was no cosy cottage. He'd done well flogging chart-topping CDs, popular DVDs, all kinds of musical instruments and top-of-the-range audio-visual equipment. His slick residence was the mark of his success. Jewel was chuffed to discover that Bill had vacated the family home to live alone—"So I can concentrate on keeping my business up to speed."

The deck spa was roomy and comfortable, and it sported several bubble speeds. The sun was drifting away on the horizon when he said, "It's extra private here, guys, almost dark. Who'd see if we all kinda peeled off."

Jewel was all for it. "Is there somewhere I can pin up my hair?"

"Me too," smiled Sophie-Rose.

"Bathroom and bedroom; first door on the right."

The girls hit an exit.

"Let's get set," said Bill. "Lose everything."

Cooper fell in with the plan. "If that's the code, I'm on it."

They lost everything in less than a minute and stepped into the spa.

"Welcome to Roma," he said, "there's a lot to like about clean country air."

"Let me tell you, Bill, the only things I miss about Melbourne are the laid-on playmates."

Bill grinned. "Quantity or quality?"

"Quality if you're choosy, quantity if you're not."

Bill hedged. "Can't you have both?"

"Better to be choosy."

"Like you?"

Cooper winked. "Works for me."

"Always?"

Cooper looked coy. "Mostly."

Jewel and Blanch returned to the spa deck with everything bathed in the dying rays of the sun. Titillating.

They stepped into the spa. Bill set the bubble speed on low and the preliminaries took off.

The first player to take things further was Sophie-Rose, who said, "I think I'm suffering from bubble overkill."

"Towels on the day bed over there, kiddo," said Bill, "if you want to let your hair down you know where the bedroom is."

Cooper took the cue, helped her towel off and led the way to the bedroom.

With Cooper and Sophie-Rose out of the way, Jewel was anxious to proceed with what she had in mind. She had never had a country stud, and she was keen to find out if what she'd heard about them was true.

"Let's quit the tub, Bill. I want to be high and dry if that's okay."

Bill cleared the spa in a flash, unfolded a couple of towels, rubbed them both dry, flicked the towels away, and flipped the on-switch of the soft amber spotlight that illuminated the deck. The sight of Jewel's delicious golden breasts sent his eyes spinning.

She closed in, cruising her nipples across his chest, and with slow disciplined moves, she slipped down to trap his love-works between her breasts. Looking up, she gently kissed and tongued his manly shaft.

"Yeah, baby!" said Bill. "This is as wild as it gets!"

"Stay cool, stud," cooed Jewel, "it's the start of something big."

Coiled around him like a carpet snake, she continued to take charge of every inch of him. His body was a trembling mass of muscle and skin and his brain, drugged by pleasure, lost control. He lifted her up into his arms and smothered her with kisses. His voice was warm brandy. "I've got to have you, kitten. My head is set to self-destruct . . . I just gotta do it, babe."

"So, what's stopping you?" The perfect question.

He yanked the mattress off the day bed, covered it with a towel and watched Jewel stretch out. Scrambling in the pocket of his jeans he pulled out a three-pack and bit the top off one of the thin raincoats. His hands were shaking so much he dropped it.

Jewel retrieved it, looked up at him and said, "Let me, butterfingers."

As soon as he was armed and ready. Jewel lay back, and she was all his.

If the ride had taken place on a racetrack it would have broken a few records. Undaunted and totally rapt, Jewel urged him on.

ON THE GENEROUS DOUBLE-BED in Bill's designer bedroom, Cooper's lust-works, filled with masculine finesse, were more refined. He held Sophie-Rose crushed in his arms, while his tooled buns rose and fell in perfect rhythm.

Cooper was an old-school lover with a raft of big city experience.

He was a late-blooming eighteen when his first encounter with a high-school debutante in the back seat of his dad's 4WD awakened him.

Since then, he'd been active, virile and discreet, until one serious love affair with an older married woman in Melbourne crushed him. He survived but the bloom had left him. Unlike his mate, Bill Harris, who never said no when the flag went up, Cooper was much more particular. He liked Sophie-Rose. She was totally feminine, she approved of him, and she liked his caring approach. Cooper was a gentleman, both in out of bed, and Sophie's family thought that as a suitor for their lovely young daughter, he was 'just right.'

When he and Sophie were done, he snapped on the bed light, checked his watch and said, "It's past ten o'clock. I'd better get you home."

He walked back to the spa deck to retrieve his clothes, and in the soft gold light, he saw Jewel dozing on the day bed. Bill was back in the spa, lazily enjoying the bubbles. He looked up at Cooper and said, "You're not leaving."

"Sophie's witching hour, Bill."

"If you're all finished, shouldn't you put something on?"

"Now that you mention it."

"Did you have a good time?"

Cooper gave him the thumbs up. "I'll sleep well tonight, mate."

"I'm just chilling, so is the lovely Jewel. When she's ready, we're gonna make some more music."

"Happy camping, Bill."

EARLY THE NEXT MORNING, as Lorrie was heading for breakfast in the hotel dining room, Jewel, looking as bouncy as a spring lamb, came skipping down the stairs. "Darling," breathed the fashion princess. "Tell Frank not to bother driving me to the airport. Bill's taking me. He's outside now, with my travel bag and hatbox in his boot, all done!"

Lorrie blinked. "Bill?"

Jewel beamed. "Bill Harris—you met him yesterday."

"Did I?"

"The spiffy one who looks like a Magic Mike recruit."

"I didn't notice."

Jewel lowered her voice register. "I did, darling, and isn't your news wonderful?"

"News?"

"Your training exercise at the McCoy Stud. Bill told me about it over coffee this morning."

"Bill told you?"

"He's Cooper's best friend."

"Is that all he said?"

"Not quite. Cooper's over the moon about you and his horse. Lucky you."

Lorrie was caught off guard. "It's strictly business, Jewel."

Jewel let out a cheeky girlie giggle. "Of course, but oh my, that pelvis of Cooper's looks like a real pleasure pump!"

"A pleasure pump?"

"Take it for a test drive and see for yourself."

With a girlie wave, Jewel said goodbye. "See you in the big city." She was out the door and Lorrie was left in a quandary. Jewel knew something she wasn't really meant to know. Did it matter? Hardly. What did Jewel care about some little training exercise in the country? She was much more interested in Cooper's pleasure pump! Pleasure pump? Only someone with a pelvis fixation could think up a tag like that! Lorrie smiled, shook her head, shrugged, and thought about breakfast instead.

AT THE MCCOY STUD, Kitty and Alice spent the next few days preparing for house guests. Two adjoining bedrooms in the west wing of the homestead were opened up and aired. French lights leading onto the wide veranda were polished to a squeaky shine. Linen cupboards were raided. Egyptian cotton sheets and pillowcases were awakened from a deep sleep. Bedspreads were shaken and hung in the sun. Floors were polished, rugs were beaten, and the connecting bathroom between the two rooms was scrubbed and dressed with towels and face washers. Herbal soaps were laid out on the marble benchtops of washstands. There hadn't been so much activity since Cooper's arrival from Melbourne, and the two homestead ladies were sky high on domestic bliss.

Kitty was taking the latest development in The Stinger episode as yet another positive sign from the outer limits. She didn't tell anyone. She held the feelings close and painted pretty mind pictures of what she felt would soon be coming true.

At the McCoy Stud, omens ruled.

13

MICHAEL J FLYNN ON THE MOVE

MICHAEL J FLYNN AND the Melbourne Cup were best friends.

It was the most important Tuesday on his calendar; the first Tuesday in November every year; one of the days that boosted his life and warmed his senses. Mickey Flynn loved the Melbourne Cup.

When he was a kid of twelve in the Sydney west, it was the day everything came to life. Mickey's father, who had never amounted to anything was a burnt-out labourer. He drifted from job to job, always found fault with the boss, picked fights with the poor slobs he worked with, and puffed on roll-your-owns while he blasted out his views on what was wrong with the world and everybody in it.

And that was probably why Mickey's mum, Dotti, was a boozer, too. After she'd taken care of her client's washing and ironing chores, she hit the sweet sherry every afternoon at four o'clock, and by seven o'clock she was too out of it to care about anything but the boneheaded current affairs stuff she took as gospel on television.

The Flynns lived in a dumpy house in a dumpy street in a dumpy suburb, and the only excitement that ever came young Mickey's way was when the low-life neighbours staged a domestic in the middle of the night, and the cops arrived. But on Melbourne Cup day it was all different.

Mickey's no-hoper dad glued himself to morning shows on television hoping to pick up tips from the 'experts.' Dotti Flynn prettied up the hat she'd bought at Kmart with the crepe paper flowers she made herself. She dolled up in what she called her 'Sunday frock,' plastered her face with powder and lipstick, and took off for the ladies' lounge at the local watering hole to party on sparkling 'Passion Pop.' Meanwhile, Mr Flynn was the loudest form tipster in the public bar.

Mickey's day hit overdrive when he and his boofheaded mates sat on the footpath outside the pub singing "Waltzing Matilda." They held a plastic bucket to catch coins the drinkers threw at them, and often collected enough to pig out at the Pizza Hut and lick up a storm on double scoops from Baskin and Robbins. By nightfall, the neighbours were always too tanked to stage a domestic. Mickey's mum and dad, too thick-headed to do anything else, were bedded down by six o'clock.

That was the green light for Mickey and his mates to watch one of the adult tapes they'd rented from Blockbuster Video with the last of their coin. They re-played the best bits, while they lowered their zippers and did their best to flog up a 'creamer.' Oh yes, When Mickey Flynn was a kid, the Melbourne Cup was bigger than Christmas. It still was. Fond memories rarely die!

MICHAEL J, RESPLENDENT IN Prada, Ferragamo and Piaget, cruised the Flemington VIP pre-Cup parties at the Victorian Spring Racing Carnival with all the élan of a northern Italian nobleman. He either lauded or trashed the catering; depending on who the caterer was. He smooth-lipped the fashionable ladies and made sure the gentlemen knew he was a man of means and influence.

On Victoria Derby Saturday, he was an A-Listed guest in the prestigious marquees that were crammed into the over-the-top Birdcage party enclosure and he favoured those serving Dom or Louis Roederer Cristal.

On Melbourne Cup Tuesday, he watched the running of the big race from a prime position in the Members Stand, shunning the Birdcage on that day for the simple reason that Mickey-speak had pegged it thus: "*Only for wankers, show-offs and fuckwits who don't give a shit about the race.*"

Melbourne Cup day had always been The Greatest Show on Earth for Mickey Flynn, and so it was for Michael J. Flemington Racetrack was where he sported his social credentials and his hard-won position as a superior being in the upper levels of the racing fraternity. There he rubbed shoulders with the international thoroughbred elite; movers, shakers and horse traders from Asia, the Middle East, Europe and the UK, and well-heeled visitors, owners and trainers from the Americas and New Zealand. In such illustrious company, there was a contingent of shrewd operators who lurked in the shadows of the sport; manipulators and fixers, masterminds and strategists, all lured by the smell of big money and ingeniously arranged victories.

They were not always easy to spot, but they were not strangers to Michael J because he was one of them, and he was rated, as they were, on the success of his latest exploits. The phrase, 'you're only as good as your last con,' was the rule by which they all lived.

The Mating Game caper should have been a triumph; a low-profile race on a low-profile race day in a warm and friendly Australian city not noted for its shady sporting happenings. But when the caper crashed, it took some of Michael J's shimmer with it.

The Mating Game failure bit the dust in the lead-up weeks to the Melbourne Cup. Instead of dumping easy cash into the pockets of syndicate investors, with their eyes on events of the Spring Racing Carnival, it had plundered their resources. Michael J felt the chill of their disappointment.

He was not ostracized, neither was he fawned over. His exalted status, like his pride, was wounded, and his vindictive attitude towards Eddie and Frank, perpetrators of the coup that trumped him, ran even deeper.

It became a vendetta. A Blood Lust!

Michael J wanted vengeance and he wanted to be back on his syndicate pedestal. In the eyes of his cold-hearted associates, he was a loser if he allowed Frank and Eddie to get away with what they'd done.

Their downfall was more important than ever. With that in mind, he cancelled his usual post-Cup trip to Hong Kong, and high-tailed it back to Brisbane the day after the big race. His jet landed at nine-ten a.m. The first person he phoned from his high-level suite in the Marriott was Jewel Blanch, who was about to leave town on a fashion assignment. The call was brief but informative. The next person he contacted was Flasher Doyle, who got a full ear-load of urgent Mickey-speak:

"Take your hand off your dick and get your useless arse up to my suite at the Marriott fast. We've got heaps to talk about!"

Flasher did exactly as he was told in the near-record time of thirty minutes. It would have been faster, but the early morning traffic delayed him.

A stony-faced Michael J greeted him. "Jewel Blanch has informed me that Eddie Edwards was at the Roma Cup, and as I understand it, he has acquired an interest in a horse called The Stinger."

Flasher looked blank. "Never heard of it."

"Hardly anyone has," said Michael J, "but according to Miss Jewel Blanch, who was at Roma in person, The

Stinger is little more than a brumby with no form, and nothing whatsoever to warrant anyone's interest."

"You've seen Jewel Blanch?"

"I've had her on the phone. She's due in Sydney on a fashion gig at Randwick and she was too busy to answer detailed questions."

Flasher held his bland look. "What kind of questions?"

"Why Edwards is interested in some broken-down nag in the bush. Do you know why?"

"Haven't got a clue, MJ."

Michael J Flynn took his habitual walk to the wide windows of his suite and looked down at the Brisbane River. He stood motionless for at least a minute, then turned to stare at Flasher.

"Those two dickheads are up to something, and we have to find out what it is."

Flasher was smart enough to know he'd better get serious, so he did his best to ask a pertinent question. "What's Jewel's word on The Stinger?"

"He's owned by a Cooper McCoy. Do you know him?"

Flasher answered, "Charlie McCoy's grandson, he lives with Charlie's widow at the McCoy Stud outside Roma, moved in some time ago."

"Charlie McCoy is the famous Charlie McCoy, right?"

"He's the one."

"Where did this grandson come from?"

"He's an ex-real estate wheeler-dealer from Melbourne."

Michael J hit Flasher with a sharp question. "But currently a wannabe in the racing game, is that it?'

"Could be just a hobby, MJ, I don't think he's serious."

"No?"

"If he wants to be in the game, maybe Edwards is giving him tips or something."

Michael J's tone sharpened. "It's the 'or-something' I'm interested in. There are a lot of maybes here. Maybe this 'or-something' is something like Saturday Night Fever. Maybe Edwards and his shady buddy, Davenport, have something happening. If so, maybe we should find out what that something is."

Flasher agreed instantly. "Yeah. Maybe we should."

Michael fired another question. "The McCoy boy had his horse entered in a race on Roma Cup day, did you know that?

"I didn't."

"Jewel Blanch tells me it ran like a dog. In the saddle was a jockey by the name of Splinter Hanson. Do you know him?"

Flasher nodded. "A good hoop, based in Brisbane."

"McCoy flew him to Roma to ride his horse. Why?"

"I guess he wanted the best hoop he could get."

"What do you know about Splinter Hanson?"

"He's a kinky cowboy, MJ."

"What kind of kinky?"

"He rides his best races with a stiffy."

"I take it you're talking about a below-the-belt stiffy."

"I reckon I am, yeah."

"He obviously didn't have a stiffy when he rode McCoy's horse in Roma. What other kinky stuff does Hanson do?"

"Smokes pot and blows other stiffies."

"That's interesting. Has he ever blown yours?'

"No, MJ, there's always a queue for his services."

Michael laughed. "Maybe he blew Cooper McCoy."

"I'd say not. Cooper McCoy is straight as a ruler."

"Nobody's that straight. Is that all you know about Hanson?"

"That's all I want to know."

"Do you know anyone who'd know more?"

"Why?"

"I'll spell it out. McCoy flew him to Roma for the race. There's a chance Hanson knows him well enough to know things about him, like what's going on with him and Edwards. Think hard, now, is there anyone?"

"I think so."

"Can you get in touch with whoever it is?"

"Sure."

"How about now?"

"Now?"

"Now." It was an order. Michael J indicated the telephone.

Flasher applied himself. He had a friend who booked jockeys regularly. He called his friend and told him what he needed to know. He was on the line for close to two minutes, then he hung up.

Michael was waiting. "Well?"

"My mate says Splinter won't spill anything on his rides. He says it's bad for his professional reputation."

"That's not good enough. I want to know if Splinter Hanson knows anything about this whole suspicious business. I have to know ASAP, and I can see now, that it's all up to me."

Flasher was crestfallen. "How will you manage that?"

"You don't need to know."

"Is that all you want from me, MJ?

"On this occasion, yes. Have a lovely day."

Flasher breathed a silent sigh of relief and high-tailed it out of the suite without looking back, and without another word.

Michael J picked up the phone and made a call.

IN A SMART RIVERSIDE APARTMENT in Hamilton, Brisbane, Mitch Brenner, thirty-two, reckless windsurfer, skydiver and social renegade, attired in his favourite gym-junkie threads and Nike Vapor Max Flyknits, answered his landline, identified Michael J Flynn's cultured voice, and purred out a deeply-masculine welcome:

"Hey there, Mike, what's happening?

"How much do you love me?"

"Give me a minute to strip down and I'll tell you over the phone."

"I'll take a raincheck on that. I need to buy your valuable assistance."

"Same rates?

"With a fifty per cent bonus."

"I'm rock-hard already. Give me a name."

"Splinter Hanson."

"Oh, yeah! Cute. Rides his best races with a boner then shows it off in the jockey's room."

"You're acquainted, then?"

"Gives amazing head."

"When can you connect with him?"

"Is this urgent?"

"Crucial."

"How about tonight?"

"Perfect."

"What do you want to know?"

Michael J explained in detail.

Mitch listened intently, took it all in, then said, "About your raincheck, Mike."

"What about it?"

"How about we call it in when I present the information tonight?"

"Will you still have bullets in the gun after Splinter Hanson?"

"He's chicken feed, Mike."

"Then you're on. Cash on delivery."

"You make me hungry, man, real hungry."

"When can I expect you?"

Mitch paused. "Around ten p.m. Will you be up?"

"Up and rearing."

Mitch purred, "Expect a thunderstorm! Where?"

"Marriott Hotel, room twelve fifty-three."

"Don't have anything on."

SPLINTER HANSON COULD HARDLY believe his luck. Here he was, showing off his valuables in the bedroom of the uber-macho Mitch Brenner, one of his favourite-ever idols. Splinter was more turned on than when he was galloping down the homestretch with a boner. Mitch, the apple of his eye, was lying back in a linen-covered armchair. He was togged in a bulging white jock while he watched Splinter showing off, his gaze firmly attached to the bulge in Mitch's tantalising underwear.

Splinter moved closer to his idol and said, "Can I help you lose the jock, lover?"

"I thought you'd never ask."

Splinter's fingers slipped inside the white waistband of the tight jock, and slowly tugged the carnal cage down. At the right moment, Mitch's generous endowment popped up and stood like a guard at Fort Knox.

Mitch rose, flipped his underwear right off, took Splinter by the hand, led him to the bed and laid him full-length on the white Egyptian cotton sheet. He joined him, held him close, gently fondled him, and murmured, "It excites me to know you mount bluebloods in this condition. Do you ever unload mid-ride?"

"I'd lose my focus. I leave the unloading to later, in the jockey's room."

"I'll bet that causes a stir."

"I was hot to try it in Roma, but the pony didn't perform."

Jackpot! thought Mitch. "You rode in Roma?"

"This horny stud flew me in especially."

"Did you get it on with the stud?'

"Nah! He doesn't play my kinda games."

"That must have been a downer."

"A big one! He's a spunk bucket. Sex on legs! I wanted him. Bad."

"You should have persevered."

"No way! He's in love with his damn pony."

"You mean figuratively."

"I don't know figuratively. I wanted to blow him, and I dipped out."

"Tell me more about Roma."

"I blew a couple of boys in the band, only once each. They were too stoned."

"Anything else?"

"What kind of anything else, Mitch?"

Encouraged by Mitch's lusty manipulations and wicked probing, Splinter spilled details of the entire Roma episode, and after tongue-worshipping Mitch's best features, he said, "Man, I want to show you how I ride a pony."

"Go ahead."

Splinter rose with his legs straddling Mitch's chest, and smoothly lowered his nether region to impale himself. After adjusting his balance, he said, "Ready-set-go, man!"

The ride started evenly, gradually accelerated, then became frantic.

"Oh, baby!" breathed Mitch, mouthing the same old cliché.

"I'm in the homestretch," gasped Splinter.

Whipping his bare flanks with his open hands, he rode to the finish line, assisted by Mitch's expert handwork on his bouncing boner.

Twenty minutes later, Splinter stirred in Mitch's arms and said, "Wanna hit the home stretch again, stud?"

"Love too, baby, but I've got an executive meet scheduled at the Marriott."

"Bugger!"

IT WAS TEN MINUTES past ten when Mitch pressed the door buzzer on room twelve-fifty-three at the Brisbane Marriott.

Michael J Flynn, adorned in a while Versace towelling robe answered the door and said, "You're late."

"I took a shower."

"Good lad. So did I."

Mitch walked into the room. Michael picked up a fat envelope from the table and said, "This is your commission. Tell me what you found out."

Mitch went into detail. Michael listened, smiling all the time, then said, "Check your commission."

Mitch opened the envelope and counted the contents. "You've overpaid me."

"After what you've just told me, it's hardly enough."

"What about the raincheck?"

"The bedroom's through there. Get everything off."

Michael waited a few minutes, then, minus the white Versace robe, he entered the bedroom. Mitch was on the bed with his head on a pillow His clothes were on the floor.

Michael smiled and flexed. "Roll over hotshot; I'm coming through the back door."

"Last time you did that I was light-headed all day."

"I'm so turned on by what you've just told me, you may be light-headed for a week."

"Good. I'll cancel my engagements."

"You're a good lad, Mitch."

"A hungry one too."

"*Bon appetit.*"

AT NINE-THIRTY NEXT morning, Flasher Doyle was seated in Michael J Flynn's suite with his ears set to flap. Michael, unusually bright and chirpy, sat sipping a cup of brewed coffee. "Right!" he said, "here are the duck's guts on Roma. According to Splinter Hanson, every stud's favourite blow boy, The Stinger is a looker in not-bad condition, a bit of early speed, ratshit stamina, won't run on. He's a four-year-old gelding who's never won a race, not temperamental, good breeding, not worth a cracker!"

"The woods are full of them," said Flasher

"McCoy bought him from a Stud owner in Dalby and is keen to train him up. Edwards offered his services on a percentage basis. There's no shortage of funds. Lorrie Edwards is on the case. That's the bit I don't get."

"Lorrie Edwards is Eddie's assistant, MJ."

"That girl trains horses?"

"Word is she knows her onions."

"I see. Can you believe she's training McCoy's no-hoper, not at the Edwards stable in Boondall but at the McCoy Stud in Roma?"

Flasher was stunned. "What?"

"The gospel according to Splinter, and you know what that means, my friend? The McCoy Stud is out of sight, out of mind. Shifty shit in the bush, where no one can see! Edwards has a caper going, Davenport is up to his nuts in it, and whether McCoy knows it or not, he's up to his nuts in it too! The bastards! Well, I've got news for them, they're going to come unstuck!"

Flasher took a risk: "MJ, we're not sure it's a caper. It could be just what it looks like; an amateur playing horse games."

Michael J sneered. "I never take anything at face value. If this is what I think it is, it could be the nail in the coffin for Edwards and Davenport, and whoever else is on the team!"

Flasher was resigned. "So, what do we do?"

"Nothing, not yet!"

"Nothing?"

Michael's chirpy mood hung on. "We could sit here all day dreaming up all sorts of ways to ambush these clowns, but that's not the way I work. Act in haste, regret at leisure. I'll think about it for a day or two. In the meantime, keep your ears open. If you hear anything let me know. I'm staying put until I get my little grey cells revved."

Flasher looked vacant. "Little grey cells?"

"Forget it, we're finished for the moment, but don't leave town."

"I won't, MJ."

Michael J flashed a wide smile. "Good man, and thanks for coming."

Flasher shook hands, opened the door and made his exit.

Michael J walked to the window again and gazed down at the Brisbane River.

He willed his little grey cells to start their motors. He had to be careful, very careful. Careful, wise and tricky—he was good at all three. Outside it was a bright, sunny morning and the waters of the river sparkled up at him. He smiled at his reflection in the broad expanse of glass, and to prove he was still on the case, Mickey Flynn smirked back.

"*Fuck yeah,*" said Mickey, "*I'd hate to be the morons who take me on! It's a loser's world when you're a fuckwit, and only a fuckwit would mess with me! The only chance those Edwards galahs have is to look for a horse-trough full of iced water to sit in, after I've shoved a bucket of hot coals up their chutes!*"

14

THE SAME DAY:
EDDIE'S MIND PLAY TAKES HIM OVER

EDDIE HAD SPENT HOURS in thought since the caper was green-lighted.

Among the things niggling him was the amount of attention given to The Stinger. Thunderdome had to be considered too. He was the superior horse, but he had to be fit enough to win when he stood in for the crucial race. Even though he'd be galloping in inferior company, he couldn't front the race unprepared.

Eddie sat in his study with a notebook and a pencil and wrote his way through the minefield of the caper. Issue number one was locking down the training sessions for the two horses. He made his notes:

> *Lorrie and Cassie: Working the Stinger in Roma. — No problem.*
>
> *Jeff: Working Thunderdome at Boondall with me supervising: Easy. We train him up, keep him fit. He's a form horse. No problem.*
>
> *Big problem: The Stinger won't run on. A badly performed galloper pulling miraculous form reversal could raise awkward questions.*
>
> *Lorrie and Cassie to address The Stinger's lazy habit of dropping out in the last stages of*

a race. Improvement in that area vital. Serious.

He underlined the next paragraph:

<u>The Stinger needs a reasonable performance profile before Thunderdome races under his name.</u>

He checked his notes again to make sure he had the right handle on everything. He added comments:

Run The Stinger on out-of-town tracks — One or two starts. Work him up to a decent showing. Improve his end-race form. He can't look like a no-hoper even on out-of-town tracks. A long-priced winner can't look dodgy! Too risky — Big trouble!

"Bugger," Eddie murmured to himself., "I'm turning into a worrywart, but I've got to get everything ironed and this is the only way I know."

When he was satisfied, he called for an urgent summit conference in his Boondall study with his four partners in the caper. He read his notes out loud and delivered a closing comment:

"If we can't come up with a working plan that addresses the issues I've written down, we may as well pull the plug now and save all our butts from a long holiday in the clink!"

Silence fell.

Eddie's notes were closely examined. All bases covered. Nothing negative anywhere.

He continued, "I reckon the bloody D–Day landing on Normandy didn't get the kind of going-over we're giving this."

"Bet it did," said Jeff. "That's why it didn't come unstuck."

Eddie's eyes swept over his charges. "Let's make doubly sure about who's doing what."

He looked at Lorrie and Cassie. "You girls are on the ground at Roma. You've got the job ahead of you; you're the key to The Stinger's performance profile. Any questions?"

Cassie piped up, "I don't know what kind of training Cooper McCoy's horse has had but it hasn't amounted to much. If Lorrie and I are on the job together, we should be able to get him to look like a racehorse."

Lorrie said, "He's the only horse we're training—he'll get the treatment."

Eddie nodded. "So, you're happy with everything?"

"As good as it gets," said Lorrie.

"Right," said Eddie, addressing Cassie. "You're The Stinger's hoop. You ride him in training, and you're aboard any of his out-of-town starts. Give him enough confidence to trust you in a race. Got it?"

"Same-old-same-old," said Cassie, a tad bored.

Lorrie chimed in. "How much time do we have?"

"Four months outside," said Eddie. "It's mid-November now. Frank initially suggested March for the ring-in race; is that still okay?"

"Has to be," said Frank. "The longer we wait, the bigger the risk." He looked at Lorrie. "All we're asking is for one or two runs for The Stinger on an out-of-town track. Can do?"

"Can do," said Lorrie.

Frank nodded. "Then March is the target."

Jeff aired his opinion. "Cooper McCoy has worked his horse too hard. He's been over-trained. He'll have to be lightened off and brought back."

"Seems that way," said Eddie. "Now let's move on to the ring-in race. Only hiccups in appearance are the powder-puff fetlocks. The Stinger has them. Thunderdome doesn't."

Cassie, still a bit bored, said, "Fetlock bandages on Thunderdome, Eddie. Like we said. It's done all the time; the only difference will be that the bandages won't be covering anything. We've already decided on that."

"Right," said Eddie, eyeballing Cassie. "You'll be aboard Thunderdome on Ring-in Day, but the McCoys have got to believe you're riding The Stinger. They can't ever twig that you're not working their horse for an outing in a Brisbane race."

Cassie stated the obvious. "Lorrie and I are way on top of that, Eddie. Way on top. Thunderdome will be an easy ride for me on the big day, but it wouldn't hurt for Jeff to give him some light work at North Point in the lead-up."

"Set in cement," said Eddie. "Agreed?"

Everyone agreed.

The room was quiet for at least twenty seconds.

Frank took over. "You guys all know your places in the scheme. I'll be looking after the offshore bets in Hong Kong and Singapore and I'll be investing a good percentage of the Saturday Night Fever money. It won't be small change and the odds will be heavy. I have a reliable contact in Singapore, and I'll be flying up ASAP to arrange everything in person. Naturally, the McCoys are in on a percentage of the off-shore betting too."

"Only fair," said Jeff.

"Any more questions?" asked Eddie.

The room was silent again. There were no more questions.

The talkathon ended. The best-laid plans of mice and men . . .

15

THE McCOY STUD: LATE NOVEMBER

KITTY McCOY WAS A breakfast person: Sensational rolled oats sprinkled with grated cinnamon and served with fresh milk and cream, plus Alice's whole grain bread with homemade marmalade and lemon butter, McCoy honey from Roma bees, and eggs from the free-range homestead chooks.

Stoked on one of Kitty's early morning breakfasts, it was possible to cruise for six hours without a battery recharge. Early morning meant six a.m. It took Lorrie and Cassie three days to adjust, but the nights were so dark and quiet that deep sleep came naturally.

Lunch was always one of Alice's fragrant barbecues; dinner, a nutritious beef stew made from rich stock and fresh vegetables. After one week of invigorating mornings, refreshing sleep, and country tucker; the city girls were ready to kick butt.

The day after she arrived at the Stud, Lorrie sat with Kitty, Cooper and Cassie to go over her methods of training as preached by Eddie, via Charlie McCoy.

"You've heard it all before, but here's a reminder; to start the day, fresh oats in his feed box."

"Blue Larner is the boy," said Cooper, "he's one of our casuals."

Lorrie nodded. "Midday; more oats if he's hungry. Your boy Blue airs his bed after the morning feed, cleans it again after his afternoon rest. I walk him for an hour after breakfast. Cassie gives him a morning trot and a full circuit canter. He's sponged down and brushed, hoofs cleaned. Cassie gives him a full circuit of the track at an even canter. No hard running. He's bathed, rubbed down, brushed again to get the blood flowing: He takes a sand bath while we have lunch, then gets a slow walk to cool him down, and he's ready to rest. He's fed again at five o'clock, hoofs packed. His clean fresh bed is waiting. After a week or so we can look at a working gallop. Standard stuff. Any questions?"

"No questions," said Cooper. "You're the boss."

THE FIRST WEEK WENT well, without anyone getting excited about anything.

The program repeated for two weeks, and The Stinger was flashing signs that he loved every minute. Cooper never interfered. Blue Larner was the A-one stable boy, and Alice noted that the farmhands had rarely looked so tidy, well-dressed, and eager to please:

"Those boys have never been so interested in what's going on here," she said, tongue firmly in cheek, "do you think it might be something we girls have said or done?"

"Which girls?" asked Kitty.

Alice gave her a wink. "Where there's life there's hope, love."

Lorrie and Cassie were invited to share the company of the Roma movers and shakers but declined. They knew were not there to flit around like social butterflies or discuss Darwin's *On the Origin of the Species* with the local studs. The days and nights rolled pleasantly on at the McCoy Stud, where the room and board were the best in the west.

At breakfast on the last day of the third week, Lorrie announced that The Stinger was ready to try a harder gallop, the news Kitty and Cooper had been waiting for.

An air of anticipation hung over Alice's bacon and eggs that morning. The Stinger was the centre of attention.

Three excited track-side groupies—Kitty, Alice and Cooper were keen to see him do his stuff. Cassie led him to the training track, and Blue Larner and the boys stopped toiling to watch the show. Cassie dressed for the big ride in spiffy riding gear with her hair tucked away under a trendy blue denim cap topped with a white pom-pom.

"Hey, Cassie," hollered Blue, "if that cap has kids, I want one!"

One momentous occasion was about to drop on the McCoy Stud. A warm day was on the way, but the sun had not begun to heat up when Lorrie hoisted Cassie into the saddle and sent her on her way for a double circuit run.

She trotted The Stinger off, increasing his trot to a canter on the far side of the oval, holding the canter until he'd completed the first circuit. As she passed the spot where Lorrie stood, she broke him into a gallop. Lorrie hit her stopwatch, and all eyes locked on the run. For once the Mitchell cockatoos were quiet, and the sound of hoofbeats rose evenly into the morning air.

Cassie kept up the pace in the backstretch and galloped her mount smoothly into the turn for the home run. She and the object of everyone's attention flashed past Lorrie. She hit her stopwatch and smiled. Cooper was beside her in a second.

"What did he clock?"

Lorrie showed him, and he let it out. "Yes!" It was more like a yelp!

"Damn!" said Cooper. "He's never been near that time before!"

Blue Larner and mates responded with a tonsil chorus.

"Sounds like they just watched the Melbourne Cup," said Alice, giving Kitty a nudge, "looks like the no-hoper isn't a no-hoper after all."

"Early days," said Kitty.

"Have faith," said Alice.

"Don't get too excited," Lorrie told Cooper, "he's not Phar Lap yet."

Cooper was the die-hard groupie. "Phar Lap wasn't always a champ."

When the excitement died down, Lorrie and Cassie talked over the gallop in private. "A good run, could he be ready for his first out-of-town sprint in three or four weeks?"

"Got your eye on anything?" asked Cassie.

Lorrie nodded. "There's a Flinton meeting in late January. What do you think?"

Cassie hit a bright smile. "Flinton? I've always wanted to visit that little track, but their race meetings don't happen all that often, do they?"

"This one's special, and it could be just right."

"Let's sleep on it," said Cassie.

Lorrie frowned. "Sleep on it? Is something wrong?"

"I'm just being cautious."

"Cautious?"

"That's all; cautious."

"Cautious about what?"

"Cautious is cautious. Give me a break."

"Cautious is not on, Cass; we're past that. Flinton looks good to me. Is there any way it's not looking good to you?"

"I guess not. Let's bite the bullet."

AFTER LUNCH, LORRIE PHONED Eddie at Boondall to report the success of The Stinger's latest gallop.

"So soon?" asked Eddie.

"We think our boy is ready to tackle a show-off race at Flinton in late January. I think the run will do him good. What's your word?"

Eddie didn't answer right away. Flinton was a deep country racetrack near Goondiwindi, a country town south-east of Roma. The track had a colourful history, and it was one of the brightest balloons on the Queensland Picnic Race scene, even though its meetings weren't frequent. But when they happened, the vibe was pure Australian outback, and the party people went ape.

Better still, Eddie knew that Flinton was way off the radar for the racing industry mainstream. If The Stinger ran well there, his confidence would get a boost, and nobody would take much notice.

Eddie took the punt. "Flinton it is. Let's lock it in."

"Will do."

Eddie was wound up. "I'm thinking about a Brisbane warm-up race for Thunderdome at Kings Park in Brisbane on the Saturday of the big Magic Millions race on the Gold Coast in early January. It's the only run he'll have."

"What about the Ring-in Race? Any decision, yet"

"There's a suitable event at Kings Park on the first Saturday in March. The prize money's not bad, so it's likely to attract a decent field. More starters, better odds."

"The timing is perfect, Dad."

"My thinking too. You say The Stinger is shaping up, so why wait?

"Come on, Dad. Is it on or not?"

"Are you and Cassie okay with everything?"

"A-okay. It's time to word Frank up. He'll need to be looking at organising the offshore bets in Singapore."

"I'll let him know today."

"What about Jeff?"

"He always fits in; I'll word him up too."

Lorries sounded anxious. "Then the first Saturday in March is D–Day?"

"Unless there's an earthquake."

Lorrie felt a rush. "I'll give Cassie the news."

"Point of no return, baby!"

"We're with you, Dad, win or lose."

Eddie knew it, for sure. Win or lose, his world would never be the same.

16

THE FOLLOWING WEEK:
FRANK DOES SINGAPORE

FRANK'S BETTING SYNDICATE FRIEND in Singapore worked as a casual barman in Raffles Hotel. He said it gave him the perfect cover. The name he used in Singapore was Anthony James Williams, the name he was given when he was born in Broken Hill, Australia thirty-nine years earlier. As Tony James, he'd had an up and down career as an actor in several television dramas shot in Melbourne and Sydney. He claimed he got out of acting because he couldn't stand the company of other actors. Whatever, Anthony was never Anthony to his close friends, and he was never addressed as Tony. He was simply 'Loveboat' a name he earned as a horny teen who boned up on cue every time he saw anything in or out of a skirt.

His first wife divorced him when he quit acting because she didn't want to stay married to 'some has-been.' His current squeeze was a beauteous Thai lady who had borne him two children, and he lived in bliss with her and their two offspring in a handsome white shuttered high-rise unit in Singapore.

He also owned an apartment in Melbourne, a house in Palm Cove in far North Queensland, and a villa in the south of France. Loveboat was not small change!

A friend got him into the syndicate game when he was appearing on stage as a fancy-pants country squire in a steamy mystery play in Kuala Lumpur. He was chosen for the job because the mastermind of the con wanted someone who could impersonate an English gentleman. Loveboat pulled off a sterling performance that netted him more tax-free money than he earned as an actor in a year, and it launched a lucrative career as a player of many parts.

When an operator wanted a showman who could impersonate a titled lord, a French aristocrat, a cockney layabout, a Manhattan millionaire, an Aussie bullshit artist, or Rhett Butler, Loveboat filled the bill. His wardrobe was vast; his make-up skills were extraordinary. In Loveboat's make-believe world, seeing and hearing were in a constant state of change.

Frank had known him for five years, ever since they pulled off a syndicate job together in Hong Kong. Because they were both free-wheeling Aussies, they understood each other. They had since become firm friends.

Frank took a stool at the famous Long Bar in Raffles Hotel, ordered a gin sling and waited for his friend to notice he was there. It took the ever-alert Loveboat no longer than three minutes to make his approach. It was brief.

"Tell me, sir, what can I get you that you haven't already got?"

"A drink in room three-twenty-eight," said Frank.

"Give me thirty minutes."

"HOW THE FUCK ARE you?" asked Loveboat as soon as Frank opened the door of room three-twenty-eight, thirty-five minutes later.

Frank's reply was to the point. "I'm about to be a whole lot richer."

"Love it, cobber. What's the job?"

Frank told him. Loveboat whistled. "A ring-in caper! Why didn't you pick something dangerous?"

Frank detailed the caper from 'go to whoa' and tied it all up with digital images of Thunderdome and The Stinger on his laptop.

"Well now," said Loveboat. "Blueblood lookalikes; and in Brisbane too. Nice innocent town; sunshine, lollipops, pretty ladies and frangipani trees. What odds on the horse?"

"Double figures."

"Give me the first digit."

"Three, maybe four."

Loveboat whistled again; louder this time.

"Glad you're impressed," said Frank. "Do you know anyone who can take those odds?"

"You're talking to him, cobber. What's my commission?"

"Seven per cent."

"How much are you investing?"

"Four hundred K, give or take."

"Have you got more?"

"Could have."

"Anything up to a half a mil; any more and I'm not your man. I prefer to stay small and discreet."

"You're my man."

"Awesome. A modest retainer for expenses, say ten K, the rest when the horse romps in. It will romp in, won't it?"

"It will."

"Who's likely to be saying it won't?"

"Michael J Flynn."

Loveboat winced. "That prick! How did you get on the nasty side of him?"

Frank gave out with the details of The Mating Game upset, and Loveboat cracked up. He laughed out loud for a full ten seconds.

"I'm making like it's funny, but it's anything but. Flynn is a mad man; a certified nut case. Watch your step, kiddo, I'm cutting you a warning, old mate. Watch your arse!"

"I always do." Loveboat was suddenly intense. "Flynn is rough company. His connection to a mob of big-money Hong Kong mercenaries, is a poison pill who goes by the name of Adrian Messenger."

"You're kidding!"

"Obviously not his real name, mate. Messenger is a rotten little Asian money mover who stitches up deals and makes sure they stay stitched. He would have been on the stitching end of The Mating Game upset, which means Flynn is not in the syndicate good books right now. If he's got it in his head that you duped him, he can't know that you're up to your knackers in a ring-in caper."

"Flynn knows nothing about it."

"Make sure he stays that way. He has a major issue with you via The Mating Game defeat, so keep on keeping him in the dark."

"I'm in with a tight team."

"It had better stay tight, old buddy. You've got the two four-footed players in place, that's for sure. Their mirror images are a gift from heaven but watch your back. I'd hate to see Flynn's knife buried in it."

"Thanks for the advice."

"Heed it. Just one more question."

"Fire away."

"Are you sure this lookalike horse is a sure thing?"

"Thunderdome is a sure thing in spades, buddy."

"That's all I wanted to know. How long are you in town?"

"I'm flying out tomorrow. I only came up here to see you."

"Love it, mate. Now let's get down to the nitty-gritty. Are you fixed up for entertainment tonight?"

"I haven't thought about it."

"You will when the bed gets turned down. Are you still doing chicks?"

"Yes."

"You never can tell anymore. I can fix you up if you like."

"Love it, mate."

Loveboat laughed again and checked his watch. "Expect a knock on your door at about seven-thirty. Be shaved and showered and ready for an experience. Prime merchandise will be the knocker, as they say."

"Cash or credit card?"

"Forget it, cobber, it's on the house. What kind of cologne do you wear?"

"Karl Lagerfeld."

"Class act! This babe loves quality cologne! You'll get two for one. It'll be a late night."

"How can I thank you?"

"Mate," said Loveboat, suddenly serious, "just tell me your plan is airtight."

Frank took clear aim at Loveboat's eyes and said, "Will the sun rise tomorrow?"

Loveboat's face lit up. "Ah yes! Confidence and meticulous planning works every time. Love it, mate, love it!"

FRANK TOOK AN ADMIRING stroll around the Singapore waterfront, dined on Chicken Parmigiana and a Caesar Salad, drank one glass of Watson Family Chardonnay in

Applecross Restaurant at Raffles, and returned to his room.

He showered, shaved, splashed his face with Karl Lagerfeld EDT, wrapped himself in one of the hotel's bathrobes, and pawed through the hotel's information booklet.

At seven-thirty, his door chimes rang. He opened the door.

A delicate Eurasian woman of twenty-something with dark hair, deep dark eyes and a sweet smile said, "Mr Davenport?"

"Yes?"

"My name is Maelyn. Mr Loveboat Williams sent me."

"Come in, Maelyn."

She entered and set the little bag she was carrying on a table beside the table lamp. She wore a pale turquoise embroidered sheath and fine gold jewellery that shone in the light of the lamp.

"Mr Williams asked me to look after you."

"Mr Williams is a good friend."

"Yes. He said that. He also said you were a gentle man."

"He meant a gentleman."

"No. There's a difference, Mr Davenport."

"Yes, I suppose there is."

Maelyn's eyes smiled. "I know there is."

She looked so lovely and so irresistible that Frank took her in his arms, felt her body welcome his, and softly rested his cheek against hers.

"Your cologne is lovely, Mr Davenport."

"Please. My name is Frank."

"Your cologne pleases me, Frank."

"Everything about you pleases me, Maelyn."

"Do you like women like me?"

"Women like you?"

"Women who like to please men like you."

"Yes, I do."

"Have you known many women?"

"Why do you ask?"

"If you haven't, I'll need to show you what to do."

"You won't have to do that."

"You are a handsome man, Frank."

"Do you think so?"

"Otherwise I wouldn't have said it."

"Are you always so honest, Maelyn?

"I'm honest about wanting to see you without your robe."

"Do you want me to take it off?"

"No. I want to take it off."

"Would you like something to drink first?'

"I'm not here to drink. I'm here to make you happy.'

"You're already doing that."

Maelyn smiled at him and said, "It's nicer to be doing this in the bedroom. Is that possible?"

"This way."

She picked up her bag, followed him, set her bag down again on one of the bedside tables, switched on the bedside lamp and turned off the room's main lights. She circled him slowly, unfastening his robe. She folded it neatly and put it on the bedside table, took a step back and allowed her eyes to journey over his body.

"You are a virile man, Frank. I like what I see."

She opened her bag, took out a black silk glove, slid it onto her hand, smiled and said in a soft voice, "I love Australian men, Frank."

"You do?"

"They respond so well when they lose their clothes."

"I responded because I'm with you."

"We're playing games."

"I know we are."

She stood close and rested her gloved hand on his shoulder. He realised then that the glove was vibrating. She moved it across his chest, down his back and over his buttocks, lingering on the cavern between them. Her face was inches from his, and she whispered in his ear, "Your cologne is exciting me."

"Your glove is exciting me."

"It's supposed to."

Her gloved hand moved lower. His whole body was tingling. His eyes were closed, his head fell back, and he lost himself in sheer delight. When he opened his eyes, he saw that she no longer wore the turquoise sheath.

Maelyn was as naked and as uninhibited as he was. The vibrating glove had served its purpose. She removed it and put it on the bedside table.

He sank to his knees, drugged by the very presence of her, and feasted on her body while she sighed and allowed her fingers to roam through his thick dark hair. He heard her say, "Do you want to pleasure me with your body, Frank?"

"More than anything, Maelyn."

She sank onto the bed and seemed to melt into it. Frank took the cue and joined her.

"You don't have to use anything Frank, it's all right."

His excitement peaked. "Wonderful."

"I'm very careful, that's all you need to know."

"I'll be careful, too."

She gave a little laugh. "You don't have to be."

Frank's performance was one of his best efforts; gentle, loving and tender. He was proud of himself.

HE FELT THE QUIET beat of her heart as she lay curled against him and he kissed her on the lips.

"Do you want to take a shower, Maelyn?"

"No. I want to wake in the morning with the scent of your cologne on my skin."

"Do you have to leave?'

"Only when you say."

MUCH LATER, AT THE door of his room, Maelyn kissed him tenderly and said, "Goodbye, Mr Davenport, I'll remember you with fondness."

"And I'll remember you."

"Then I'm satisfied."

He slept like the proverbial baby. His flight was due to leave at ten a.m. He showered and shaved, and when he splashed Lagerfeld cologne on his face, he grinned at himself in the mirror and said, "I'll sure have trouble forgetting you, Maelyn."

17

THUNDERDOME AT NORTH POINT: CRUCIAL QUESTIONS

EDDIE'S NERVES WERE KEEPING him on edge. Jeff had just ridden Thunderdome at a track trial at North Point, and he was ready to dismount when Eddie walked over, and said, "Bloody great trial. He's a stayer in the making, Boss. I ask him for an effort, and he gives me Richard Branson."

Eddie didn't need to be told. He knew the stallion had to be trained as a distance runner; he had the blood for it. There was another plus. He performed well when he was lightly raced, an indication he'd run well fresh. He hadn't started since he arrived at Boondall, and Eddie felt he needed a Brisbane race before he ran as the ring-in.

The chosen race was on the Saturday of the Magic Millions Carnival on the Gold Coast, a seventy-minute drive south from Brisbane. The Carnival ran through the first week of January; a glittery event on the southern Queensland racing calendar, and it attracted huge crowds.

Eddie asked his question. "Have I picked the right race?"

Jedd frowned. "What's up, Boss? Are you worried about something?"

"We only need one little thing to go wrong, and we're in deep shit."

Jeff dismounted and unsaddled his mount.

"It's like this, Boss. Thunderdome needs a Brisbane run to tone him up for the Ring-in Race. But if the smart arses get him in their sights, it will be almost impossible to race him under another name."

Eddie nodded "And?"

"The race you've picked is on the same day as the main Magic Millions race on the Gold Coast, which means the media and most of the big blokes in racing will be down there, and they won't be in Brisbane where they can get a good look at him."

Eddie grinned. "You're not a dickhead, are you?

"No, Boss. It's never been one of my ambitions."

"We'll only have a token bet on him; nothing more."

"Good thinking," said Jeff. "Like we're just giving him a run."

Eddie nodded. "And for insurance, we'll have Cassie in the saddle."

"What about Bart Anderson?" asked Jeff. "He's got a sharp caller's eye and he'll get a good look at our big boy."

"Bart Anderson is calling for the Magic Millions on the Gold Coast that day. Brisbane's copping his stand-in, a guest caller from Newcastle, who won't be here on Ring-in Day."

"Then that takes care of that," said Jeff. "What about the race stewards?"

Eddie couldn't see a problem. "It's a big field. Twenty-two starters with a swag of good horses. It's early January, two months away from Ring-in Day. Who'll remember one horse who ran in one unimportant race?"

Jeff flashed a wide smile. "Then what's the worry, Boss?'

"You think it's all sounding okay?"

"As good as those Three Tenor blokes singing 'Santa Lucia.' Anything else on your mind?"

"Ring-in Day!"

"What about it?"

"There's a perfect race at Kings Park on the first Saturday in March. The Stinger is eligible, but I want to make sure that when Thunderdome runs in his place, he'll be set to take it out after one Brisbane start."

Jeff spread his arms. "With nothing on his back, he'll kill it!"

Eddie grinned. "I had to ask."

"Bloody hell," said Jeff. "I'm glad we've got that sorted. Now I've got something you'll want to hear."

"Let's have it."

"A good mate of my dad's has bought that old wine vineyard on the way to Nudgee Beach. It's a fifteen-minute drive from the Boondall Stud, the grapevines have gone, and the bloke is using it as an exercise space for riding school horses."

Eddie caught on. "And that's where we hide The Stinger on Ring-in Day?"

"We don't want him at the Boondall stable. He'll have to be well out of the way."

Eddie thought for a moment. "So how do we play it?"

"It's a safe bet that the McCoys will be in Brisbane for the race."

"I'd say so, yes."

"We'll have to be careful about how we switch the horses. When I found out about the vineyard, I've worked something out."

"Go on," said Eddie.

"On the Thursday before the race, I drive our Range Rover to Roma, stay overnight and leave early Friday morning with the Range Rover hooked to Cooper's float with The Stinger on board."

"Right," said Eddie.

Jeff got right down to business.

"I'll arrange for the McCoys to leave Roma for Brisbane an hour or so after me. Cassie and Lorrie can follow a bit later. The McCoys will hit Brisbane at about two p.m., give or take, and book into their hotel. Cooper can look in on his horse at Boondall on Friday afternoon, and again on Saturday morning. As soon as he leaves on Saturday, I'll drive Stinger to the Nudgee vineyard hideout. While I'm doing that, Cassie and Lorrie can bandage Thunderdome's fetlocks, and load him into the stable float. When I get back from the vineyard, I'll drive Thunderdome to Kings Park, and settle him in the horse stalls."

An eager Eddie, said, "So where are the McCoys?"

"They'll be invited to the Committee Room Luncheon with the racetrack bigwigs."

"Who invites them to the Committee Room?

Jeff had it covered. "Kitty McCoy is a Race Club member, and because of good old Charlie, she's a celebrity. If you let the club heavies know she'll be at the track with Charlie's grandson, they're a moral to turn on the hospitality."

Eddie nodded. "I'll attend to that right away."

Jeff had both thumbs-up. "Problem solved. Kitty and Cooper will be getting the VIP treatment in the Committee Room, and they won't be anywhere near the horse stalls to see Thunder standing in for their horse."

"Perfect," said Eddie, "now what about your dad's friend at Nudgee. Is he likely to ask questions?"

"Not on a Saturday, Boss, he's away at Brookfield with the riding school groupies, and he stays there all day."

"There's no one at the vineyard?"

"The caretaker; a nice old guy who loves horses."

Eddie was bowled over. "Looks like you've got all bases covered."

Jeff beamed. "I have to earn my share of the spoils, Boss, so I sat down and figured it all out. Switching the horses had me stumped for a bit. Not anymore. We're looking real good."

"By the way," said Eddie, "I didn't know you liked The Three Tenors."

Jeff winced. "Gimme a break, Boss. I don't like 'em at all, but this wild chick I knew thought they were the Mickey Mouse. What's a bloke to do, start an argument and dip out on the rock 'n' roll?"

18

MICHAEL J FLYNN AND LILLIAN ST CLARE: GLAMOUR PLUS ONE

IF MICHAEL J HAD KEPT a dossier on his vendetta progress it would have been a book of empty pages. He sat in his Point Piper apartment gazing out at Sydney Harbour; same old, same old ferry boats; same old hydrofoils; same old bridge; same old Opera House, and same old North Shore high-rises. He was not in a good mood.

He was even having bad sex. When he should have been giving all his attention to pumping out a hot time in the bedroom, his brain was thinking vendetta. Michael J had never been a bad lay, but he was fast turning into one.

The Magic Millions Carnival in early January was one of his favourite racing gigs of the year, and he always looked forward to it. It was a shining light on his social horizon; another chance to preen and pose for a glittery audience of hedonistic racegoers. It was closing fast, and he was finding it hard to whip up enthusiasm for it. Instead, he was fretting like a kid whose packet of jelly babies had been nicked.

He turned away from the boredom of the harbour; picked up the Magic Millions program that had been mailed to him, and idly turned the pages.

"Same-old-same-old," he said to the empty room.

Couldn't someone think of putting a new spin on it?

It was unlike him to be negative about something he'd always been positive about and he knew it.

He went on absent-mindedly turning the pages of the program. He suddenly stopped. He had turned a page, and one image caught his eye. He recognized the woman in the picture and read the scanned caption:

> *Lillian St Clare, glamorous editor of Ultimate Cool, south-east Asia's leading fashion monthly, will be one of the VIP visitors to the Gold Coast for the Magic Millions.*

He read the first few paragraphs of the copy to learn that Lillian would be reporting on the Magic Millions fashion scene and that she was also 'extremely keen to know more about the Australian fashion industry.'

"Bet your arse she is," he said out loud, "her magazine is starting to score with Down-Under readers, and she's hot on the subscription trail."

When he heard his own voice again, he said, "Damn! I'm going to have to stop talking to an empty room!"

He took another look at Lillian's image; not bad for a forty-five-year-old career girl. She was based in Hong Kong where her magazine was published. He had met her a few times at promotional soirees and cocktail parties.

"Lillian baby," he whispered, "you're such a damn operator. Why aren't you here when I need you?"

He tossed the program on a chair and heard it land. Two minutes later he was taken by an incredible idea that shot like a Roman candle into his brain. For days he'd been challenging his little grey cells to come up with ways to get someone on to the McCoy Stud at Roma to give him a lead on what Lorrie Edwards and Co were doing with Cooper McCoy's brumby.

He'd thought about Jewel Blanch, but he wasn't sure she'd report back without asking awkward questions. Now, in one bright beautiful flash, he had been presented with the answer to his dilemma!

Lillian St Clare could well be his ticket to the McCoy Stud! Yes!

Michael J's little grey cells were re-booting—spark plugs were sparking, motors were revving, a scheme was hatching! It would take work. It would have to be carefully grey-celled and meticulously planned, but out of it would come the answer to the riddle of what Edwards and Davenport were doing with Cooper McCoy's hopeless brumby!

"Yes!" He said the word out loud with a holler and a shout.

Michael J Flynn, after a depressing hiatus in the doldrums, was cranking up!

He made himself a dry martini, walked to his wide window, and thought how fantastic the harbour looked; ferry boats ferrying; hydrofoils racing; the Opera House in all its glory, and in the distance the high-rises of the North Shore, rampant and erect against the cloud-streaked summer sky. Yes! High-rise hard-ons! He had some serious thinking to do, and for the first time in days his mind was on sex; not on his vendetta.

All lusty smiles, he opened his little book of available playmates and picked up the telephone again. Ah yes! Mickey Flynn was back!

"*Fucken ripper!*" said Mickey as he dialled and waited for a couple of his casual acquaintances to answer. "*It's been a while since I rocked and rolled with these two, and I'm in the mood for a walk on both sides of the wild side!*"

CINDY AND DAN CURTIS were a couple of married-to-each-other-entertainers Michael had met on a luxurious cruise through the Panama Canal. Cindy was a cute blonde, with pert Venus de Milo breasts, a Scarlett O'Hara waist, and adorable hips.

She was as inviting as a birthday cake, and as accommodating as Mamie Stover. Dan resembled Ryan Gosling, with thick dark hair. He had discovered his dick at the age of five and he'd been obsessed with it ever since his father told him he could make it grow to the right size if he kept yanking on it.

On-board the luxury liner, Cindy and Dan delivered their Captain and Tennille versions of chart-toppers of the seventies in their nightly concerts and they went over big. They didn't have to think too deeply about anything, which was just as well. Thinking deeply was not one of their best features, but they had other talents, one of which they shared in frequent depraved sexcapades with Michael J in his first-class A-deck suite.

They were now back on call.

While Michael J waited for them to ring his doorbell, he was busy in the kitchen rustling up culinary surprises.

CINDY AND DAN ENTERED Michael's abode, and admired the 'lovely views.'

Michael grinned a wicked grin. "A view is a view. We'll have much better things to look at, so let's get down to the nitty-gritty."

Dan asked his question. "Is this the super-luxury cruise, or budget-priced hanky-panky?"

"I don't do budget-priced anything, dude. I break the bank at Monte Carlo. Your fee is a win at the blackjack table, and I'm the dealer."

"Fucken ripper," said Dan.

"Let's get cracking," said Michael.

One naked-skin fest was at the starting gate.

Michael stretched out, back down, on the flat sofa in the middle of the room and delivered his opening proclamation. "You can forget ordinary, I'm too primed for same-old, same-old."

"Call the shots then, mate," said Dan.

"You'll find the guacamole, the Monterey Jack cheese, and the soft tortillas on the bench behind you. Slap some guacamole on my Mexican lollipop, wrap it in a tortilla, and pretend it's a south-of-the-border hot dog."

"Cute," beamed Cindy. "What are we calling this?"

"What's Mexican for 'as wild as it gets'?"

Cindy was rapt. "Gee, Mikey, I haven't had that before."

Michael J was full of beans. "You'll love it, honey-chile. Beat's jambalaya and chile gumbo, hands down."

With that, he picked up a remote-control beside the bed, aimed it at the high-res audio on the wall, pressed the button, and whadda ya know? One second later, Marty Robbins was singing, "El Paso."

"Gotta have atmosphere," sighed Michael, as Cindy and Dan munched on the tortilla. "The Monterey Jack cubes are to cleanse the palate. Eat up, guys, and don't hold back. I like it hot!"

When the guacamole, tortilla, and Monterey Jack were history, Michel J lifted his legs, opened them for business, and directed phase two. "Your move, Danny boy, plugin down below. Go for broke, while Cindy rides me side-saddle and lets me play touchy-feely with those gorgeous little boobies."

"Where did you dig up that move?" Dan asked.

"I'm told the Badlands of West Texas were rife with wild stuff just like it. The Apaches are said to have patented the recipe after Santa Ana screwed The Alamo."

And Marty Robbins sang on.

When the phase three romp took place, it certainly wasn't boring, but it was more in line with tradition, so Michael J jazzed it all up by adding Mitch Miller's "Yellow Rose of Texas" on the audio.

Way after sunset, he graciously dispatched Cindy and Dan with two chilled bottles of Perrier-Jouët Rosé, and a fat embossed envelope containing a pile of hundred-dollar bills.

"Thanks for everything, guys," he cooed. "Next time you're on for a culinary cruise, I've got a great act with strawberries and cream."

"Good one," chimed Mickey Flynn. *"Now what I gotta do to Eddie Edwards and Frank Valentine is what I've just done with Cindy and Dan!"*

19

PRE-CHRISTMAS AT THE McCOY STUD:
A TRUTH DAWNS

IN THE MID-DECEMBER heat, Lorrie worked The Stinger for an hour from five a.m., took a break for breakfast then gave him a light workout until lunchtime, cooled him off with a long walk, and rested him through the afternoon.

Ten days into December a thunderstorm broke over the Stud at dawn, and it rained heavily until mid-morning. The rain brought a drop in the warm temperature, and at eleven a.m. Lorrie decided to give her charge his second full gallop. The storm had blown a mess of dead branches and undergrowth all over the place.

Cooper had Blue and the boys on clean-up detail with the tractor and stable generator. Lorrie, Kitty and Cooper stood by while Cassie saddled up and covered two laps of the track, the last half at full gallop. Lorrie clocked the run and registered disappointment when the time was slower than expected.

"He was lazy today," she told Cooper, "could be the weather."

Cassie heard the remark, dismounted, and said, "Don't think so."

"Then what do you think?" asked Lorrie.

"On the day he recorded his best time," Cassie explained, "there was something different about the way he handled the turn. He didn't stall."

"Do you know why?

"It threw me a bit at the time, but I've thought about it. It was the silence."

"What silence, Cass?" Cooper asked

"The Mitchell cockatoos were quiet for once, the boys were watching the gallop, everything was still. All through the run, I could hear him breathing, clear as could be. I could hear the rhythm of his hoofbeats and I heard them pace up when he rounded the turn."

"I'm not getting it," said Lorrie.

Kitty, who had been listening to the exchange, spoke up, "I think I am."

Cooper gave her a questioning look.

"That horse is easily distracted," said Kitty, "he's a sticky-beak. If something distracts him when he's running, he loses focus. Couldn't that interfere with his coordination?"

For a few moments nobody said anything; then:

Cassie spoke up. "I'm sure you're right, Kitty."

"And?" said Cooper.

"It's like this," answered Cassie. "If he loses focus when cockatoos are screeching, and a noisy tractor is on the job, why wouldn't he lose it on a racetrack when the punters start yelling?"

"It doesn't add up," said Lorrie, "whether punters are yelling or not, racetracks are not quiet places."

"True enough," said Cassie, "but when a field closes on the home turn, the noise levels pump up 'cos the punters are going off their heads and there's the amplified sound of the race call as well. I reckon that's enough to throw this horse off balance. He's sensitive to noise and that could be why he doesn't run on in races."

Kitty spoke again. "Charlie had a horse that trained lazy, but on the track, he was a star. Every time he won, he came from near last at the home turn, and Charlie said it was the cheering that got him to the post. He was a crowd freak."

Cooper picked up on that. "What you're saying is that if one horse can buzz on cheering, another horse with a different temperament could go the other way."

"Seems possible to me," said Kitty.

Cooper agreed. He suddenly turned hyper. Before anyone could say anything, he sprinted to the homestead, grabbed a rifle and fired a couple of shots that sent the cockatoos flapping into the bush. He yelled for the boys to stop working the tractors, to turn off the generator, then with everyone still staring, he ran back to the track and said, "Silence made to order, girls. Can we give the theory a shot?"

"Let's do it," said Cassie.

She mounted The Stinger, cantered him to the far side of the track then broke him into a gallop. He covered the backstretch, ran smoothly to the turn, accelerated around it, and finished the gallop. Cassie trotted him back to the waiting watchers.

The suspense was palpable. "I didn't clock him because it wasn't a full run, but he looked great," said Lorrie, "how did he feel?"

"Awesome," said Cassie.

"How awesome?" asked Cooper.

"I heard his hoof beats pace up when he took the turn."

"No pulling back?" asked Lorrie

"You all saw it," said Cassie, "he took the turn like he did the other day."

More   excitement.   More   optimism.   Smiles everywhere.

"Okay," said Lorrie, "we've got a challenge happening here. We'll have to find a way to keep him focused."

"No pushover," said Cassie.

Cooper snapped to attention. "Gotta go!" he said. "Hold the fort, don't do anything until I get back, and don't wait lunch!"

Kitty said, "Come again?"

Cooper didn't answer. He sprinted to his Jeep Renegade, jumped in and took off. Twenty minutes later he roared into Roma's main street; parked outside the Bill Harris New Millennium Sound Shop, skipped through the front door into Bill's office and told him what he wanted.

Bill listened, nodded a few times and said, "No problem, when do you want this stuff?"

"How about right now, Bill?"

"You mean right now?"

"We're best mates, mate; wouldn't ask anyone else. Just remember who got you the knockdown to the glamorous Jewel Blanch, and the best night you've had all year."

Ben blushed. "Well, when you put it that way."

ALICE'S BARBECUE LUNCH UNDER the pepperina trees was on its last gasp when Cooper's Jeep stopped on the edge of the shady courtyard two hours later. Cooper opened the driver's door and got out. Bill Harris alighted from the passenger seat with the eyes of four curious females all over him.

Cooper joined Bill and opened the car's rear door.

"Are you going to tell us what this is about?" asked Kitty.

"In a sec," replied Cooper. He put his hand on Bill's shoulder. "Bill, you know Kitty and Alice, right?"

Bill nodded and smiled.

Cooper continued, "The cute young chick is Cassie Morgan, best damn jockey in the country, and you remember Lorrie Edwards, best damn trainer in the country."

"We met at the Roma Cup barbecue," Bill said to Lorrie, "how's your friend Jewel Blanch?"

Lorrie asked the loaded question, "You're asking me?"

Bill grinned. "We're not engaged, yet. She'll need another barbecue to pull that off."

Everyone giggled while Cooper unloaded two bulky audio speakers from the rear door of his 4WD and set them up on the Jeep's bonnet while Bill fiddled around with a battery and leads.

A couple of minutes passed, then Cooper gave out to his captive audience. "My friend Bill is the best damn audio freak in the great south-west, and he deserves full credit for what you are about to experience."

Everyone waited patiently. Cooper waved at Bill and said, "Ready?"

Bill nodded.

"Check this out," said Cooper.

The speakers erupted, first with muffled crowd sounds then with the clear voice of a race commentator calling a race. There were more crowd noises as the race call continued, and finally, rowdy sounds of cheering and yelling when the call reached its peak and the race ended. The McCoy Stud had become a racetrack.

Cooper struck a triumphant pose, indicated Bill, who joined him, and said, "How's that?"

"Just like the Roma Cup," said Alice.

Cooper qualified. "That's exactly what we're going to make Sting think. He's not going to pull his lazy tricks anymore. From now on he's going to be working for his room and board."

Bill took over. "We've made six CDs, all different; tomorrow's Phar Lap won't get bored."

Kitty looked chuffed. "I take it that it's your intention to play those CDs while your horse works out?"

"Trackside," said Cooper, "we can start on low decibels; pump the volume up, then pump it right up when he takes the turn."

Cooper addressed Lorrie. "That's the plan, but the final decision is yours, Boss."

Lorrie hesitated. "What do you think, Cassie?"

Cassie's face was all lights. "We're nuts if we don't give it a go," she said.

"Have you boys had lunch?" asked Alice.

"Take the seat beside Cassie," Cooper said to Bill, "and do your best to behave like the gentleman you are. I'd like a word in private with my star trainer, then I'll roar you back to town."

Cooper escorted Lorrie across to the row of stables. "I don't want you to think I'm horning in here," he said as they walked. "If you don't think my idea is any good, I'm not going to freak out or anything, but I had this flash see, and I went for it. Have I upset the apple cart?"

"I would like to think about it."

"I'm not coming on like some hillbilly smart aleck, am I?"

"You're anything but a hillbilly, Cooper."

"The last thing I want is to offend you."

"You're not offending me."

They had reached the stables, and the clean fresh pine-scented aroma was heavy in the air. Blue Larner had everything spotless. The Stinger's stable was four or five down. The top of his Dutch door was open, and as they approached, his head appeared.

Cooper patted his horse's forelock. "Give me five, boy."

The Stinger let out a little whinny and nudged his head against Cooper's hand three or four times. Cooper smiled at Lorrie. "We're best mates."

Lorrie had been around horses for long enough to know about the bonds that linked them to the men who understood them.

Cooper kept his hand on The Stinger's forelock. "When I first saw him in the horse stall at Dalby, I felt he was special. He hadn't done anything on the day, but I felt he wanted to. When I was a kid my granddad told me that man-horse language has nothing to do with talking, it's all about feeling, and when I saw The Stinger that day, I felt somehow, he wanted to be something but didn't know how. That's why I bought him."

"You bought him on a whim?"

"I bought him on instinct. I've learned to trust mine. I honed it over five years of wheeling and dealing in the cutthroat world of big-city real estate. You get a lot of timewasters in that business. Lookers aren't always buyers, and if you're not careful they'll cost you money."

"Really?"

"I had my share of them until I learned to trust my instincts. I got so good at separating the lookers from the buyers that I never tripped up."

"Never?"

Cooper smiled. "Sometimes."

His bright blue eyes spelled out his message. "But only if the looker was a looker."

Lorrie got it. "Why did I ask?"

Cooper went on. "I've been haunting racetracks since I came to live with Kit. I saw a lot of horses, but not one I wanted to own until I saw Sting. The guy who owned him wanted to sell him, and I wanted to buy him, but I sure didn't buy him on a whim. Are you with me?"

"I am."

Lorrie had heard talk like that before. She remained silent, allowing Cooper to tell her everything he wanted to say.

"My horse was born to run, Lorrie, and I'm sure he knows it. He's intelligent. I don't think we'll have any trouble getting him used to the faked-up sound of racetracks. He might get a bit of a fright at first, but I think he'll settle when he figures they're racetrack noises, not tractors or Mitchell cockatoos. I think we can teach him the difference."

Lorrie was coming around. "It's possible."

Cooper gave her a long look. "You think so?"

"It sure won't hurt to try it."

He turned then, and with his hand still fondling his horse's forelock, he said, "You've got a new friend Sting, and she's on your case. All you have to do is chill out and let it happen."

Lorrie was almost mind surfing on the emotional waves coming from Cooper. She'd never known a young man quite like him. Here was an ex-real estate yuppie from the Big Smoke turned horse owner, and he was not only giving her lessons in horse psychology, he was opening the door to his deepest feelings, so she could understand just how much he appreciated what she was doing for him and his horse. What was she supposed to do? There was only one answer. She had to get on with her job, and her job was to get The Stinger's form up so Thunderdome's win as the ring-in would not arouse the suspicions of the racing industry.

That was it, and that was all there was. Nothing more. Nothing less. She was committed. Four other people including her father were involved; six counting Kitty and Cooper, and she could not let any of them down. She felt her conscience niggling her.

Get it together, and play the charade, dummy! So, she did.

She let Cooper know that she and Cassie had thought seriously about entering The Stinger in a race at Flinton in the last week of January.

He was stoked. "I've heard all about that little Flinton track. Will he be ready by then?"

"Maybe not ready to win, but we'll get a chance to find out if his training program is working and to see if we've nailed why he's been failing to run on in his races."

"It's your call, Lorrie."

"Cassie and I believe we should go ahead."

"Done," said Cooper. "I'll call the Flinton Race Club and set it up."

Lorrie had a final word. "Don't get your hopes up, Cooper. Either way, the race will be valuable experience."

"Do I book Splinter Hanson?"

Lorrie shook her head. "I'd like Cassie to ride him."

"That's just perfect!" said Cooper.

"She thinks so too."

Cooper faced his horse. "Hear that, hotshot? You're in another race, and in the saddle is your new best friend, Miss Cassie Morgan!"

Lorrie's conscience niggled her again. She had a word with herself:

Stay on top of it and remember what you're here for. This is not real! This is only play-acting! The only thing that's real is the caper, and this game is the key to the caper! That's how it is, so keep on playing the game!

As Cooper and Lorrie walked back to the barbecue terrace, Kitty, sitting in the shade of the pepperina trees, watched them and felt a little thrill.

It's happening, she thought to herself, *it's going to be all right. The Stinger is going to make it.*

COOPER'S AUDIO TRAINING KICKED off the next day.

At six-thirty a.m. Cassie had The Stinger saddled and ready for his early morning trot. The sun shone dimly in a cloudy sky. Cooper had the speakers set on the bonnet of his Jeep with the CD at the ready. He kept the decibels at a low level, but The Stinger did not work well. After thirty minutes, Lorrie decided he'd had enough and switched the audio off. The experiment was too soon for judgement.

"A bit like roller-blading," said Cooper, "your butt takes a beating from too many falls, but when you find your feet, you're breaking the speed limit."

Lorrie had to smile at that. "I think we'd better stay with the audio, Cooper, somehow I can't see The Stinger on roller-blades."

She and Cassie persevered. Five days later there was a definite improvement. No plain sailing but definite improvement. Hard yards are hard yards!

Slowly but surely, the audio treatment was working.

DECEMBER 25 LOOMED LARGE at the McCoy Stud. The Stinger's program had plundered everyone's time, and Christmas seemed to come out of nowhere. Cassie arranged to have two days with her family in Brisbane. Eddie was spending Christmas Day with his elder sister on the Sunshine Coast as he always did. Lorrie usually went with him, but because she was so committed in Roma, she decided to stay put. Cooper had been invited to spend time with Sophie-Rose and the Hadleys, but his plans were uncertain.

Mr Smooth, Frank Davenport, was already in residence at Palazzo Versace on the Gold Coast for The

Magic Millions Carnival which was still over a week away. Frank was in the mood for the beauteous flesh of the silly season, but the caper was rarely out of his thoughts. Eddie was keeping him up to speed with the moves, and Frank knew that the financial arrangements were in the experienced hands of Loveboat Williams in Singapore. All was well.

20

BILL AND COOPER: BOY TALK IN THE SPA

O N A WARM ROMA night in the lead up to Christmas week, Cooper sat drinking a cold beer with Bill Harris in the bubble-zone of Bill's spa. The beer was nicely chilled, and the cool water tingled and teased their naked skin. Cooper wasn't behaving like the normal stud Bill had come to know, and he asked what was wrong.

Cooper unloaded: "It's Sophie-Rose, mate."

"Damn," said Bill, "she hasn't got a bun in the oven, has she?"

"I use raincoats, you know that."

"Okay; then what?"

"She's too sure of me, and it's getting awkward."

"Awkward how, Coop?"

"She's hinting at an engagement ring, and her parents are talking like I'm already part of the family."

"And that's not in your plans?"

"It might have been once."

"What happened to cool it?"

Cooper took a deep breath. "Lorrie Edwards happened."

"That's understandable. Does she know how you feel?"

"I'm confused, Bill, I honestly don't know. Sometimes I do, other times I don't, and it's making things difficult for me. Sophie and I have been getting it on fairly often, and it's been good, but now when I'm with her, I'm thinking about Lorrie."

"Oh, man! That's as bad as it gets."

"Tell me about it."

"So, what are you going to do?"

"Sophie's oldies have invited me to spend Christmas week with them on some ritzy island in Fiji."

"And you don't want to go."

'You got it."

"Because Lorrie Edwards is staying put at the Stud?"

"That's it."

"Then be brave and tell Sophie that Fiji is out."

"I think I should."

"Then like I said, mate, be brave!"

After a pause, Cooper said, "You've talked me into it."

"Please! I haven't talked you into anything."

"I guess not, Bill."

"What are you going to do about Lorrie?"

"Keep pitching of course."

"The town is full of alternatives, you know."

"I guess it is."

Bill's solution: "I can set you up if you like."

"I guess you can."

"I grew up in Roma, Coop, need I say more?"

"I've got the message."

"Best advice, mate," grinned Bill, "otherwise—"

"Otherwise what?"

"Boys will be boys, Coop, you'll wear your friggin' palm out!"

Cooper smiled. "Jingle all the way, mate."

21

CHRISTMAS AT THE McCOY STUD

ALICE AND KITTY SPENT busy hours in the homestead kitchen preparing for the Christmas Day dinner in the pepperina courtyard.

Cooper and Bill Harris took two days to ribbon the trees with fairy lights, and they set up a giant audio-visual screen to showcase Bill's selection of music DVDs on Christmas night. Kitty and Alice's Christmas Day guest list included a handful of their best friends, and a dozen close acquaintances; an informal gathering.

With Cassie on her two-day break, Christmas Eve was a quieter night for the four McCoy regulars in residence. Alice and Kitty dressed for it, so did Lorrie, who wore one of her floaty mushroom pink summer numbers. Her honey-blonde hair was loose and shiny, and her strappy high heeled shoes added a touch of sass. She looked so unlike Lorrie the horse-trainer that Cooper looked twice when he saw her walk into the fairy-light fantasy of the pepperina terrace.

Alice nailed his reaction. "Your eyes will fall out in a minute, love."

The meal Kitty and Alice prepared was introduced by Cooper's little speech.

"Tomorrow's lunch will be a big deal, so this is our night from us to you, Lorrie. We didn't quite know what to buy you, so we've splurged on Cristal champagne, Sevruga caviar, chilled lobster, and Alice's knockout ice cream cake. You don't get stuff like that in Roma every day."

"Knock it off, love," said Alice, "we know how to bung it on if we have to."

Lorrie had no time to think about Christmas presents either, but it didn't seem to matter. Cooper popped the champagne cork and poured. When the banquet was past tense, he made another little speech.

"It's now time for the main event! It's your night, Lorrie, and this surprise comes to you with the able assistance of my good friend Bill Harris."

Standing by the audio-visual machine, Kitty pressed the start button.

The giant screen lit up with the Metro-Goldwyn-Mayer logo, and a fanfare announced the name of the famous movie, *National Velvet.*

Lorrie felt a tingle. Her favourite film of all time. As a kid, she'd never tired of watching it on television, and here it was on a giant screen among pepperina trees and fairy lights on the barbecue courtyard of the McCoy Stud in western Queensland. She said a quiet thank-you to Cooper who took the comfortable chair beside her.

"How did you know?" she asked him.

"I bribed Cassie."

When the film ended, and its famous star, teenage Elizabeth Taylor, had ridden her horse, The Piebald, to victory in the film's Grand National, and Lorrie had stopped sniffling, Alice and Kitty retired to the kitchen to clean things up; dismissing offers of help.

Cooper poured two more glasses of Cristal and passed one to Lorrie.

"Merry Christmas," he said, "and it is, thanks to you."

"Merry Christmas," said Lorrie, touching his glass with hers.

"I've watched you with my horse, Lorrie, and even if he doesn't amount to anything, you're giving him a chance. I honestly couldn't ask for a better Christmas present."

Lorrie took a breath to reply.

He stopped her. "You don't have to say anything."

"At least let me thank you for the wonderful night."

"The McCoys know how to be sociable. It runs in the family."

"Your grandfather again?"

"Charlie was quite a guy. He died too soon, but I think that was meant to be. He wasn't born to be old, and I miss him. He was one of those special people. You'd have liked him, Lorrie. He loved horses big time!"

"Horses are my family too, Cooper. My dad wants to win a Melbourne Cup, and he thinks he has the horse that can do it."

"Because it's every Aussie trainer's dream."

Cooper was trying hard to hold the moment. Now that he had Lorrie all to himself, he wanted to keep her there. He knew he was manufacturing conversation, and the champagne was helping. Lorrie was relaxed and chatting. She remarked on the pleasant atmosphere of the homestead, and he asked, "You're not missing Brisbane?"

"I haven't thought about it, but no, I'm not missing it at all."

He stayed on track: "What about your friends?"

She thought for a minute before she said, "I don't have a lot of friends. I'm a working girl. When my mother died, I looked out for my father; not because I had to, but because I wanted to, and heavy socialising was out."

"So, you got interested in horses instead?"

"Dad taught me a lot. He's still teaching me."

"And you obviously love it."

Lorrie said nothing, but she nodded and smiled.

Cooper took a risk. "Is Frank Davenport a part of your stable team?"

"He's Dad's friend. They get on well."

Cooper then made a mistake. "How does he get on with you?"

Lorrie, sensing where the talk was leading, calmly put everything in perspective.

"We get on fine, but like I said, Frank is Dad's friend, not mine, and right now, my most important friend is your horse. I think I'm a good trainer, and I need to keep remembering why I'm here. I have a job to do, and I'm doing it, but I'm grateful that it's all so easy, because I like everything here; tonight's company included."

Cooper knew enough to get off the track. He had to admit he was a tad disappointed, but no doors had been closed, and he was content to be told that he was one of Lorrie's 'likes.'

They talked on, drinking champagne and sharing thoughts while Alice and Kitty worked effortlessly in the kitchen.

"I like that girl," said Alice, "there's nothing average about her. I like that."

"I do too," said Kitty.

"What about Cooper?"

"What do you mean 'what about Cooper?'"

Alice rolled her eyes. "That was no ordinary night we just had, not ordinary at all. It wasn't just fancy champagne and sticky fish eggs and a soppy old picture on a great big screen."

"Then what was it?"

"Cooper's love song to that lovely girl."

"You think so?"

"I know so, Kit, so now we wait for him to make his move."

"Cooper won't move until he's on sure ground."

"And you don't think he is?"

"He had a broken romance in Melbourne. Apparently, it was serious."

"And it left a scar?"

Kitty shook her head. "Scars heal, Alice, they always do, but that's not why Cooper came to live up here. He's making a new life for himself in Charlie's world, and if what you say about tonight is true, he'll move when he's ready."

That was not good enough for Alice. "I notice he didn't go to Fiji with that Sophie-Rose Hadley and her gang. Bully for that!"

"You don't care for Sophie-Rose?"

"Her mother's a flitter gibbet, her father is only interested in money, and she's nowhere near as right for Cooper as Lorrie Edwards. If you ask me, Little Miss Sophie-Rose-Whatsit is just someone to fill the gap."

"Fill the gap?"

"Share the sheets, Kit, whatever. His late nights are not spent solving the world's problems in the Roma Pizza Parlour. I'll say no more, except this; I don't want to see Lorrie walking away after four months. What do you think of that?"

"I think you're an old softie, Alice, but I never had you pegged as a matchmaker."

Alice laughed. "How do you think I got my own boys settled? Not that I interfered, I just pushed and shoved in the right direction at the right time."

Kitty glanced at the kitchen clock. "What do you know? It's past midnight. Merry Christmas, Allie, and did I ever tell you how wonderful it is to have a friend like you?"

Alice had the last word. "That's always been a given, and Merry Christmas back, but I'm giving you fair warning, Kit, I'm not giving up on those two, so you better get set for some nice quiet pushing and shoving."

Kitty had no further comment. *She admitted to herself that she'd had thoughts about Cooper and Lorrie ever since The Stinger had brought them together, but she wanted things to happen in their own time. Still, she thought, it's nice to know I'm on the same wavelength as a powerhouse like Alice.*

22

THE GOLD COAST MAGIC MILLIONS

MICHAEL J FLYNN WAS on top of the world. After hours of scheming and plotting, his head was full of his top-secret Lillian project. He knew it would take time to put everything together, but it was a happening! Certified.

His excitement was back on track for the Magic Millions.

The famous Racing Carnival incorporates several days of high-end yearling sales. It explodes on the Queensland Gold Coast every year on the hangover heels of New Years and ricochets in on a slew of big spenders, show-offs, hot talkers, smart arses, empty vessels, fashion flashers, assorted hangers-on plus an A-List of genuine international connoisseurs of the Thoroughbred world.

It has no pretensions. No one ever accused it of being Royal Ascot.

The word carnival suits it to a T. Circus may be an even better word. Fun is probably the best one.

The Gold Coast's business operators welcomed each year's Carnival with open arms; taking it for what its worth with well-planned pitches to lift as much cash as possible from the pockets of the hedonistic hordes.

For show-ponies of Michael J Flynn's ilk, The Magic Millions provided a perfect platform—a networking bonanza par excellence. Michael J's favourite bed-down in seasons past was the Gold Coast's glittery Palazzo

Versace, on the shores of the Southport Broadwater, where his demands were ever-graciously met.

In return, he unloaded megabucks in the hotel's bars and restaurants, often entertaining the A-Listers he wanted to impress at soirees in his luxurious private suite. But when the fickle MJ discovered that *Ultimate Cool* editor, Lillian St Clare, was accommodated elsewhere, Palazzo Versace bit the dust.

If St Clare was at Hotel Conrad, so be it. MJ would be at Hotel Conrad too. He was fast on the blower to Martin Olson, his long-suffering travel agent in Sydney.

"I want to cancel my reservation at Palazzo Versace and re-book Conrad."

That hotel's location was on Broadbeach Island, a vibey spot on the Gold Coast's central hub. Its twenty-four-seven excitement had a lot to do with Conrad's in-house casino, the Gold Coast's pumpy money magnet. The hotel was also one of the sponsors of the Magic Millions, and it was playing host to several of the Carnival's splashy social events.

"It may be difficult to get preferred accommodation at this late date," said Martin Olson.

Michael J was ready. "Tell the people who run that hotel who I am, that they'll get all my business for the whole time I'm there, and that all my business will include lavish entertaining in my top-level suite. An early flight tomorrow would be best."

"Mr Flynn, top-level suites at Conrad are booked months ahead at this time of the year."

Michael J was not a whit deterred. "What do you expect me to do? Entertain high-end guests in some pokey little double bedroom on top of the car park?"

Martin remained calm. "I can't promise anything, but I'll see what I can do."

Not good enough for the great Michael J. "Fine," he said. "If it's too difficult to get me preferred accommodation at Hotel Conrad, I'll see what I can do with another travel agent, and when I find one who can get me what I want, I'll see what I can do about giving him my business."

That said, Michael J hung up like the prize bully he was, and Martin Olson, motivated by the possible loss of the major commissions his testy client paid him every month, went seriously to bat; sweet-talked the Conrad management into playing ball, thereby saving his professional life. Michael J was already assembling his Magic Millions wardrobe when Martin called back with the good news forty-five minutes later.

MJ's reaction was predictable. "How could they afford to turn away a drawcard like Yours Truly?"

Martin Olson nursed his cool. "I've booked you on a flight to the Gold Coast tomorrow morning at nine-thirty a.m. You'll arrive at Coolangatta Airport approximately an hour later, and the Conrad limousine will be waiting."

Michael J was impressed. "Perfect, old sport. See what you can do when you really try?"

"Enjoy your trip," said Martin, "and as always, Mr Flynn, happy to be of service."

Michael J's grunt of approval signalled the end of the communiqué.

Martin Olson hung up, instantly calculated the size of his commission, and smiled. "Okay, he's a big head and a wanker, who cares? Sooner or later he'll get his, and don't they all?"

MICHAEL J PICKED UP his telephone and called Flasher Doyle in Brisbane. "Any new developments?" he asked when Flasher picked up.

"Not a murmur, I reckon Edwards and Davenport have gone to ground."

"I reckon you reckon wrong. They're keeping a low profile, and that is suspicious. I'm checking in at Hotel Conrad at Broadbeach tomorrow, and I'll be there until the end of the Magic Millions."

"I'm checking into the same hotel tonight."

"Good. You know where to contact me if anything comes up."

"Right as rain, MJ."

THE NEXT MORNING, THE great man landed on the Gold Coast. He was met by the Conrad limousine, delivered and deposited. It was one of those beautiful cloudless days that Gold Coast tourism heavies rave about. After unpacking his wardrobe of shirts, ties, suits, shoes, sports and evening wear, he slid open the wide glass doors to his generous balcony suite high above the glistening Gold Coast, and stepped into the sunshine.

His suite faced east, overlooking the resort's sweeping north-south panorama: golden beaches, rolling surf, busy highways and towering high-rises. A gentle breeze blew in from the south-east, bringing with it the salty freshness of the sea while it brushed against Michael J's face, and ruffled his thick dark hair.

"Yes," he said, taking a deep breath, "this is the way to go about urgent business."

Indeed. On the suite's dining room table sat a complimentary bottle of vintage Taittinger in an ice bucket, a bowl of fresh strawberries, a platter of imported cheeses, and a crystal bowl filled with hand-made chocolates, together with a warm welcoming note from the management.

This was the life that the VIPs of the world had grown to accept; a world Mickey Flynn had never dared dream about; now second-nature to Michael J Flynn. After fifteen minutes of feeling like one of the gods on Mt. Olympus, Michael J left the balcony, popped the cork in the Taittinger bottle, poured some of the champagne into a crystal glass, sipped the sparkling liquid, crunched away on a strawberry or two, cut a wedge of camembert, and let it melt on his tongue.

He parked his butt at the table, uncapped his Mont Blanc fountain pen, composed a welcoming note to Lillian St Clair in his practised handwriting, sealed the note in an envelope, wrote Lillian's name on it, and called the concierge to arrange delivery.

Still seated at the desk, he took time to go over the plans for his visit. He wrote everything down:

> *Tonight: The official Magic Millions Cocktail Party on the landscaped pool court of the hotel. Tomorrow: Ladies Day at the Gold Coast Turf Club.*
>
> *After the races: A VIP soiree in my suite with a roster of special guests drinking Taittinger champagne. I'll supervise the catering with hotel's Executive Chef, and Lillian St Clare will be my guest of honour. Buckingham Palace can eat its heart out.*

After another glass or two of vintage Taittinger, MJ decided it was time to prepare for the Magic Millions Cocktail Party. Wouldn't the guests be lucky?

LILLIAN ST CLARE READ Michael J's hand-written note twice and smiled.

Michael J Flynn's notes were always worth reading. His writing was so individually formed it could never have been done on a computer. Right. What did Michael

J want? She could not imagine, but she knew she'd have a whole lot of fun finding out.

Lillian, as the cocktail party's guest of honour, arrived at the Conrad pool court early enough to be briefed on the evening's program. She did a sound check with the audio guys, and a lighting check with the LX guys. She had spent the afternoon going over her speech and had committed most of it to memory. By six-thirty p.m. when the invited guests began filing onto the pool court, Lillian was composed, confident and ready to embody the philosophy of *Ultimate Cool,* the fashion magazine she had worked so hard to establish.

UPSTAIRS IN HIS SUITE, Michael J, ablaze in his best Prada after-five wear, scrutinised his reflection in a full-length mirror.

Mickey Flynn grinned back at him and said, *"Fucken shit-hot, mate!"*

Satisfied with Mickey's eleven-out-of-ten rating, Michael J sprayed his closely shaved face with Ferragamo EDT, and decided it was time to give the cocktail party the pleasure of his company.

The official guest list numbered 400, but by the time sneaky gate crashers had talked their way past the security heavies, the crowd swell was likely to be more like 450; an uneven mix of sophisticates, racing heavies, fat cat bureaucrats, savvy investors, horse traders, and fashionable swans, plus a slew of rag bags and touts connected in one way or another to the Carnival.

It was not exactly an exclusive melee, but Michael J figured if he dropped anchor with the right folks, he was safe from the rag bags and touts who relentlessly dive-bombed the wine waiters and attacked the paraded platters of canapés as though one of the Biblical famines of Moses would soon be upon them.

MJ was carefully late, arriving forty-five minutes after the time indicated on the invitations. By then the starving louts had stopped attacking the waiters, and the rag bags had settled into a sort of joyous frenzy of boneheaded racing trivia and wine-fuelled hilarity.

A waiter offered him a drink. He cast his eyes over the flutes of suspicious sparkling liquid on the tray, turned up his nose at what appeared to be domestic fizz, and waved the waiter away. Standing quite still at the security checkpoint, his eyes swept the crowd, finally lighting upon the svelte form of Lillian St Clare.

She was in conversation with a small group of guests: standing out like a petunia in an onion patch. Michael J advanced slowly. As he closed on her, he took in her appearance: She wore a full-length sheath cut from some fine fabric embroidered all over with tiny gold bugle beads. The effect was pure magic—when she moved the sheath shimmered like ripples on a sunlit pond. Falling from her neck to the strapless bust of her sheath, was a soft cascade of silk organza ruffles, cleverly covering the approaching signs of age on her naked skin.

Her make-up was a work of art that had probably taken time, yet it looked natural and becoming. Her chestnut hair, loose and shiny, was the perfect frame for her mobile face. Lillian was not in the first bloom of youth, but as a bundle of feminine finery, she was undeniably admirable.

Michael J caught her eye, and as he came nearer, her lips broke into a wide bright smile. He knew a couple of the people in her small group. There were exchanges of "hellos" and other fatuous utterances.

At the right time, he took Lillian aside and said, "Thank God you're here, this bash could rightly be mistaken for a wombat convention."

"You're such a snob," Lillian said. "It's a sporting cocktail party, not a catered affair on Victoria Peak."

"More's the pity."

She smiled. "I'm having a lovely time, and I'm so glad I flew in for this Carnival. I'm busy-busy but looking forward to everything."

Michael J staked his claim. "I hope you'll save some time for me."

"Goes without saying. I just loved your sweet note. How thoughtful of you."

He nodded. "If you're doing fashion coverage you won't have time for me at the racetrack, but I'm having an exclusive little champagne soiree in my suite after the races tomorrow."

"Sounds marvellous, I've been to your champagne soirees."

"I'm staying in the hotel, same floor as yours, just down the hall."

"How convenient. Who'll be at your soiree?"

"People like us."

Lillian laughed. "Michael, you really are a terrible snob, but you do it so well, and at least you're honest about it. What time?"

"Five p.m." He paused. "And do I have to tell you how absolutely stunning you look tonight?"

"I'm flattered." In return, and right on cue, Lillian ran her professional eye over Michael J, not missing a thing. "And how good do you look? I'd say George Clooney, but he has none of your inventive flair, you've got him on the ropes."

The game-playing had started. Rule One: Flatter each other. Rule Two: Keep everything even, all attempts at superiority are out. Rule Three: Play it cool until the object of the exercise is clear. Rule Four: Never negate anything until the cards are on the table. Rule

Five: Always remember the most important question: What's in it for me?

One of the men in Lillian's group excused himself to remind her she was due to make her official speech. "They're about to introduce you."

The gushing introduction that followed made Lillian sound as if she were the most important fashion identity in the world, and the lower echelons whooped it up when she mounted the steps to the stage and stood shimmering in the spotlights.

"Holy shit," said one of the younger wild-eyed racing types. "If that's what fashion cougars in Hong Kong are like, I'm on a flight tomorrow, right after a shopping spree at Condom Kingdom."

Michael J thought seriously about letting Mickey Flynn loose on him but changed his mind. He was there on a mission and it didn't include Mickey's ripping into guests at an official function. Not a wise move.

Lillian's well-presented soliloquy was winding down when the man who'd excused himself to her ten minutes earlier edged closer and offered Michael J his hand.

"How do you do, sir, my name is CK Dexter Beaumont." The man's lazy drawl suggested roots somewhere in the Deep South of the United States.

Michael J took the proffered hand. "Michael J Flynn."

"Call me Dexter. I'm Albuquerque, New Mexico, USA, here for the Magic Millions Yearling Sales. Where are you from?"

"I divide my time between Australia and Hong Kong."

"Are you in the racing game?"

"I'm on the edge, old sport, a sort of passionate observer."

Dexter's next comment caught Michael J off balance. "I'm only asking because my friend over there, says he's sure he saw you in Brisbane the day a horse called The Mating Game lost him a small fortune."

Michael J's eyes narrowed. "The Mating Game?"

"Should have won, according to my friend, the best of good things beaten by bad luck. You can't win them all, can you?"

"I don't know that it was bad luck," said Michael J, full of bitter recollection.

"No? Tell that to my friend, you may make him feel better."

Dexter called his friend over and introduced him. "This is Mr Roger Bannister; he's here for the horse sales too. He's a Brit but he spends a lot of time running around the world."

Roger smiled politely, shook Michael J's hand and said, "How do you do?" His voice sounded as fruity and rich as a barrel of ripe plums.

Michael J replied politely, adding, "Your friend Dexter says you saw me at the track in Brisbane the day of The Mating Game fiasco. I was there on the losing end just like you."

"Damned unfortunate, to say nothing of costly," said Roger, "I went for the doctor on good advice and lost the lot." Roger paused for breath and looked Michael J in the eye. "I heard whispers that the win wasn't quite pukka."

"I've heard that, too, and I believe it," said Michael J.

"Too late to do anything about it now," said Roger, "I suppose we just leave well enough alone."

Michael J smiled a thin smile. "There are ways of evening scores, old sport, and this particular score is anything but settled, but on a more pleasant note, I'd like both of you gentlemen to accompany Lillian to my suite for some champagne and caviar after tomorrow's race meeting."

"If it's at all possible we'll do our best to accept," said Dexter.

Michael J presented his card. "Call me on my cell phone and let me know."

Dexter returned the gesture and presented his card. "I move around quite a bit, but I'll always get a message if you call that number."

Loud applause and appropriate gushing followed Lillian's opening speech. The beautiful people and rag bags were rapt. Lillian was the star of the night, acknowledging compliments as she slowly pushed her way through the crowd. Michael J felt a tap on his shoulder. He turned to see a slightly tipsy Flasher Doyle clutching a half-empty bottle of domestic beer.

"Been hobnobbing with the big boys, hey, MJ?

Michael J, doing his level best to be tolerant, said, "Big boys?"

"Those two blokes you've been talking to have been chucking huge coin at prime horseflesh at the yearling sales. Holy shit! They must both be loaded. Who are they?"

The word loaded did it. Michael told Flasher who they were and that he'd invited them both to his suite the following night.

Flasher was duly impressed: "Shit! You sure can pick 'em, can't ya? Did they tip you any winners for the Carnival? They'd have a clue or two, wouldn't they?"

As luck would have it, Michael was rescued by a greeting from one of Flasher's lower life acquaintances:

"Flasher! Where the fuck have you been? We've saved a plate of calamari for ya! Bloody hell, mate! We can't keep it guarded all night."

Flasher grinned at Michael and said, "Keep up the good work"—then allowed his friend to drag him away.

Lillian had managed to shake off her doting fans—and clutched Michael's arm. "I think I've had enough. I was supposed to be joining the officials at dinner but I'm not hungry and I begged off."

Michael seized his chance. "How about a quiet drink upstairs?"

"Pure heaven," said Lillian.

He paused at the concierge desk, ordered a fresh bottle of Tattinger to be delivered pronto, and piloted a grateful Lillian to the bank of elevators.

They were safely behind the doors of his suite when the champagne arrived. The waiter opened it, poured two flutes and made a polite exit. Dispensing with the small talk with as much grace as possible, Michael got straight to the point. It was time to give Lillian the details of his secret proposal.

"You'll love it, Lillian, it has your name all over it."

"I'm waiting, Michael."

If he'd had a trumpet, he would have blown it.

"It's a glamorous fashion shoot, photographed on location at the McCoy homestead in Midwestern Queensland. Your magazine will be the star, and it will be great PR for you. I can promise all the cooperation you'll need."

"How interesting."

Lillian had questions. Michael had all the answers.

He would deliver the project into the capable hands of Jewel Blanch. She would hire models, supervise photography, arrange transport and accommodation, coordinate and source the fashion, the accessories and make-up, and anything else required.

"You've thought this out, Michael. It's not a flash in the pan, is it?"

He lied like a trooper. "I want it for Queensland Racing. I'm a big fan!"

"Tell me more." The more Lillian heard, the more tempted she became. "I met Jewel Blanch this morning," she said. "She's my assistant at Ladies Day tomorrow, and she was not at the cocktail party tonight because she's at the track putting the finishing touches to the fashion contest; her choice. So far I'm impressed."

Michael J rode his advantage, stressing every plus he could think up, including the undying gratitude of the magazine-reading population of Australia.

"Think about that, Lillian. When has a prestigious fashion magazine made such a generous gesture to the talented designers of this country? This one story, together with your coverage of the Magic Millions, will make you the Down-Under media name of the moment!"

Michael J had hit the right nerve. "I want everything on paper," said Lillian, "the proposal, all the details and the extent of my financial commitment."

Michael was fast. "Forget the financial commitment. That's my gift to the project but I don't want it broadcast."

Lillian was genuinely surprised: "Since when have you become a financial patron-saint, Michael?

"Since this minute. Do we have a deal?"

Lillian correctly read the unspoken motivation. "What are you getting out of this?"

He was honest because he knew she'd want him to be. "Do you have to know?"

"Not really."

"Then focus on what this little exercise is doing for you. Can you detect a flaw anywhere?"

"Not at the moment but I'll be reading the fine print."

"Provided you're satisfied when you've read it, and you will be, do I assume we have a verbal agreement on which to brief the unprincipled legal desperados?"

"We do."

"May I say how much I admire you?"

"We're birds of a feather, Michael, you don't have to gild the lily."

"More champagne?"

"I have a huge day coming up, do you mind if I say no?"

He walked her to the door and said, "Have a wonderful time tomorrow."

She smiled sweetly. "You're not only a snob, Michael, you're a fully-fledged con, but you're so good at both you're irresistible. Goodnight and thanks for the champagne."

He closed the heavy door, walked to the telephone and called Jewel's mobile. "Are you still at the track?" he asked when he heard her voice.

She answered affirmatively.

"Right!" he purred. "Don't say anything, just listen. I've got something important to discuss with you, but I cannot do it on a mobile phone. Will you be too beat to come to my suite when you've finished?"

He smiled at her positive answer, then said, "I'll wait up for you, and the champagne will be chilled."

He walked out on to his balcony and surveyed the twinkling night-time panorama of the Gold Coast. He took several deep breaths of the cool fresh air and knew he wouldn't sleep a wink. He was far too excited. He thought about Jewel and knew that after he'd given her his good news she'd be just as excited. Even so, it was not going to be one of those whipped cream nights. This was strictly business. Michael J stood for some time on the balcony working it all out:

He would pitch the McCoy Stud fashion shoot as Lillian's idea. Jewel would have to believe that any involvement on his part would steal Lillian's limelight! He was merely the contact, the conduit to the grand gesture—nothing more. The shoot would be Jewel's baby. Michael J sighed into the night sky. His trick was shaping-up a sure thing. There was only one more ingredient—the most important one.

He heard the door buzzer and looked at his wristwatch. He knew when Jewel Blanch walked into his suite that his vendetta would step up another rung on the ladder to fulfilment!

Jewel, openly impressed, listened intently to the proposal. Michael J laid it on with a trowel, finally reaching the most sensitive part of the deal:

"I want you to understand I'm getting involved as a favour to Lillian. I don't want any credit, but anything I can do to help will be done."

"That's wonderful, Michael, but I just can't walk onto the McCoy Stud with a trailer load of models and a couple of photographers and expect to take over the place without permission."

"Of course not."

"I'll need permission, and insurance. The shoot will take three days at least."

"You're friendly with the McCoys. You met them at the Roma Cup, didn't you?"

"I did, and I got on well with them."

"And you're friendly with Lorrie Edwards?"

"I get on well with her too, I like her."

"She's training a horse at the McCoy Stud. Won't this add to the story?"

Jewel took the bait. "You think I should be the one to talk to the McCoys?"

"With Lillian's blessing!" It was a proclamation. "You'll be seeing her tomorrow, and you'll find out first-hand how keen she is to have the whole thing bedded down."

Jewel gave him a happy smile. He suggested a celebration glass of Taittinger. She agreed.

"A small one only, I have an early morning, and a big day tomorrow."

"Get used to big," said Michael. "Tomorrow is the beginning of your world of bigger things, but only if you know how to make them happen."

When he picked up the chilled champagne bottle, Michael J heard Mickey say, "*You're a dead set killer, mate, but it is so fucken easy when you're dealing with boneheads.*"

23

THE MAGIC MILLIONS ON TRACK

LADIES DAY WEDNESDAY WAS in full swing when Frank Davenport weaved his way through the throng in the Gold Coast Turf Club's Dome Marquee; a permanent air-conditioned glass-enclosed structure that barely held the rollicking crowd. Frank was almost submerged in a surging sea of mobile females, delectable darlings, flamboyant ensembles, shell-shocked gentlemen, and a collection of hats that could easily have come from the costume wardrobe of *La Cage Aux Folles*.

He had a place at one of the tables but preferred the freedom of wandering about, taking in the sights. The big buzz was the fashion parade and the choosing of Best Dressed, Best Hat, Best-Dressed Gent and Best Couple. Chief Judge was Lillian St Clare, who was already on view, adorned in a delicious ensemble that had most of the female population of the dome green with envy, the middle-aged gents breathing unevenly, and the younger guys conscious of that certain feeling.

Lillian's assistant, Jewel Blanch, wasn't overshadowed. She had youth and freshness on her side and flashed seductive smiles when anyone complimented her on her crisp navy and white frilly frock, her red panama and her strappy red shoes. Frank thought he'd never seen her looking so much like a sparkler on a birthday cake. She waved at him and he waved back, but he could see she was busy and moved on.

He had just about finished his sight-seeing trip in the marquee when he felt a touch on his right arm.

He heard the masculine voice say, "How the Dickens are you, mate?"

Frank recognized the voice immediately. He glanced in the direction of the voice, and his cheeky Singapore friend, Loveboat Williams smiled at him. Frank took a good look. Loveboat had Loveboat's voice, but he looked all wrong. It was like he'd borrowed someone else's clothes, someone else's hair, and someone else's be-whiskered face.

Loveboat winked at him. "Disguise too much for you?"

"You don't look like you, neither does that suit."

"Armani, mate; shirt, tie, socks, and under jocks too. Wanna see?"

When it occurred to Frank that Loveboat was playing one of his many parts, he asked the question, "Who are you supposed to be?"

Loveboat struck an impressive pose—and spoke in a mint julep accent. "Sir, you are addressing none other than renowned Albuquerque horse trader CK Dexter Beaumont."

"Albuquerque?"

"Albuquerque, New Mexico, USA, home of the famous Hot Air Balloon Festival."

Frank was swept away. "You're making that up!"

Loveboat explained: He and three other professional imposters were hired by a mega-rich Middle Eastern Thoroughbred owner to be present at the annual Magic Millions Yearling Sales to outbid one of his serious rivals for the best of the current crop of yearlings, without the rival knowing.

Loveboat was the mastermind. He created the characters and directed the production. For himself, he invented Dexter, 'a suggestion of Rhett Butler'—Roger Bannister was one of Dexter's Brit-born friends from the '*jungles*' of Park Lane, and the third character, due to appear later in the week was Christopher Coburg, 'a South African diamond millionaire.'

The gig was three weeks of well-financed luxury, with accommodation at Hotel Conrad, extravagant expenses and designer wardrobes. The Middle Eastern owner knew his rival was a tightwad, with restrictions on his financial outlays. The brief to Loveboat and his two buddies was decisive: "Stay in the bidding until the tightwad drops off!"

To up the ante, the imposters were told to bid against each other to further cloud the deception and to keep the bids out of reach.

"It is a dream assignment," said Loveboat. "As of now we've bought ten prize yearlings, and the sales have another twelve days to run. Splashing money around can be a whole lot of fun especially when your name is CK Dexter Beaumont, and you can lead big heads like Mike Flynn up the garden path!"

"You mean the one and only Michael J Flynn?"

"The one we all love and adore."

"You yanked his chain?"

"Till it rattled, mate. One of the most delicious things I've ever done."

Loveboat then launched into a description of the trick he and Roger Bannister, his Brit buddy, played on Michael J Flynn at the cocktail party, quoting background information Frank had blurted out about The Mating Game fiasco to him in Singapore.

"We gave him the works, old mate, and he went for it, but here's yet another a word of warning—He's gunning for you and your friend Eddie Edwards, so put on your bulletproof vest, and buckle up tight. Flynn is one dangerous dude, and he's after you, body and soul. In short, he wants to do you in."

"What happens if he finds out you've kidded him?"

Loveboat shook his head. "Our credentials are bona fide—I covered our backs as soon as I accepted the gig. I engage professional operators all the way, up front and back. Flynn even has my card."

"He has your card?"

"A bone fide Albuquerque horse trader can't expect to be taken seriously without a business card, old buddy. I have a service that takes messages, and if Flynn asks questions, he'll find out that Roger and I are exactly who we pretend to be. But I can't say this often enough, Frankie. Don't let him find out what you're up to. Lock it up tight, mate, or you'll be a trophy on his wall."

"I hear you, Loveboat."

"I did some checking. After The Mating Game screw-up, Adrian Messenger, that rotten little poison pill, bad-mouthed Flynn to the syndicate as a risky player, and Flynn's radar has picked up on it. The only way he can get back in with the syndicate is to take you and Edwards out of the game!"

"For good?"

"Wise up, Frank, you've been around. You were playing with the big boys when you iced The Mating Game, and if I miss my guess you weren't exactly playing fair. Your winning horse had help, yes?"

Frank thought for a second. "Yes."

"You don't have to be coy with me, cobber. I'm as shifty as they come, and I'm living dangerously doing what I'm doing down here, but I always walk softly. If you want to beat the system, walk softly too, 'cos if someone hears you coming, the system will beat you. Have you had time to work on your caper since we met in Singapore? Just how tight is it?"

Frank was wary. "Should we be talking turkey with all these people around?"

Loveboat laughed. "Best place to tell secrets is in a crowded room. Everyone assumes you have nothing to hide, so top me up and be brief."

Frank did as he was asked, carefully covering all points. Loveboat took it all in; treated it to a brain scan, had a few queries, then delivered his verdict:

"Damned it if isn't daring. You've sure got the nuts and bolts in place and it looks like you've got the holes plugged up, so I'll go ahead and fine-tune the betting strategy. Mate, this single caper could grow roses all over our future nights and days."

"That's the grand plan," said Frank.

With a wave and a flourish, Loveboat excused himself and moved off to be instantly swallowed up by the bouncy crowd.

Frank turned toward the marquee's main exit door, caught a pungent whiff of Ferragamo EDT, and stared straight into the searching eyes of Michael J Flynn. Frank was a deer in the headlights, momentarily startled.

Michael J was not. Oozing velvet charm, he said, "Hello, Frank, fancy meeting you here."

Frank recovered pronto. "Not so fancy, Michael, we both belong on racetracks."

"Well put," said Michael J. "I couldn't help noticing that not so idle conversation with the man from Albuquerque, CK Dexter Beaumont, wasn't it?"

"Correct," said Frank, sensing he was under investigation.

"I didn't know you indulged in earnest verbal exchanges with mega-rich horse traders, Frank."

Frank was speed thinking, making up a story on the spot. "I met Dexter Beaumont at the Karaka Yearling

Sales in New Zealand last year. He had never been to Australia and he was interested to know more about it."

"And you were wearing your tourism hat."

"Waving a flag top, I was happy to clue him. Dexter's a nice guy."

"Rolling in money I hear and making expensive noises at the yearling sales."

"He is."

"What does he intend doing with all the horse flesh he's investing in?"

"He hasn't said anything to me about that."

Michael J smiled. "I thought you may have been urging him to pass over a couple of his expensive purchases to your trainer friend Eddie Edwards, who could no doubt teach them all the tricks of the track, and I do mean all."

Frank caught the implication and quickly reached for an out. "We didn't discuss that; we were talking about winning chances in today's big race."

"Did he have any suggestions for a wager?"

"He's not a tipster, Michael."

"Wise man. Give my regards to Eddie. I thought he may have been here."

"He's in Brisbane. He has a runner at Kings Park on Saturday, and he's all tied up."

"As tightly as he should be, I hope. Do say hello when you see him. Nice to run into you, old sport, and try to have a good day."

Michael J moved away, edging easily though the packed marquee, nodding and smiling as he went. It was his best imitation of Cary Grant in *To Catch a Thief,* Michael J Flynn was a man who wore two faces, and there were times when even he didn't know which face he was wearing.

Frank Davenport breathed easy. The last person he'd wanted to run into was Michael J Flynn, and his stress level dropped when the short meeting ended.

IN A QUIET CORNER of the model's dressing room in the crowded Dome Marquee, Lillian St Clare was lending her ears to Jewel Blanch, who gushed excitedly as she delivered all the details of the proposed fashion shoot at the McCoy Stud in Roma. Lillian was impressed.

"I'll need the proposal in writing, and my legal people will go over it for approval but that's standard procedure."

"The proposal will be in your hands before you leave for Hong Kong," said Jewel.

"Darling, it seems you've thought of everything."

JEWEL CALLED LORRIE AT the McCoy Stud two minutes after she walked into her Conrad suite that evening. On the telephone in Roma, it took Lorrie a few minutes to understand what was being thrown at her. When she did, she was caught off-field. A fashion shoot that sounded like a Las Vegas blockbuster.

Jewel pushed her barrow with a breathless plea: All she wanted was a 'yes.' Everything would be taken care of by professionals. The models, crews and assistants would be accommodated in Roma and be driven to the site. The catering would be negotiated, clothes stored in a dressing room on wheels, technical setups slated from eight a.m., models from ten a.m. until four p.m. Minimum two days, maximum three, plus a generous fee for the use of the Stud.

Lorrie didn't answer right away but Jewel was impatiently hanging out for an answer. "Lorrie? Are you there?"

" I'll put the idea to the table at dinner and get back to you."

"I'll wait for your call, honey. Fingers, legs and arms crossed! Okay?"

DINNER AT THE MCCOY'S that evening was another of Alice's nutritious bombshells, but it was upstaged by Lorrie's ten-minute delivery of Jewel Blanche's unusual request. Midway through her pitch, she realised her audience was anything but indifferent. Alice's eyes were shining, Kitty's eyes never wavered from Lorrie's face, Cassie was showing signs of excitement, and Cooper was a picture of thoughtful interest. When Lorrie stopped speaking, the table was silently agog.

"Well?" she said, "what do you all think?"

Kitty answered first, "If everything's going to be arranged, and all we have to do is supply the location. I can't see why it couldn't happen."

"They wouldn't have to get caterers," said Alice, "I can ask the CWA ladies to help me take care of that, all for the cost of the food and a donation to the club."

"The farmhands will never be the same," said Cassie.

Everyone looked at Cooper. "What you're all overlooking," he said, "is that we're trying to get The Stinger familiar with the hustle and bustle of the racetrack. We've already got the audio, but a bit of extra activity going on would sure assist the cause."

"You mean you're for it?" asked Lorrie.

"Boots and all," he answered, "but if you think it will affect The Stinger's program it's no deal."

Everyone looked at Lorrie. "I honestly can't see that it will."

"Is there anything to sign?" asked Kitty.

"Standard procedure only," answered Lorrie, "Lillian St Clare's people will take care of that."

"What do we do now?" asked Cooper.

24

CLICK ROBERTS: THE ONE AND ONLY

MICHAEL'S VIP SOIREE IN his suite went as planned but it was a minor event on his social card. Lillian and his elite horse traders sent their apologies so he lost interest, wound everything up as soon as he could, and took to the shower.

As soon as Jewel clinched the deal with the McCoys, she hung up and dialled Michael J's suite. He took the call in the shower. When he heard the good news, he barked out a wet response, hung up, grabbed for a towel, dried off, and called his favourite paparazzi shooter, a money-hungry eager beaver by the name of Click Roberts.

"Where are you?" asked Michael, when Click answered his mobile.

"Up a fucken tree outside Palazzo Versace. I'm stalking that dickhead who does that telly talk show. He's here cheating on his girlfriend with his latest root."

"You said Palazzo Versace. You do mean the hotel on the Gold Coast?"

"Where else? Its Magic Millions old buddy, old mate, the joint is full of wankers, and I'm on the dough-ray-me trail—like, you know, show me the money, honey."

"I'll do just that if you get out of that tree and pay me a visit, I've got a big budget assignment with your name written all over it."

"How big is big?"

"Michael J Flynn big. I don't talk small-change and you know it."

"You're the man, Mikey. Where are you?"

"Hotel Conrad, Broadbeach, twenty minutes away from you. If you come right away, I'll pay you a consultancy fee for the visit, and you can forget the dickhead you're stalking."

"Sounds like a plan. I've been up here for two hours and I'm starting to feel like a kookaburra. I'm on the way, Hosay!"

Click Roberts knew Michael J's assignments meant hard cash. Life as a pap shooter had its ups and downs, but he was one of the best. His downfall was money—he had trouble holding on to it, but in Click's little black book, Michael J Flynn was listed under 'Easy Cash.'

Good paps didn't play the rules. His no-rules rule also ran to cars. He drove a dusty old Ford Falcon because he didn't want to be conspicuous! He was out of the tree and into the seat of the Falcon in a flash. The trip took fifteen minutes. He took the turn from the highway on a yellow light, roared past a Volvo and a BMW into the driveway of the Hotel Conrad, alighted like a VIP, and politely asked the concierge to valet-park his dusty wreck.

When the concierge hesitated, Click said, ever so nicely. "I'm here on an assignment for Mr Michael J Flynn, would you like to check with him? He's waiting for me upstairs."

The concierge was back in two minutes. "Everything's fine, Mr Roberts."

He handed Click a plastic key card. "You'll need this to get you to the twentieth floor. Just swipe it when you get into the elevator. Mr Flynn would like you to go straight up."

Click said, ever so nicely, "Shit! I thought I might have time for a root in the bar first, but when duty calls, duty calls."

He smiled, handed the concierge the keys to his Ford, swaggered through the front foyer to the bank of elevators, rode to the twentieth floor, swaggered along the corridor to Michael J's corner suite, knocked on the door and yelled, "Room service!"

Michael opened the door, invited Click in, sat him down, poured him a vodka and orange from the mini bar, and detailed the assignment.

Click took it all in. He'd be on-site at the McCoy Stud and accommodated in Roma in the best possible digs. The actual fashion shoot would be handled by a commercial photographer. Click's job would be to shoot atmosphere—the models on call, interesting action in and around the Stud itself, Jewel Blanch in producer mode, lunch under the pretty trees, coffee breaks, and all the other fancy images wanky magazines love to present to their adoring readers.

A smiling Michael added, "That's just the window dressing."

Click smiled back. "So, what's the real-deal? Gimme the duck's guts."

"Record what's going on with Lorrie Edwards, Cassie Morgan, Cooper McCoy and McCoy's dud blueblood. That part of the assignment has to be carefully handled."

Michael paused and fixed Click with a hard stare.

"Carefully means carefully, Click! It can't appear that you're interested in anything happening on the track. Understand? You're to be nothing more than a friendly lens man employed by *Ultimate Cool* to cover the glamour aspects of the story. Jewel Blanch, the bird in charge of everything will be briefed. Got it!"

Click was all savvy. "Got it by the knackers, man. Do you want me to pick up any titbits of info, too?"

"The only things I don't want you to pick up on are the models. They're off-limits."

"Fuck! If I've gotta give up sex for three or four days, it's extra."

"You'll be well paid for your abstinence. It's already included in your fee."

"Okay. I'll screw myself silly before I hit Roma."

Michael J rose from his chair. "I'm not interested in your screwing agenda, I want results, and you're on a retainer—starting now."

"Hot cha-cha," said Click, "just one hitch."

"Which is?"

"I'm covering for a buddy on a commercial shoot in Brisbane this Saturday. That's not going to get in the way is it?"

"Saturday in Brisbane is not a problem. Do you have anything else happening in the very near future?"

"Nothing I can't get rid of. When can you confirm all this? Like dates and stuff."

"The shoot is confirmed as of this minute, all other details by the end of the week. Are we all clear?"

"Like a sunny day at the beach."

"You're a true professional, Click. I'm chuffed to have your services."

Click finished his vodka and orange, put the glass down and stood. "No need to bullshit, Mike, we're both cowboys and we both play dirty when we have to. I don't lose sleep over that. You're paying me, I deliver, and the best thing about me, old mate, old buddy, is that I don't ask questions."

"That's exactly why I pulled you out of that tree."

"And exactly why I don't have to climb back up the fucker. Some other pap can shoot that telly dickhead. My heart wasn't in it anyway."

Michael J Flynn felt like flying. *Yes!*

25

THUNDERDOME AT KINGS PARK

THUNDERDOME'S SCHEDULED RUN AT Kings Park in Brisbane had become a minor problem for Lorrie. Kitty and Cooper knew Cassie would be in the saddle and they were keen to watch the run. No way could that happen! If they noted Thunderdome's curious likeness to The Stinger, the caper would crash.

But Lorrie's dilemma disappeared when Jewel called to say she was anxious to visit the Stud to blueprint the fashion shoot. Lorrie cleverly arranged the visit to coincide with the weekend of Thunderdome's race. She also alerted Jewel's eager young friend Bill Harris, who let out a Tarzan yell when he heard the good news. It didn't take much urging for Bill to persuade Cooper to turn on a welcoming party.

Lorrie breathed easy; but as Ring-in Day drew nearer, she realised the magnitude of what she was involved in. She was constantly on the alert watching for slip-ups, anxious to avoid mistakes. At the same time, she had to carry on as if things were normal and above board.

In Brisbane, Eddie was still jumpy.

Thunderdome's race was timed for mid-afternoon. As ordered, Jeff delayed the horse's arrival at the track to lessen his exposure time for racegoers who liked to cruise the Kings Park horse stalls.

On the morning of the race, Lorrie drove Cassie to the track.

It was not a big crowd. As Eddie predicted, the regular groupies and hotshot punters were on the Gold Coast for the last big Magic Millions race, and the horse stall cruisers were fewer than usual. As luck had it, there was an unexpected diversion that grabbed the attention of the punters.

A commercial television channel was shooting a promotion for the year's Winter Racing Carnival in May, and one of their on-camera stars was hogging the limelight, talking to the crowd and pumping the catering facilities. He had no permission to shoot the horses before or after each race.

Thunderdome, wearing the number 4 saddlecloth, looked a picture when Jeff led him into the saddling paddock, where promotional camera coverage was banned. When it was time to mount, Cassie arrived with her saddle.

"He's real fit, Cass," said Jeff, "the race is a bit too short for him and he needs the run, but if we wanted to be serious, he could shake the crap out of this field."

Cassie smiled. "Can't oblige this time, Jeff."

"Don't let him get away from you," said Jeff, as he hoisted Cassie aboard.

"Like I said; not this time."

"Good girl."

Eddie was in the Members Stand in conversation with veteran racetrack journalist, Ray Douglas, a seasoned judge of horseflesh.

"Your runner looks fit," said Ray.

Eddie kept it light. "A bit too fresh today, Ray. He needs the run."

"Nice looking horse, Eddie. I don't think I've seen him before."

Eddie covered instantly. "Looks aren't everything, Ray. He's on trial."

"Oh?"

"He's a bit of a barrier rogue."

"That's a shame."

Lorrie waited on the edge of the saddling paddock while the horses paraded, and she joined Jeff at the trackside after the runners left the paddock.

The starting signal sounded, and the field jumped. The only part of Bart Anderson's call Jeff heard was, "*Thunderdome missed the start and Cassie Morgan has taken him to the rails.*"

Jeff was relieved. "We're in the clear, Lorrie, all good."

It was a fast run race on a perfect track. Thunderdome finished fifth in the centre of the track. In the Members Stand, Ray Douglas gave Eddie's shoulder a friendly pat.

"Your horse might have won that race if he hadn't been for that bad start. When are you saddling him up again?"

Eddie was casual. "He's bloody hard to train, and he needs a lot more work."

Ray flashed a grin. "Good luck, then"

Eddie sensed that Ray was in the mood for more horse talk, so he made an excuse to get away and hurried to meet Jeff, who had Thunderdome covered, and waiting at the horse stalls.

"Damn great run," said Eddie.

"Told you, Boss. He's gonna kill that ring-in field."

Eddie was still nervous. "Let's load him into the float and get him out of here."

Ten minutes later, Thunderdome was safely aboard the float on his way back to the Boondall Stud, with Jeff and Eddie in the Range Rover.

Cassie and Lorrie were following in Lorrie's Subaru. "You're all quiet, Cass," said Lorrie, "are you unhappy about something?"

"Not really, I'm thinking about how fantastic it's going to be when all this stuff is over."

"Having second thoughts?"

"No time for that. We're both in for the long haul and I've just had a practice run for the big day."

"How do you feel?"

"I don't really know."

"You're not tense about anything, are you?"

"Nothing as simple as that."

"Then what is it?"

"What we're doing is not your everyday racing exercise, Lorrie, it's a lot more than that, and I guess I'm a little edgy."

"You're not alone, kiddo."

Cassie gave her a look. "We're pushing boundaries you know."

"It's too late to get off the train, honey."

Cassie didn't say anything right away, then it came out.

"Who said anything about getting off?"

JEWEL'S VISIT TO THE McCoy Stud went swimmingly. She talked up the fashion shoot, won everyone over, and went wild over Alice's idea of having the CWA ladies help with the catering. Jewel was the star of Cooper's party, a Saturday afternoon barbeque that ticked all the boxes for the Roma groovers. An excited Bill Harris had a quiet word with Cooper.

"Mate, Jewel's all set for another bubble session in the spa. I've lined up a playmate for you if you wanna come along."

"Oh, yeah?"

"One of the numbers I told you about. Interested?"

"Why not?"

"She's A-one merchandise."

"Sounds good."

"Get excited, Coop. Like I said, I'm looking after you."

"How can I thank you, Bill?"

"Just cool it, and have a good time."

"Bet on it, mate."

AS THE SUN WENT down in the aftermath of the party, Alice and Kitty were cleaning up in the kitchen.

"I didn't take to that Jewel girl when I met her last time, but I like her. She's a real do-er, Kit, and this fashion shoot of hers is going to be fun. Roma hasn't had anything like it since I can't remember. It's like the first time I saw Ashton's Circus when I was a kid."

26

ULTIMATE COOL IN THE OUTBACK

ALICE'S ASHTON'S CIRCUS-WORD-PICTURE bore an element of truth. The procession that entered the McCoy Stud on the Monday of January's third week was no minor event.

The fashion whirlwind got off to a flying start early on the morning of the first day, when a huge silver and white mobile home was towed into the property by a cream Land Rover driven by a snappy looking dude in blue jeans and a khaki shirt. Jewel, who had taken up residence with the models in Roma the day before, was on-site to meet him.

He parked the mobile home on her indicated spot close to the barbecue court, told her where to contact him in town if she needed him, then leapt back into the Land Rover and took off.

Blue Larner and the farm boys had arrived early to see the sights and were pretending, with little success, to go about their business; not in their ordinary everyday work duds either. They all wore crisp clean shirts, spiffy jeans, shiny boots, Akubra hats and a bandana or two.

In the kitchen, Alice and Kitty were busy with four of the CWA ladies. Together they made a no-nonsense sextet with their minds on the job. The aroma of freshly baked bread drifted into the early morning sunshine along with the faint sounds of Glenn Campbell's greatest country hits. The pink-breasted Mitchell cockatoos, lured by the aroma of the bread, were dancing in the pepperina trees or pecking at the big bowls of wheat and corn Alice had set for them.

The Brisbane fashion photographer, Scotty Malone, was scouting suitable shot spots, checking light meters, looking creatively thoughtful, and wording up his young assistant, who was making like Steven Spielberg on location for *Raiders of the Lost Ark*.

The three make-up props and wardrobe girls arrived in a cream van crammed with goodies; frocks, accessories, footwear, handbags, umbrellas, make-up, and all sorts of things to have and to hold. Like an army of sassy worker bees, they ferried it all to the imposing mobile home, while the farm hands tripped over each other.

Click Roberts roared up in his dusty Ford Falcon, hopped out, slung his camera bag over his shoulder, took in the scenery and introduced himself to Jewel Blanch.

"I'm guessing you know what I'm here for," he said, hauling out his fancy camera and patting it, "I got a brief from Lillian St Clare to aim this baby at anything that looks like hot stuff. You cool?"

Jewel's answer was, "I'm cool."

Click gave her his best macho-dude grin. "Anything special you need, just ask. I'm at your beck and call, and when Click Roberts is on your beck and call, baby, no beck or call is too extreme. Are we together on that?"

"We are," said Jewel.

"Hot-cha," said Click. "If I get in the way, you're on call to tell me to butt out."

"I'm sure you won't get in the way," said Jewel.

Click was on the verge of making a move on what he'd instantly identified as scrumptious merchandise when he reminded himself of Michael J's stern warning to stay away from the shapely feminine talent. He withdrew into his lusty shell and flashed a great wide smile instead.

Jewel smiled back. "It's great to have you on board, Click," and walked away.

Click watched her departure and threw a meaningful look at the attentive gallery of farmhands. "This is gonna be one horny assignment," he said, "and it's gonna be all a man can do, to stop doing what only a man can do."

Click's words connected with nineteen-year-old Blue Larner, the youngest and chirpiest of the farmhands, and their official spokesperson.

"Welcome to our world," said Blue, "we got sleepless nights coming up too."

"Hazards of the game," said Click.

On the track, Cassie was giving The Stinger his morning workout, with Lorrie and Cooper standing by. For once, Cooper's attention was not on his best mate. Realising what the distraction was, Lorrie summed it up.

"You wanted a fashion shoot; you got a fashion shoot. Is this what you expected?"

"Not quite," Cooper replied, "but I'm sure the fascination will wear off."

Lorrie's eyebrows rose. "Wait until the sophisticated visitors get an eyeful of The Stinger doing his thing to Bill's masterful audio."

"I'm hanging out for that," said Cooper.

Looking over his shoulder, Lorrie caught the approach of a second cream van that had just turned into the McCoy Stud driveway.

"Here's something else to hang out for. I think the models have arrived."

Cooper turned around, saw the van glide to a stop, and watched the six models emerge—silken haired, long-legged and satin-skinned—prime examples of what every wannabe Aussie model could ever hope to be.

The farmhands stirred restlessly, shifting weight from one foot to the other. When a couple of the models unleashed pearly smiles and friendly waves at them, the healthy country lads registered a heartbeat rise and a tremor in their loins. For once, Blue Larner had no comment.

The reaction did not escape Lorrie, who glanced Cooper's way and said, "I think your boys have just flown to la-la land. You too?"

Cooper nailed her with a wicked look. "I've seen girls before, and just for the record, I've logged a few flight hours, too; trips to the moon on gossamer wings, corny stuff like that."

Lorrie was itching to keep the conversation on that track but reminded herself that it was neither the time nor the place to be playing games.

"We'll do our thing with Bill's audio after lunch," she said. "It's a cloudy day. It looks like the sun is going to stay in hiding so it shouldn't be too hot."

"You're the boss," said Cooper, registering a pang of disappointment. He'd wanted to keep the cute-speak happening and as usual, he didn't quite understand why it stopped.

Under Jewel's direction, the fashion whirlwind revved up. She was on top of everything, issuing orders, constantly conferring with Scotty Malone and the prop girl, checking on make-up and wardrobe in the mobile home, and keeping up the flow of the fashion changes. The models were clockwork examples of how a shoot should happen. There was a short mid-morning refreshment break under the pepperina trees. Alice's ladies were all over it; coffee, tea, fresh juices, chilled water, sticks of homemade shortbread, and fresh-from-the-oven pumpkin scones with homemade rosella jam and clotted cream. Everyone hoed in!

Lorrie took the time to tell Jewel how impressed she was, and Jewel responded.

"This will be a magic shoot. It will look marvellous in print, and it's just too fantastic that you could make it happen."

"Who's the adrenalin junkie with the camera?" asked Lorrie; "The brash one in the Rolling Stones T-shirt."

Jewel identified him. "Click Roberts, he's shooting the atmosphere; background stuff that will feature in the layouts. This place will look sensational."

"Some team," said Lorrie.

Two minutes later the break was over, and the shoot cranked up again.

CLICK MOVED ABOUT LIKE an oiled grasshopper, skipping in and out of the action but never getting in the way. He was in such constant motion, and it was so hard to figure where he was aiming his camera that he was dizzying to watch.

Click never missed a trick, he caught it all—image after image, and like a bird of prey stalking a potential snack, he eagle-eyed the track, and shot what was happening there too. Every now and then he took a break to check his camera or to recharge his adrenalin machine, but he was no slouch.

Lunch came and went with a flurry of small talk, funny patter, and tasty things to eat and drink. The catering teamsters were on the mark with a banquet of the honest-to-goodness granny tucker.

Despite the movement and dazzle of the fashion shoot, the main event of the afternoon was The Stinger's show-stopping performance. After a warm-up circuit of the track, with the audio providing the appropriate background, Cassie broke The Stinger into a gallop. As the pair approached the turn, Cooper upped the audio decibels, and the watching audience lost it.

Photographers, assistants, models, Blue Larner, his boys, and the resident McCoy groupies let loose with an unexpected outburst of vocal encouragement.

Unaccustomed to the wild reaction, The Stinger broke stride to go into what appeared to be a pretty gleeful take on a rap dance, then instantly recovered to finish the gallop. Cassie brought him back to the gate to loud applause.

Cooper summed up the performance. "We don't want him doing that on a racetrack."

Cassie saw the humorous side. "Come on, Cooper. He was just showing off."

Lorrie's comment was no-nonsense. "He's not getting away with that. Take him around again, Cassie."

She turned to the gallery. "Okay guys, he's going again. Can we have the same reaction please?"

"Betcha!" yelled Blue Larner. "Tonsils at the ready, fellas!"

This time the gallery was augmented by the CWA ladies. Cassie repeated the run; slow trot, canter and a full gallop. When she had The Stinger ready to take the turn, up went the audio and the real-time outburst. The Stinger took the turn in his smooth stride and finished his run.

Lorrie turned to Cooper. "Your four-legged friend has a sense of humour, Cooper, but he's got to learn that fun is fun, and work is work."

Cassie trotted The Stinger back to the gate. "That's it for today," said Lorrie, "we'll sponge him down and brush him up." She looked over at Cooper and said, "He's lucky we're not brushing him off."

Cooper walked over to her. "You're upset."

Lorrie didn't know whether she was, or she wasn't, but she couldn't help smiling anyway. "I'm only doing my job, Cooper. Do you mind telling that to your best friend?"

Cassie had unsaddled The Stinger, and his bridle was off. He looked in Cooper's direction and trotted over to him. "Give me five, boy," said Cooper.

The Stinger did his familiar trick.

"I've got news for you," said Cooper, "your trainer is browned off. Work is work, feller, you can have fun when you're rich and famous."

The Stinger nodded again, and Lorrie caught Cooper's cheeky grin.

"I'm getting confused here," she said, "I don't know whether I'm supposed to be training your horse, or you."

Cooper didn't miss a beat. "Either way, we're both receptive."

The exchange did not go unnoticed. Alice, who'd been standing with Kitty, gave her friend's arm a little nudge with her elbow. "Don't say I didn't tell you. That boy is chomping at the bit, and I don't mean the horse."

Bill Harris called in later in the afternoon with a pile of barbecue chops, a tray of sausages, a bucket of coleslaw, a carton of sparkling wine, and made an announcement:

"Dinner's on the New Millennium Sound Shop, guys!"

Jewel glanced at the tray of goodies. "We intended going back to town for a light meal and an early night"

"What's the point?" countered Bill. "You can eat here and still have an early night."

Kitty sealed Bill's offer. "No trouble at all, we'll fire up the barbecue."

Day One was over by seven-thirty, Jewel, with her Production Manager's hat firmly in place, organised the transport back to the motel. If Bill had anything else in mind, it was not on the agenda. Jewel was fashioned-out.

DAY TWO WAS A by-the-numbers repeat of Day One, with a couple of exceptions.

Lorrie had decided it was time for the bandages to appear on The Stinger's fetlocks, and after lunch that day, she quietly discussed the move with Cassie.

"Thunderdome will have to wear bandages for the Ring-in Race. They just can't appear on at Kings Park on the day."

"Of course, not," said Cassie, "that's something nobody thought of."

"I did, Cass, but I've been putting it off."

"Have you thought of an excuse?"

Lorrie explained, "My story will be that as a lightly raced novice in a big field, The Stinger could take a knock or be shuffled in the run to the turn."

Cassie nodded. "Things like that do happen, and fetlock injury is not uncommon."

"True enough. If we take the precaution of applying bandages in training, he'll be used to them when he runs bandaged at Flinton. How does that sound."

Cassie nodded again. "What about Thunderdome?"

Lorrie had the answer. "Jeff can work him in bandages a few times at North Point. With a light weight in the Ring-in Race, he'll be out of trouble anyway."

The deal was done. The bandages were applied. When they came to Cooper's notice, he accepted Lorrie's reasoning without question.

Better still, on The Stinger's afternoon run that day, there was no replay of the rap dance, something Cooper noted with a kind of mischievous pride:

"No rap dance today, coach; looks like he liked the bandages. My mate's a quick study, he usually fits in without causing a fuss. Want me to tell him anything else?"

Lorrie squared up. "Tell him he's a good boy."

Cooper couldn't help himself. "Anything you want to tell me?"

"Yes. I think you're both doing nicely."

"You too, but you should try to take time to enjoy yourself, you're working too hard."

"Efficiency buys results, Cooper."

Lorrie refused to play. It was not on the agenda. She knew the situation could not get out of hand. She'd had the moves put on her before and she was skilled at handling them. She reminded herself again that Ring-in Day was only weeks away, and that she was the key player.

Cooper was baffled. He knew there was chemistry between them, and he couldn't work it out, so he took it on the chin and backed off.

Cassie dismounted and unstrapped The Stinger's saddle. She was no dope, she saw what was going on with Cooper and Lorrie, and she wanted to open the door for Lorrie to walk through, if she needed. She qualified. "Maybe when all this is over, you can come back here for a holiday or something, you know, just to have some fun with nothing else on your mind."

Lorrie registered the message. "Might be an idea at that—sometime."

Cassie played cute: "You know the best thing about Cooper McCoy?"

"What's that, Cassie?"

"He's not Frank Davenport."

Lorrie frowned. "You've never told me you don't like Frank."

"I like Frank just fine, he's Joe Cool. He's a smart act, but he's Hong Kong and you're not. He'll never sing your song, kiddo, he doesn't know the words."

"We're together on that," said Lorrie.

"I just wanted you to know that I know—okay?"

Cassie changed the subject abruptly. "Our four-footed mate went well today. He's getting there, and damn it if Cooper isn't right about him. He's got this thing, it's hard for me to say what I feel, but there's a kind of yearning about him."

"I hear you."

"I like him. I really do. When I'm working him, he's always with me."

Cassie broke off for a second. "You know what he is? He's a learner. If we had him for a few more weeks I honestly think we could make him into something."

Lorrie faced her. "Like letting him run as himself in the big race?"

Cassie said nothing.

"Forget it, Cass. He's too inexperienced to let loose in a big field on a major city racetrack, and there's too much money on the table. Besides, we don't have a few more weeks. He runs at Flinton next week, and depending on how he goes, we'll give him another run somewhere else, but we're only training him to look good—that's all. We're not training him to win."

Cassie let out a sigh. "Thanks for reminding me."

"Sorry."

"No. I needed that."

27

THE 'COSY COMFORT BED AND BREAKFAST' THAT EVENING

MRS ROBERTA SANDERSON'S COSY Comfort Bed and Breakfast, two blocks east of the Roma Hospital, was her pride and joy. Her ex-hubby, Lucas, fell for a mega-rich Gold Coast widow he'd sweet-talked on the Internet. Realising he was on a good thing, he left Roberta to live with the widow. He became a kept man.

With the swag of money Lucas's new lady paid Roberta to agree to a divorce, she tricked-up her big old-fashioned county house as a four-suite overnighter with 'Luxury Country Breakfasts.'

Roberta's prized assistant was Angelique Jones, twenty-three, a salubrious young lady who had given up her job as a barmaid in one of Roma's older hotels to take a well-paid job with Roberta, whose optional add-on, was a 'Bumper Three-course Evening Meal'; Chicken and leek Soup, Roast of the Day, and Sweet Sherry Trifle.

Currently installed as Roberta's star border, was Mr Click Roberts, whose roving eye had a habit of roving wickedly over the buxom charms of Angelique Jones.

All Click needed to press his point, was one glimmer of interest. It came at the evening dinner table after the second day of Jewel's fashion shoot. Click had finished a generous serve of trifle, and he was anxiously rubbing what appeared to be a dodgy shoulder. Observant Angelique noticed and volunteered assistance.

"If you've got a problem there, Mr Roberts, I can take care of it."

Click wasted nary a second. "I think it's a stiff muscle. I've been shooting all day."

Angelique was all innocence. "I know all about stiff muscles. As a matter of fact, they're my specialty."

"Fancy that, now. What's your treatment?"

"The best one is a rub with Red Papaya Elixir."

"That sounds like some wanky cocktail."

"Cocktail's the word. Do you want to try it?"

Click followed through. "Are you the masseuse?"

"You got it. Warm-up under the shower and you're on."

Click went to his room, showered, dried off, and towel-wrapped his flanks. Minutes later there was a tap on his door. Angelique barged in. With her came a large bottle of Red Papaya Elixir and a fluffy towel.

"Hit the bed, baby-cakes," she said. "Face down, hands by your side."

Click obeyed, and the rub began—shoulders, neck, upper back. Click was stoked. The aroma of the warm elixir filled the room.

"I can smell paw-paws," he said.

"That's what papaya is, honey. You should know that, you're a city boy."

Click was heating up. "What else can you teach a city boy?"

Angelique kept rubbing. "Got anything in mind, Mr Roberts?"

"Click's the name, babe, and Click's in the market for a chick."

"You don't say."

"Any ideas on how I get a chick in the market for Click?"

"How many times have you used that pitch?"

"Lost count."

"I can believe that. Okay, let's get a look at the merchandise."

Click lost the towel and rolled on to his back.

Angelique sized everything up and looked again.

"Does it come with a guarantee?"

"Certified."

"Well, now, aren't you cute?"

"Qualified, too."

Angelique put the elixir bottle on the bedside table, unbuttoned the shirt frock she was wearing, took it off, along with the rest of her gear, folded everything neatly, piled it all on the table, then stuck a fetching pose. Aphrodite rising from the mist.

Click's eyes popped. "Wow! Do I ever need some of that!"

"Not so fast. Off the bed, please."

He was on his feet in an instant. She stood behind him, pulled him close, scooped up a palm-load of elixir and began moving her hands over his chest, his abdomen and his thighs. He felt her hard nipples sweeping across his back in sensuous passes and moaned a lusty moan.

"That's *Blazing Saddles*, chick! This is as wild as it gets."

Her perfumed hands moved down to fondle his major reason for living, and another moan escaped from his lips.

Angelique was on a roll. "The object of this exercise is to get you off. I like long rides and I don't want you losing it too soon when you're in the saddle."

"You're playing my song."

She upped the action and Click steamed up for the home run. That old feeling took over, and in no time at all, his senses hit ecstasy mode and he was up, up and away.

He sank to the bed and said, "How much wilder can it get?"

She joined him on the sheets. "Stick around, that's one down."

"There are more games on the roster?"

"You're in Roma, honey, we play hard."

"Who's complaining?"

"It's nice to connect with a fella who knows the value of first-class action. There are heaps of cowboys out here who saddle up, ride rough, and hit the road without so much as a thank-you. I had you picked as a no-sweat stayer, the minute you checked in. Just relax. You don't have to do anything, you don't have to say anything, all you gotta do is play it cool, recharge the batteries, and start counting. You know how to count, doncha, Click?"

"You stole that dialogue from an old Bogie movie."

"I did. It was *To Have and Have Not*."

"I'm having it all."

"Foxtel is replaying *Basic Instant* tonight. We can watch it on and off while we're waiting for you to recharge between bouts. Maybe you can pick up a few clues."

"I'm an old movie freak. Keep 'em coming."

"Okay," said Angelique, "Try this. I want you to imagine you're a visitor to Tombstone and you walk through the swinging shutter doors, and see me waiting at the bar."

"Cockfight at the OK Corral"?

Now firmly in focus, Click topped her on the bed and said, "Fasten your seat-belt, Angie baby, it's gonna be a pumpy flight."

"*All About Eve*?"

"All About Click, and if you're still in the mood we can hit the replay button and play it again, Sam."

WHEN CLICK FINALLY HIT the slumber trail at two-thirty a.m., the count was four and he was a happy resident in Satisfaction Central.

Four hours later, he arrived at the homestead; chirpy, sparkling and ready for another busy day. Alice handed him a steaming mug of coffee, sniffed the air and gave him an interested look.

"Why can I smell red paw-paws?"

"My favourite midnight snack while I'm watching old movies."

28

A FASHION SHOOT IN THE BAG

DAY THREE OF JEWEL'S epic was a piece of cake. It was all over by midday; the signal for a long lunch. Kitty, Alice and the CWA girls excelled themselves. By two p.m. the *Ultimate Cool* blockbuster was wrapped up for the drive back to Brisbane. Scotty Malone and his assistant left first. They were followed by the make-up props and wardrobe girls, who had their mobile home and its cargo of goodies ready to move out on cue. The models were booked on a late afternoon flight to Brisbane.

Jewel had elected to stay in Roma overnight to 'thank Bill for his help.'

Click Roberts took off in his dusty Ford Falcon after profusely thanking the grateful catering company. "I'm full of beans," he beamed, "and you ladies have made me re-think my diet. I'm off the junk stuff and into the good stuff. I'll probably live to be a hundred."

That said, Alice sent him packing with a cardboard carton loaded with 'good stuff' just in case he felt like a nibble on the way home.

With an exhilarating sigh, the McCoy Stud returned to normal, the fashion shoot was in the bag, all prettied up and waiting to rattle the world.

Alice watched the exit of the last van. "Kinda lonely," she said to Kitty, "funny the way good things come and go."

The party was over. Not without a slew of side effects.

29

THE AFTERMATH OF ULTIMATE COOL

ON THE MORNING AFTER Click Roberts drove back from Roma, he rode to the fifteenth floor of the Brisbane Marriott to deliver his CD to Michael J Flynn, who had flown up from Sydney to receive the evidence in person. The CD contained ten folders packed with images; close to five hundred in all. Click had edited his shoot to sharpen the pictures; deleting double-ups. He confined the actual fashion shoot to one folder, because he didn't think it was all that important.

Michael J fondled the CD as if it were the Treasure of the Sierra Madre. He had the rest of the day free to pore over Click's evidence.

"Now tell me," he said to Click, "what was your impression of what's going on out there in the Wild, Wild West?"

Click was on the spot with no real answers. He had shot himself silly for two and a half days without really forming any opinions. "What you see is what you get" was his on-the-spot take, and he'd seen it all.

That was not good enough for Michael J, not good enough at all. "Were you on the job all the time?"

"Check my images. Every one says when it was shot, exact time to the second. All there, from seven-fifteen a.m. through, two days and a bit, old mate. I don't dud clients, I take the cash, I do the job, I deliver, no worries."

"You picked up nothing?"

"I picked up everything. Hot models with long legs, far-out mother hens with far-out tucker, one horse with two horny birds on its case, one class-act cowboy, a well-greased fashion shoot whipped into shape by a sharp-shooting photographer getting prodded along by a red-hot babe who kept heating my rocks. Anything else?"

Michael J Flynn was not a happy man. He was sure something was missing. He did not get where he was in the world by ignoring the fine print. And somewhere in the fine print of the *Ultimate Cool* gig was the answer he was looking for. The same question niggled him. Why would Eddie Edwards have his daughter tied up for three months training a dud horse in Hicksville? It made no sense.

All right, all right, then. Edwards may not be a bright spark in the grey cell department; maybe he would have gone for the Hicksville deal to wave a flag for the grandson of a famous trainer, maybe that was it, except there was a fly in the cream pie and the fly's name was Frank Davenport!

Could it be that Davenport has the hots for Lorrie Edwards? Easy to understand, but is a tout like Davenport ready to hook up with a low-rent operator like Edwards, just to give his dick better aim at the jackpot? No way!

Click broke into his thoughts. "I know you're pissed off, Mike, and I'm sorry, but honest, I saw nothing but good stuff out there, and there's nothing on the CD that tells a different story. Check the images; all you'll see is outback Disneyland, because that's all there is!"

Michael J cooled off, and for a few minutes, he allowed himself the rare privilege of appearing human. "Okay, Click, and thanks. Sorry to be a sore head."

"She's apples mate, I'm on my mobile. It's never switched off, if you want to check on anything on the

CD give me a call. If I'm in the middle of a root or anything, leave a message and I'll call back ASAP, okay?"

Michael J said his thanks again, showed Click out, then loaded the CD into his laptop. It was nine-seventeen a.m. By twelve-twenty p.m., his head was whirling, his eyes were bleary, and his thoughts were more tangled than a bowl of spaghetti. Click was right. Outback Disneyland it was. He stood, walked to the telephone and ordered coffee and a Caesar.

"I want the coffee in a plunger, fresh, no cream, no milk, the Caesar dressing on the side, no egg, don't forget the anchovies. I'm serious. If the order's not right the waiter wears it." Down went the phone.

"I've had a gutful of this shit!" snarled Mickey Flynn. *"Getting fucked over by a couple of amateurs is not my idea of prime time. This is pissing me off, major!"*

For once Mickey was on the ropes, so he backed off to heed Michael J's good advice. When in doubt, relax, feed everything to the little grey cells and let them work it out. That's what they're for. Have they ever let you down? Michael J was so confident in the workings of his little grey cells that he actually smiled at the room service waiter, who had been warned to expect a scorpion, but walked out with a tip; in cash!

Michael J had just finished swirling the last of the crisp lettuce in the excellent Caesar dressing when the call from Lillian St Clare came through from Hong Kong. After the obligatory 'howdy-doody' and game-playing had gone by the board, Lillian got down to business.

"What I really want, Michael, is to tell you I'm gobsmacked."

"Gobsmacked?"

"A frightful word I know, but Scotty Malone's Roma images came in this morning, and we're over the moon up here. Click Roberts e-mailed his atmosphere coverage last night and it's too marvellous for words."

"Too marvellous for words?"

"We're tossing out most of the material we had planned for the May issue and we're going big on this. We've also decided on a mainstream promotional campaign in Australia, and Jewel Blanch will head it up. I thought you'd be pleased."

Michael J was bordering on a boredom attack. "I'm glad it turned out."

Lillian went on. "I won't say it was completely unexpected, but I was not prepared for what has been delivered, so I'm saying thank you."

There was a pregnant pause. "That's great, Lillian."

"My! Where did that little boy voice come from? Don't tell me you're embarrassed! For once in your life, you don't know what to say?"

Michael felt a prick of panic. "Nobody knows I had anything to do with that shoot, do they?"

"I don't dishonour confidences or break promises. Understood?"

"Understood."

"I don't know what you're involved in down there, but I can only hope that what you're getting out of it is as impressive as what I've got. I can hardly say anything more."

"You don't have to."

"Take care, darling, and please, when you're up here next we must get together. I'm absolutely insisting."

The call ended.

The great Michael J Flynn was humbled for an instant only, but that was the second time in one morning, and twice was too much. He took a deep breath and went back to the laptop. Two hours later he felt like throwing it at the wall. Something would come up. If you believed that, it always did; always!

30

THE STINGER'S BIG DAY AT FLINTON

AT THE McCOY STUD, it was all shoulders to the wheel. The Stinger's Flinton debut was only days away, and the pace was on to get his performance up to the mark. Cassie and Lorrie were on his case early every morning, and they kept up the daily routine without missing a beat. Cooper stood by without interfering. Bill Harris checked the audio every day, and the interest of the farmhands ran to replays of their carousing every time their hero ran a circuit of the track. It became a ritual; like going ape at a U2 concert.

Kitty and Alice kept everyone nourished, and the Mitchell cockatoos were having a ball.

When Flinton Race Day dawned, excitement rose with the sun. Alice had a big breakfast ready at six-thirty and everyone dived in.

The minibus hired to take the McCoy groupies to Flinton waited in the driveway. At seven-thirty, Cooper and Bill Harris loaded Sting into his float, hitched to Cooper's Land Rover, and drove off. A few minutes later Kitty, Alice, Lorrie and Cassie, splendid in their Sunday best, joined Blue Larner and the farm boys in the minibus, to follow the float.

It was not a long trip. After passing through Roma, the bus turned south, ran through the town of Surat, then turned south southeast, to head for the small town of Flinton, north-west of Goondiwindi. In Alice's opinion, if you lived in the west and you'd never been to the

Flinton Races you had every right to be ashamed! She had a point. Flinton Races had been an institution since way back, and they were kept alive by the warm spirit of the outback. Like the kookaburras, kangaroos, emus, and Mitchell cockatoos, they existed because they were supposed to!

The January 26 meet that year was a staged picnic for Australia Day, with a card of five races. The Stinger was running against seven other Thoroughbreds over a short distance; his first race since Lorrie and Cassie had taken him on. Excitement in the minibus ramped up as Flinton drew nearer. Blue and his boys were primed. As The Stinger's official task force, their enthusiasm could have powered the bus.

By the time the McCoy contingent arrived at Flinton, the Australiana bubble was bouncing all over the racetrack. Flags wearing the stars of the Southern Cross waved in the breeze, a country band played. The bar was open, drinks and picnic tucker were going down, and a bush poet, bleating out the infectious rhyming rhythms of Banjo Patterson, held his listeners in the palm of his hand.

The racegoers of the west habitually dressed for mainstream picnic race days. Prizes for 'Fashions on the Flinton Field' were generous incentives that resulted in colourful examples of How the West is Dressed. A couple of talent scouts tricked up as 'Fashion Police' ran their mischievous eyes over arriving racegoers and handed out entry forms to anyone who made their grade.

Lorrie and Cooper got an instant thumbs-up. She was in one of her favourite floating mushroom pink ensembles with a hat, strappy shoes and a shoulder bag to match. Cooper was sporty GQ, in blue jeans, a crisp white shirt, blue tie, navy jacket, fawn Akubra and tan boots.

The sassiest Fashion Police chick was taking entry details, no great shakes, nothing more than names, places of residence and corny stuff like. "Did you make your outfit yourself, or did you get it from which Flea Market?"

Filling out Cooper's entry, she smiled a wicked smile and said, "There's a bonus if you give me your telephone number."

Cooper fell into the trap. "What's the bonus?"

"I'll tell you when you're putting your boots under my bed."

Lorrie had trouble restraining herself. "Not so easy," she told the chick, "there's a long queue in Roma."

Cooper sure didn't miss that one. He gave Lorrie a look. "I can always make room for one more."

By now he knew better than to expect an encouraging answer, but he continued to live in hope. The Stinger was entered in Race Three. Cassie changed into her jockey silks for the race. She was Aussie to a fault in Eddie's stable colours of gold and green, sporting a gold satin cap with a white pom-pom on top. She caught the eyes of the local lads in the bar and they ripped into a rowdy chorus of "Waltzing Matilda" when she trotted her mount into the saddling paddock.

The Stinger looked regal; all shiny, sleek, and happy to be where he was.

In the company of Thoroughbreds, he was as blueblood as any of them. Blue Larner edged close to Cooper and said, "Our mate is all McCoy class, Coop, and we're real bloody proud of him."

Cooper smiled a wide smile. "Your mate is aware of that, Blue."

"Yeah, well, me and the boys wanted you to know we're with you and Sting all the way. All the way, Coop."

The seven runners moved around to the starting gate at the far side of the track, and the McCoy groupies, glued together by team spirit, stood hushed and still, all eyes on the white pom-pom on Cassie's gold cap. She had The Sting standing alert and calm, responding to her every touch of the reins; reassured by the weight of her young body in the saddle. She patted his forelock and he gave her a knowing nod. Together, they were ready.

"Let's do it, boy," she said, "let's show 'em who you are."

He answered with a nod, and she patted his forelock again. The field lined up. Cassie focused, and concentrating on her horse, moved him to his place, and sat statue still. When the bell sounded, she jumped him into the race and felt him hit his stride. He was out from the rails when he took the back turn, and with five horses in front of him, he settled into an even gallop. Still out from the rails, Cassie had him holding his ground. When she saw the home turn coming up, she took a deep breath, leaned forward, and got him ready to make his move.

Watching trackside, right opposite the winning post, Lorrie could see Cassie's gold cap on the outside of the small field. She crossed her fingers. The home turn was scant metres in front of the leaders, and it was The Stinger's big test.

The crowd was stirring. "Get ready, boys," said Blue Larner, corralling his cheer squad, "he's our mate, and he's got to know we're with him."

Easing her weight up and packing it all into the stirrups, Cassie leaned her head closer to The Stinger's mane and whispered, "Come on, baby, this is it."

The other jockeys were yelling at each other, but she took no notice. When The Stinger hit the turn, Cassie shifted her weight toward the running rail. He felt the move and curved into the straight like a snow goose on the wing.

"Go!" yelled Blue Larner, and the farm boys started the chant they'd perfected at the Stud: "Go, Sting! Go! Go! Go! Go, boy!"

Cassie heard it over the yelling crowd, so did The Stinger. Instantly quickening his pace, he stretched out for the short run to the post. The McCoy groupies lost it. The object of their excitement passed three runners to take on the two leaders. He downed one of them, but the post came too soon. He finished full of running, only half a head second, and Cooper McCoy felt his mind explode. Standing beside him, Lorrie felt the mist flood into her eyes and quickly blinked it away. Kitty and Alice were pulp, Blue Larner was dancing and his farmhand mates were hugging each other.

"We did it!" yelled Blue. "Two more strides and he would have won. True story boys; true story!"

It was only a run on a colourful fun day on a racetrack in the west, but as far as the McCoy groupies were concerned it was the Stradbroke, the Ten Thousand and the Victoria Derby all rolled into one! Lorrie grabbed for one of the tissues in her handbag, patted her eyes, and felt her heartbeat returning to normal.

Kitty, with her back to Lorrie, had Cooper in an embrace, and she was trembling. Her eyes were closed, and she was whispering, "Yes–yes–yes."

When she released him, he took the step that put him at Lorrie's side. His arms opened to take her in. Closed inside she felt the warmth of him, and stayed there to hear him say, "That was just the start, Lorrie, all that time and all that patience and look what it's done."

She was all but out of control. It took moments for her to recover. When she did, she backed out of the embrace and said, "It was a good run, Cooper."

Again, he felt it, the chemistry was there, so why wasn't she giving in to it? Again, he could not figure it out, but it was not the time to try.

Cassie trotted The Stinger back to scale, there was more "Waltzing Matilda" with lots of "Good on yous," encouraging cheers and handclaps. When the short speeches were over, and Cooper had accepted the second prize envelope, Fate stepped in and smiled.

The Race Club's special guest of the day was Sam Hutchinson, a national television sports commentator whose wife, Jenny Preston, was a well-known way-out fashion designer. Her labels hung on the racks of the local boutique, and she was at the track to do her bit as the official fashions judge. Sam was her sidekick for the day.

When Lorrie and Cooper were nominated for the finals, Cooper made it clear that they were not at Flinton to win fashion prizes.

"The way your horse ran today," Sam said to Cooper, "I predict you'll be in line for more than fashion prizes before much longer."

Nice comment, and as it turned out; not without clout.

On his sports program three nights later, Sam included a rave about the rousing time he and Jenny had in the Queensland West. Mentioned in the mix of things they did together was the Flinton Race Day. At the end of the rave, Sam dropped this gem:

"Cooper McCoy, the grandson of iconic Aussie trainer Charlie McCoy, had a starter, The Stinger, in the main race. I don't know what he's got in mind for the gelding, but I'll tell you this, his horse is showing signs of becoming a McCoy treasure."

Sam's weekly show, aimed at the sporting world in general, was informative and well-respected. His rousing flag-wave for The Stinger was worth its weight in gold.

It was respectful recognition for a winner in the making, and it came from a know-all's mouth on television. Word ricocheted around Roma's racing circles and filtered into the streets. Eddie, who had not watched Sam's program that week, heard about it on the grapevine in Brisbane and called Lorrie.

"You told me about The Stinger's great run, but you didn't tell me that Sam Hutchinson had seen it."

"I didn't know Sam would bring it up on television. I took it as an on-the-spot compliment; you know how television people carry on, Dad."

Eddie was on the ceiling. "Doesn't matter why he said it, he said it. We have the word of a hotshot on telly that The Stinger is not a no-hoper. That's all the credibility we need. You know what it means, don't you? Now we won't have to start him in another race before Ring-in Day. It's a miracle!"

"Exactly that at the McCoy Stud, Dad. Why don't you and Jeff come on up to see for yourself?"

Eddie got the message. "Good public relations, huh?"

"Can you spare a day or two?"

"How about we bring Frank to make up the team?"

"I'll book you in at the School of Arts Hotel."

"Let's look at something else while we're at it," said Eddie. "Cassie will be on Thunderdome on Ring-in Day. She should have at least a week with him down here at North Point before the race, so why don't we leave Jeff up there with you while that's happening?"

"Can we find an excuse for that?" Lorrie asked.

"How about this: We'd like Jeff's feedback, nothing more. He's worked with some great horses and we value his opinion on The Stinger."

"Why do we need his opinion, Dad? The Stinger is not racing in Brisbane, Thunderdome is."

Silence, then: "Yes, I'm forgetting. Jeff can still stay up with you. The break will do him good."

31

MICHAEL J AND THE REVELATION

Eddie was not the only one who missed Sam Hutchinson's show. Michael J Flynn considered the program beneath him and never watched. Not so Flasher Doyle, who hung on it every week. Michael J was back in his Sydney penthouse, still smarting about the non-event of the *Ultimate Cool* fashion extravaganza. He was hardly interested enough to listen when Flasher called to report on the positive bell-ring Sam had given The Stinger.

"What?" thundered Michael, "some television moron talks up the brumby's star gallop at some wallaby paddock in the bush, and we're supposed to start frothing at the mouth? Those camera clowns wouldn't know which end of a horse eats the oats. They spend all their time grinning into a mirror or ploughing through ratings books!"

"Sam Hutchinson is well up on the game, MJ. He picked the winner of the Melbourne Cup."

"So did the old bird who does my laundry. She pinned the form guide to the wall and threw a dart at it. The way things are not happening in my world, I might have to throw a few darts at Edwards and Davenport."

"Still nothing on the Roma fashion stuff in the bush?"

Michael J was mildly embarrassed. "Nothing, damn it. I'm going cross-eyed looking at the files Click Roberts shot, but I'm not giving up! Never! I don't have it in me.

I've just had a new computer monitor delivered, the biggest they can find, and I'm trawling through everything again; mega-sized this time!"

"Good luck," said Flasher with a weak try for sincerity.

"Luck has nothing to do with anything. There's only patience, resilience, determination, and little grey cells, and I've got the lot!"

"Little grey cells? You're always talking about them, MJ. I don't know what you mean."

"Don't let it bother you, Flasher, you haven't got any."

With that, Flasher was off the wire, and with a shrug of resignation, Michael J walked into his office, took his padded seat, switched on his computer and watched the giant screen boot up. He loaded the CD, let out a sigh, and psyched himself into another session.

Here they come again; three times bigger this time. The models beside the track, yeah, yeah, Cassie Morgan mounting the brumby at the Stud. She's in the saddle, trotting, galloping. Cooper McCoy talking to Lorrie Edwards; what an arse this chick's got! I wonder if that cocky McCoy jock has had it yet?

Mad if he hasn't, and if I ever got the chance, I'd have both of them—anytime.

With a bored nod, he went on with the job. *Here's that bunch of old birds clucking about in the kitchen; lunch under the trees, cowboys cheering; what the hell at? More models, Jewel giving directions, yeah, yeah, some idiot setting microphones up. more galloping, the brumby in fetlock bandages dancing on the track. Big deal!*

It went on, the fashion photographer aiming his camera, more old birds holding loaves of bread, shit! Cowboys yelling, more models; great legs, great! Cooper

McCoy trying not to look like a big city yokel slumming in the bush. And here comes that really boring file again. Thirty images of yawn!

Some nitwit mugging at the camera. What was he doing in Roma? More pictures of him. Why was Click Roberts wasting time on this moron? He's in this file's every shot!

But wait, wait—wait!

Isn't that Cassie Morgan in jockey silks on board the brumby somewhere in the background? Is it? Looks like her—is it?

Yeah, and there's Lorrie Edwards in the background looking hot in a short skirt and fancy hat, more Cassie Morgan in jockey silks trotting around on the brumby. And who is that idiot mugging at the camera? Where did he come from? Some stupid camera hog!

This isn't the Roma Racetrack, is it?

Then, with a sudden jolt, Michael J Flynn's little grey cells exploded; sending a delicious shiver through his body, and his whole consciousness lit up.

"Wait one minute!" he bellowed to his empty room.

Have I been missing something? Click didn't tell me about a race at the Roma track. He didn't say anything about any horse race anywhere. Where was this? Why is Cassie Morgan in jockey silks on board the brumby? Why is she in jockey silks on a hillbilly training track in the bush? And I didn't notice all this background stuff before. Is there something I don't know? Is there something Click didn't tell me?

Michael J picked up the phone and dialled Click Roberts on his mobile.

"Click Roberts Media; talk to me."

Michael J identified himself.

"Hey, Mike!" said Click, "what can I do for you, old buddy?"

Michael J asked his questions about Cassie Morgan in jockey silks, Lorrie Edwards in racewear, and the mugging idiot in the foreground of some of his images.

"Oh, yeah, I meant to tell you about that file, Mike, sorry, forgot to mention it."

"Mention it now."

"It was that job I told you about on the Saturday of the Magic Millions, the job I covered for my mate, remember?"

"I do recall that. Where was it?"

"It was at Kings Park Racecourse in Brisbane."

"You're sure of that? It wasn't at the Roma Racetrack?"

"No way, Mike. It was in Brisbane."

"Who was that idiot mugging at your camera all the time?"

"Some dumb fairy from one of those wanky travel shows on television. He was there promoting the Winter Racing Carnival in May. The channel wanted still images for the print media. I included that file with your stuff by mistake. Sorry, Mike. No charge. You got a freebie. Are you cool?"

Michael J felt his little grey cells singing and dancing. "As a box of cucumbers, Click. You can get back up your tree."

"Not in a tree, Mike. I'm on a balcony on Hamilton Island picking off a mob of star triathletes in training. You should see the bodies on the chicks. I'm on the job with a half-hard boner! Have a good one."

Click hung up.

Michael sat staring at the computer monitor. He didn't know whether to laugh or cry or dance all over the room, so he just sat there. Finally, he stood, clenched his fists and said, "Yes!"

He leapt at the telephone, dialled Flasher Doyle, and barked out a command when Flasher picked up.

"Don't say anything, don't do anything! Just listen and answer questions, right?"

Flasher answered automatically, "Right."

"On the Saturday of the Magic Millions, Eddie Edwards raced a horse at Kings Park in Brisbane. Do you remember which horse it was?"

"The Edwards newbie, Thunderdome. He missed the start but put up a good finish in the straight."

"Who told you that?

"My stand-in in the bookies' ring. I was at the Magic Millions."

"Did your stand-in say who rode him?"

"Cassie Morgan was up."

"Was Lorrie Edwards there?"

"She could have been, MJ, but my mate said it was a small crowd."

"Have you ever seen the horse?"

"Edwards trains at North Point, I never go there."

"You said the horse that raced that day wasn't the McCoy brumby, right?"

Flasher was adamant. "No way. It was Thunderdome, and he's no brumby. He's a class act."

"A class act that missed the start and put up a good finish in a class-act field?"

"According to my mate, yes."

"That's all, Flasher. I'll be in Brisbane tomorrow. I'll call when I get there, but I want you to get me all the nominations for maiden and novice races coming up in Brisbane in the near future. Bring them with you when you meet me."

"What's this about, MJ?"

"It's about a nuclear explosion. See you tomorrow and make sure you have those nominations with you!"

Michael J hung up and scanned the racehorse images again. Yes. The evidence was staring him in the face! Cassie Morgan was not in jockey silks riding the brumby in Roma, she was on Thunderdome in Brisbane. The Kings Park shots were not as clear as the images at the McCoy Stud but some of those shots clearly showed The Stinger's fetlock markings. In others, obviously shot on a different day, his fetlocks were bandaged.

Michael J checked the Kings Park shots again. No fetlock markings on Thunderdome. He closed his eyes and shook his head. The little grey cells had done it again! A one-in-a-million miracle; twin bluebloods, perfectly matched in every way but one: one with fetlock markings, one all clear.

A scrubber and a well-performed runner, both being trained by the crooked Eddie Edwards! The shifty bastards! They gave their class act a run to tone him up. But to make sure he didn't win the race they made sure he missed the start.

Then what do you do? Switch the horses! Let the goodie run with fetlock bandages that hide nothing at all! Race him under the brumby's name, then grab enough cash to put a deposit on the Taj Mahal! Brilliant! The biggest sure thing of all time! Fantastic! Awesome!

And who do you think thought it all up? Fancy Frankie Davenport, that's who!

Well, guess who's got them on toast? Come into my parlour said the spider to the fly! I knew it! I damn well knew it! Talk about a triumph!

Michael J picked up the telephone, dialled Martin Olson, his trusty travel agent, and in a voice dripping organic honey, he gave his instructions. "I'd like a flight to Brisbane late this afternoon or early evening; no airline preference, plus a suite in the Brisbane Marriott for tonight and tomorrow night. On the following day, a flight from Brisbane to Hong Kong, direct, first class of course; Cathay Pacific preferred. I'm expecting to spend a few days there, and I'll call you when I need to return."

"All noted," said Martin Olson, wondering if he was actually on the blower to the real Michael J Flynn, "any specific instructions?"

"None that I can think of. If you feel like adding anything, feel free and let me know."

"With pleasure, Mr Flynn, I'll confirm everything within the hour."

"Thank you for that, Martin; as usual I appreciate your professional attitude."

When the call ended, Martin Olson sat back in his chair, took a deep breath, stared into space, and said to no one in particular, "Michael J Flynn has finally flipped his lid. Send in the clowns!"

Little did Martin know that the biggest circus in the racing game was about to blast the centre pole right through the big top!

32

THE McCOY STUD:
THE CALM BEFORE THE STORM

WITH HIS INITIAL ELATION for The Stinger's strong run at Flinton in perspective, Cooper was not naïve enough to think it was anything more than it appeared to be, a promising pointer of things to come; proof that Lorrie's program was working, and that his horse had finally been cured of dropping his bundle in the run to the post. Kitty and Alice were hardly duped either; they'd both been around horses for too long to be conned by a pleasant surprise. Still, their hopes had been given a lift by The Stinger's encouraging jump out of the no-hoper closet.

But for Blue Larner, the McCoy farmhands, and Sam Hutchinson's Roma fans, the Flinton run was a sure indication of The Stinger's golden future. Overnight he loomed large as Roma's answer to Gunsynd, the stout-hearted Goondiwindi grey that galloped into racing history in the late sixties and early seventies, to be immortalised, for as long as Goondiwindi is on the map, by a statue erected in the hometown racing park named after him.

Lorrie and Cassie, with Ring-in Day rushing at them, realised they had to announce their wonder horse's next bid for glory. They advised Kitty and Cooper of Eddie's decision to enter The Stinger in a race at Kings Park on the first Saturday in March. As Lorrie expected, the announcement was met with a mixture of rapture and nervous speculation.

"Do you really think he's ready for Kings Park?" asked Cooper.

"We'll make him ready," said Lorrie.

Cassie's optimism backed her up. "He's on a roll. He's felt his wings, and he wants to fly."

That fancy cliché instantly hit the right note. The Stinger was green-lighted to take the Brisbane Big Smoke in his stride with the full blessing of the McCoys. There was further excitement when Lorrie announced her father's impending visit to the McCoy Stud. Accompanying him would be Frank Davenport and Jeff Dysart; both of whom played an important part in launching The Stinger's emergence from the limbo world of the brumbies!

As Lorrie told it, these three racing heavies were busting to take another look at the horse that was sparking the interest of the Roma sporting set.

All done.

The visit was scheduled for the coming weekend. It was four weeks to Ring-in Day. The Stinger's program continued. To keep her mind on the job in hand, Lorrie had taken to thinking about the program as Play Training. She cast herself in the role of Play Trainer; but even so, it was a near impossibility to cut off from the excitement of the daily routine at the McCoy Stud. It took some doing. It was doubtful that the grandest optimist on the planet could have predicted the Roma fever that was swirling around The Stinger's Brisbane debut. It was a hullabaloo that was never supposed to happen, and it had caught Lorrie and Cassie in a web of deceit.

The illusion the two girls were forced to maintain was that The Stinger was being trained to take the Big Smoke by storm. But the truth was another story.

Despite the adoration being heaped upon him, The Stinger would be nothing more than an imposter hero. It would not be his win at all. The victory would belong to his twin! Now more than ever, the ring-in was a secret that could never see the light of day! Never!

Frank drove Eddie and Jeff from Brisbane in the rented Ford Falcon. It was an easy drive, and they arrived in time for Alice's barbecue lunch; the usual nutritious treat laid out under the pepperina trees with the Mitchell cockatoos for colourful company.

The conversation focused on The Stinger and his chances in Brisbane, and it predictably turned to the business of betting.

Cooper made it clear. "My horse won't run without my money. I'd feel like a traitor."

Frank took advantage of the opportunity to suggest that perhaps Eddie could take care of an investment for the McCoys, in lieu of paying them a leasing fee for their horse.

"But you've all done so much," said Kitty.

Eddie took over. "I have confidence, Mrs McCoy, and I have had it from the start. You and Cooper have agreed to share any winnings your horse may earn, and I feel that a respectable wager on your behalf, is very much in my quarter. I hope you see it that way too."

"That's awfully generous, Mr Edwards," said Kitty.

At which point Alice piped up, "I'm OC betting for the CWA ladies who helped with the fashion shoot, and Kitty will sure be betting some of her own money."

"Best of luck," said Frank.

It was an understatement. Luck takes a back seat when a sure thing really is a sure thing, and money is the name of the game. Lorrie and Cassie said nothing.

The barbecue was travelling well when Jeff asked Cassie if she'd mind introducing him to The Stinger.

"I'm impatient to meet the horse I'll be working with for a week," he said to the table, "anybody mind?"

Nobody did. Cassie and Jeff walked across to the stables, which were fresh as always with the aroma of Blue Larner's pine-scented disinfectant. Cassie opened the door of The Stinger's stall, walked in, strapped on his bridle and led him into the sunshine. Jeff stared without saying a word.

He spoke, finally. "I'm winded, Cass, I'm seeing double here. He's the same."

"Almost," said Cassie, "except for the powder puffs on his fetlocks, and he's maybe an inch or two shorter, but yeah, he's Thuderdome's twin; right on."

Jeff was bright-eyed. "He looks wonderful, Cass. I mean look at him."

"He gets treated like royalty here. Want to take him for a run? I'll saddle him up if you like."

"Well, yeah. I mean, yeah! Damn it, Cass, I can't believe it."

Cassie saddled The Stinger and walked him across to the training track gate.

"He knows the routine," said Cassie, "trot him around to the back stretch, he'll canter for a bit then break into an even gallop. Don't push him; he's already had a workout this morning."

Jeff mounted, took off, let the horse dictate the pace, returned to the gate, and dismounted.

Cassie smiled. "What's your verdict?"

"Fine piece of horseflesh, Cass, and he's supposed to be a no-hoper?"

"He was never that, he just didn't know how to behave like a racehorse, and it fooled everyone except Cooper McCoy."

"Eddie should take him on, afterwards. What do you think?"

That was the one question Cassie didn't want to answer.

She'd thought about it, and she figured Lorrie had too, but neither had brought it up because nobody was thinking beyond Ring-in Day, which was now the point of no return. In Singapore, Loveboat Williams was driving engines in the shady world of the wager rogues who cashed in on inside information. He and Frank had it worked out. Money had been transferred; big odds had been taken, the plan was in place, and a cloud of hope hung over the McCoy Stud. But Cassie was aware of something that had never been discussed; she didn't like giving it mind space, but Jeff's remark had brought it to the surface.

It was doubtful that Eddie could ever have anything to do with The Stinger after the caper race. If the smart thinkers discovered he was Thunderdome's twin, it wouldn't take long for them to do the arithmetic. Suspicious minds could turn the win into a scandal that would be punched up, exaggerated, and swept into the vortex of a media backlash. Cassie knew, and no doubt Lorrie knew too, that The Stinger's career could well be over the minute Thunderdome flashed past the winning post bearing his name.

To protect the secret of the caper, one of the two horses would be forced to disappear, and it didn't take much guessing to figure out which one.

Jeff stood eyeing Cassie, waiting for the answer to his question. When she didn't answer right away, he suddenly realised why.

"It can't be on for him can it, Cass?"

"It's not on the cards."

"What will happen?"

"You know what will happen."

"When?"

"Soon after the ring-in."

"Is there another way?"

"You know there isn't."

"Nobody thought about that, did they?"

"We were all too busy thinking about the caper. Sting is a great horse, Jeff. Cooper's right about him, he's special, he's got a soul, and we've all fallen in love with him."

"It will break Cooper McCoy's heart, Cass, yours and Lorrie's too, right?"

"I don't want to talk about it. It's too late and we can't think about it."

Cassie misted up. Close to breaking down she took a deep breath, pulled herself together, and said, "Everything will go as planned because it has to. I'll be in Brisbane next Sunday. I'll spend a week with Thunderdome while you're up here. Okay?"

Jeff left well enough alone. "You'll find the Thunder boy in great shape, Cass, and he's easy on the track."

"I'm looking forward to working with him, honest," said Cassie, giving The Stinger an affectionate pat on the flanks. "Look after him for me, Jeff, I'm going to miss him while I'm away."

She took hold of The Stinger's bridle, and the three of them walked back to the stables together.

Jeff put his arm around her and pulled her close. "Stay cool, Cass, it will all work out. We'll have to think of something."

"Whichever way it goes, Jeff, there's a hurt at the finish."

33

THE BRISBANE MARRIOTT & HONG KONG

FLASHER DOYLE SHOOK HIS head in a forlorn attempt to clear his brain.

Seated once again in the Flynn suite at the Brisbane Marriott, he held a cup of strong coffee in his right hand, and every few seconds he gulped at some of the black liquid. It didn't help much. He was struggling to believe what Michael J Flynn had just told him. Somehow it was out of his sphere of understanding, but he realised it had to be true.

"A ring-in. Shit! It can't be a bloody ring-in!"

"That's the third time you've said that," snapped Michael J, "and it's the third time I've said it is. What are you, a new species of talking parrot?"

"What is Edwards going to do with twin horses?"

"Wake up! There won't be any twin horses."

"Thunderdome just disappears?"

"One of them has to. Who the hell cares?"

Flasher let that sink in, then said, "So, why don't we tell them we're onto the trick and spoil everything?"

"Get it right, Flasher! I want them to go ahead with their bloody smart-arsed con. I want them exposed and ruined, out of the game with no chance of ever getting back in!"

"That's heavy, MJ."

"It's supposed to be."

Michael J continued with a list of his sinister predictions. "The McCoys will be tainted accomplices.

Edwards will be eyeballing a bleak future. Cassie Morgan and Lorrie Edwards will be answering ads for restaurant kitchen hands, if they're not locked up, and Davenport will never again get his butt back into the Hong Kong Jockey Club. Bingo! Clean sweep! All of them washed up. When they messed with me, they made the biggest blunder of their lousy lives!"

Totally overtaken by the vengeful drama of it all, Michael J wheeled on Flasher Doyle and just about frightened him out of his chair.

"Now Listen! Here's where you come in—I want you to round up a team of protestors, a collection of out-of-work actors or layabouts. I want them to stage a demonstration right after the running of the race in question."

Sitting stock still, Flasher said, "What kind of demonstration, MJ?"

"When the three placed horses hit the winners circle, I want calls of, 'Ring-in! That horse is a ring-in! That horse is not The Stinger!' and I want it repeated until the stewards are forced to investigate. Now, who can you get to do that, Flasher?"

It was more like a command than a question. Flasher, on the spot, thought fast. "I know a bloke. He set up a mob of loudmouths who turned on a real big show when one of those rock bands flew in to play at the Stradbroke last year.

"It worked. You'd have thought the band was The Rolling Stones. This bloke is good, but he asks top dollar."

"Pay him what he wants! Tell him his people can't look like lowlifes and bums. I want about twenty of them and they've got to look like genuine racegoers."

"What if they don't want to do anything as shady as this sounds?"

"I've thought of that. They're to be told it's for a location scene in a movie that's being shot at Warner Studios on the Gold Coast. That should clear the air."

"Is that what the organiser is to be told, too?"

"If you show him the money and tell him what you want, why would he ask questions? One more thing; these layabouts will need someone to answer to on the day."

"This bloke takes care of that in person."

"Then buy him! Cash in hand! Tax-free!" Michael J threw a deadly stare right at Flasher's face. "Can I rely on you to do that?"

"What about the budget?"

"There's no budget. Whatever it takes! I repeat; can I rely on you?"

"Yes! Of course you can, MJ. Yes!"

"Fine! Now there are strict instructions. Are you listening?"

"I'm all ears."

As soon as he knew he had Flasher's abject attention, the determined Michael J Flynn detailed the details of his planned vendetta.

To make sure nothing was leaked, the team of demonstrators could not be on the racecourse until ten minutes after the running of the race before the ring-in. They had to be briefed off-track beforehand. Once on track, they would be positioned on the lawns close to the winners' circle, and their demonstration would begin as soon as the winner and the two placed horses leave the track to file through the gate.

Their outbursts must be strident enough to alert the stewards and race officials and to trigger questions at the right level. Then the team had to immediately disperse and be lost in the crowd. Once done, the demonstration would slip out of focus, and the attention would automatically shift to the unmasking of the race's imposter and his shyster connections.

Michael J almost blinded Flasher with a triumphant smile. "And that," he announced, "will be one of racing history's grandest moments, delivered by Yours Truly for the glory of the game, and its ongoing integrity."

Flasher was bowled over. "Crikey! I gotta be there to see that!"

"You won't see it. You'll be on your stand in the bookies' ring. In the lead up to the race, you will be posting The Stinger at longer odds that anyone else to lure the Edwards stable bets. If the brumby is posted at twenty-fives, you offer thirty-threes. If it's at thirty-threes, you offer forties. Why would you worry? The ring-in will be disqualified, you'll keep the Edwards stable bets, and you won't have to pay out a red cent. But you will be able to give evidence of stable support for the ring-in horse. Have you got it all, Flasher?"

Flasher was genuinely excited. "Yeah. I have!"

"On the big day, I will be in the Members Stand with Colin Clive, the Manager of the State Racing Authority, plus a small contingent of celebrities and racing VIPs. When that horse is exposed, I will be outraged at the revelation, as will Mr Colin Clive! He will no doubt be prompted to summon the Storm Troopers!"

"Or Steven Seagal?"

Michael smiled. "He's past tense. We better get the dickhead with the hammer."

Flasher missed the point. "Thor?"

"With his hammer!"

Flasher nodded. "Oh yeah! One more question, MJ."

"Ask it."

"It's pretty common knowledge that you only make personal appearances at racetracks on very important days. Last time in Brisbane it was okay because the media printed you were in town to check on The Mating Game's chances at the Spring Carnival. What's your excuse this time?"

Michael J smiled. "I'm loving this. Go on."

"If anyone catches on that you were there to watch a ring-in caper run off the rails, they'll guess you knew about it beforehand."

"Yes?"

"And if you knew about it beforehand, why didn't you do your duty and blow the whistle?"

"Is that it?"

Flasher looked as if he'd scored a trick for once. "That's it."

"And you think I missed it? Well, I haven't missed a thing. I've got it all worked out, and because I never count my chickens before they hatch, I'll tell you how I'll be dealing with that little problem when everything has been arranged."

Flasher backed off. "Okay, I'll get the demonstration end of the deal on the way."

Michael J was on a roll. "That's my boy. Now I've got ends to tie up in Hong Kong. I'm jetting out tomorrow for a few days, but I'll stay in touch. Are we on the same page here?"

"Yes, and I've never known a page like it!"

"And you never will. It's payback time!"

As soon as Flasher left, Michael J called Adrian Messenger in Hong Kong, on his direct line. "I'm on a flight out of Brisbane tomorrow. Are you free to meet with me at my Victoria Peak address at any time that suits you the day after?"

He listened to Adrian Messenger's positive response and said, "Three p.m. it is. I'll look forward to the meeting."

MICHAEL J FLEW CATHAY PACIFIC to Hong Kong the next morning and met with Adrian Messenger at the appointed time the following day. The impassive Asian gentleman sat facing his host on the brocade covered couch in Michael J's office. He wore his customary white suit, cream shirt, off-white tie and cream leather shoes. His white panama hat sat beside him on the couch.

His hands rested on his knees; his fingernails were buffed to a dull shine; his gold wristwatch was barely visible under the starched cuff of his shirt. Apart from the intermittent up and down twitching of the little finger of his right hand, Adrian Messenger could easily have been an alabaster figurine. He listened attentively while Michael J outlined his strategy to bring down the perpetrators of The Mating Game fiasco.

When Michael J had finished, Adrian Messenger asked his first question. "Do you have everything in place?"

"It has all been worked out and arranged."

"My connections will not be involved in any way?"

"They will not."

"A great deal of money was lost when The Mating Game failed to honour your promise. You are at present not in good standing."

"Which is why I am taking steps to make sure these people will pay dearly for The Mating Game upset, and that they will never be able to interfere in any of your future operations."

"A wise move, if you desire any further involvement with us."

"If there's one thing I'm good at, it's wise moves."

"I will advise my connections accordingly, Mr Flynn."

"No doubt, news of my upcoming success will reach you in Hong Kong."

"Mr Flynn, you realise that it is rare for any of the people with whom we do business, to be given a second chance. We never offer a third."

"I understand I'm privileged. I will not need a third chance."

"That is fortunate. May I also point out that if you fail in this enterprise, your name will be stricken from our list of trusted international contacts. You will no longer be welcome to be involved with us. In plain language, Mr Flynn, as far as we are concerned you will have ceased to exist."

"When we meet again you will have reason to congratulate me."

"In which case, I will do so with pleasure."

Adrian Messenger picked up his panama hat and said, "Thank you for your time and understanding. I wish you a safe trip to Australia." He stood, turned, walked to the office door, opened it and quietly made his exit.

Mickey Flynn was fuming. *"Up yours you little shit! When I've got Edwards and Davenport knackered, I'll shove that fucken white hat of yours right up your friggin' cracker!"*

But Michael was too ecstatic to give in to anger. Mickey's fume was put on hold while his alter-ego phoned Lillian St Clare at *Ultimate Cool*. After the usual fatuous gush and prattle, Michael J dealt out his latest pack of lies.

He was arranging a VIP luncheon at Kings Park on the first Saturday in March to celebrate the Brisbane debut of The Stinger, the horse that appeared in the accompanying shots of the McCoy fashion shoot.

"It will be the most auspicious of occasions, and I am insisting on the pleasure of your company."

Lillian was intrigued; even more so when Michael J offered to fly her to Australia to be accommodated at his expense. Suspecting a red herring, she said, "Is this part of your little sideshow, Michael?"

He did his best to sound shocked. "I thought it would be the perfect time to launch the publicity for your May issue, and to meet Kitty and Cooper McCoy in person. Jewel Blanch can get cracking with the press releases as soon as you say yes."

Lillian immediately recognized the positives. "Beautifully put, Michael. I'm accepting of course, which does not mean I'm not suspicious."

"We're true soul mates, Lillian, we should play together more often."

"I could never cope with you too often, Michael. Let me know the flight and accommodation arrangements as soon as possible, so I can alert Jewel Blanch."

"Consider it done."

Michael J allowed the receiver to drop gently into its place. "Yes! Lillian's in. I knew she would be. There's just one more important person to add to the mix, then the magic potion will be brewed and bubbling, and I will have a legitimate excuse to be at Kings Park on a nothing race day."

He gave out a nasty little chuckle. "But it won't be a nothing day for Edwards and Davenport after I've driven nails into their coffins, with long sharp nails!"

"Right on," said Mickey Flynn. *"Fuck with me, and your dick's a brick!"*

Michael J sorted through his prized collection of VIP business cards, found the one he was looking for, and lifted the telephone receiver.

It was seventeen days to Ring-in Day.

34

THE McCOY STUD PREPARES

THE BIG DAY WAS closing fast, and there was a tingle in the air at the McCoy homestead.

It was heating up the kitchen, where Kitty and Alice talked incessantly of Race Five at Kings Park on the first Saturday of March. Kitty and Cooper were booked into the Brisbane Hilton. Alice planned her own party at the homestead. Bill Harris was setting up his giant screen in the barbecue court for the television coverage of the race. Alice had invited the CWA ladies and their families to lunch, they were Sunday-dressing, and a bag-load of their Stinger bets would be hitting the Roma TAB.

Alice had it summed up: "We'll send the place broke!"

Kitty's bets were in place. She thought it only right for all the money she'd won on Saturday Night Fever to be invested on The Stinger. It was magic money she'd put aside for this very special event. Her dreams for Cooper's horse were coming true.

Blue Larner and the boys were on the job, adding their rowdy cheering on cue whenever Bill Harris's audio pumped up during training sessions. Blue had booked a minibus to take them to Brisbane for the big race, but the response had been so positive, he was forced to cancel the minibus for something bigger—an eighty-seat Volvo that was rapidly filling up.

Meanwhile, Jeff's working visit to Roma was ending.

He had taken over the homestead's guest room, but the McCoy Stud had overtaken him. He was, after all, a country boy at heart, and what with Alice's cooking, the thrill of walking in Charlie McCoy's footsteps, and the infectious atmosphere, he was a goner from the start. He had taken to The Stinger, and the horse had taken to him.

He and Lorrie had worked together before. Their current training sessions in Roma were no-nonsense workouts that bore every resemblance to the real thing, and the eyes and ears of Roma were all over them. There was no mention of what would happen to the town's favourite horse after Ring-in Day. Jeff did his best to keep his mind off it. He slipped up once. At the end of one workout session, he said, "It's a real shame this horse has nowhere to go."

Lorrie pulled him up. "It's out of our hands, Jeff, and I don't like it any more than you do." That was it. Nothing more was said.

Cassie returned to the Stud with glowing reports of Thunderdome's ability, and she and Jeff exchanged notes; a couple of professionals behaving like professionals.

Jeff said his "goodbyes" and "thank-yous" to Alice and the McCoys, gave The Stinger a farewell pat, packed up, hugged Cassie and Lorrie, climbed into the driver's seat of the Range Rover and drove back to Brisbane.

Somehow, Lorrie and Cassie managed to ignore the buzz in the air to stay focused on the complex machinery of the caper. Not once did they waver. So ran the days:

The sun came up and the sun went down, and the only place that existed on the planet was the McCoy Stud in Roma. The real world was another place altogether.

It was ten days to Ring-in Day.

35

AT THE BOONDALL STUD

Eddie was having restless nights.

The weight of the caper hung heavily on him. He'd taken to waking in the middle of the night to pore again over every detail of the strategy. He had visited the old vineyard at Nudgee Beach to make sure it was a suitable holding place for The Stinger on the big day. He came home satisfied, and by the time February had turned into March, he felt he was as ready as he'd ever be for the big ask.

Jeff returned from Roma with positive news of what was happening at the McCoy Stud. Lorrie and Cassie had done their job well. The McCoys were delighted, and although it all seemed too good to be true, they were optimistic about their horse's chances in the Big Smoke; wishing is as whishing does.

"They'll soon be a lot richer," said Eddie. *"And that's something,"* he said to himself.

On the second day of March, Frank Davenport turned up at Boondall with an interesting snippet of news that came to light during a telephone call from Loveboat Williams in Singapore. He had received word from his message service that a call had been made to CK Dexter Beaumont from Michael J Flynn in Australia. Curious to find out more, Loveboat put on his best CK Dexter voice, and returned the call to discover that Michael J was inviting him to be present at a VIP luncheon at the Kings

Park Racetrack in Brisbane, on the first Saturday in March.

The invitation was issued on the off-chance that Dexter would be in Australia at the time. When Loveboat inquired further, he was given the relevant details of Michael J's exciting event: Lillian St Clare, editor of *Ultimate Cool* magazine, was flying in from Hong Kong, her May issue would be featuring a cover story about the fashion shoot at the McCoy Stud, and her Brisbane representative, Jewel Blanch, was arranging advance publicity.

Michael J further fleshed out details of his event. It came over like a garden party at Buckingham Palace. How could Dexter, a strong supporter of the Gold Coast's Magic Millions, not be there in the esteemed company of Colin Clive, CEO of the State Racing Authority, and a gilt-edged gaggle of A-Listers?

"I wouldn't miss this for quids," Loveboat told Frank, "I want to see this wanker's face fall into a whirlpool of his own stirring, when your horse nails the prize." Loveboat paused for a moment. "That will happen, won't it?"

"Guaranteed, mate," Frank replied.

"Then expect to see me in my CK Dexter glory on the day in question. All systems go! After all, the best moment of a con is watching it kick arse."

WHEN WORRY-WART EDDIE heard about Flynn's grandiose plans, he had doubts and expressed them to Frank.

"Should we be worried about Flynn being at the track?"

"He's big-noting. He'll be at the track to impress racing industry big wigs, and to show his cheesy support for Lillian St Clare, and her Roma homestead fashion blitz. He'll probably claim to be a friend of Cooper's horse!"

Eddie, still edgy, said, "You don't think he's twigged to anything?"

"We've been too careful, Eddie."

"You and Jeff worked out a schedule for the McCoys. Is it in place?"

"Everything confirmed; all bases checked and rechecked, so take it easy and stop worrying."

It was seven days to Ring-in Day.

36

THE CLINCHER

THE NEWS FROM ROMA was huge.

Blue Larner's eighty-seat Volvo bus was a sell-out. On top of that, three minibus loads of businesspeople, and countless private cars were all Brisbane bound. Trains and flights out of Roma were booked solid. Alice's party at the homestead had grown into a major ninety-guest rage, with the CWA Ladies whipping up bring-your-own goodies to back up the catering.

In accordance with his plan, Jeff drove the Range Rover to Roma on Thursday afternoon, stayed overnight, and at dawn on Friday morning he loaded The Stinger in Cooper's float, and took off for Boondall. Blue Larner and the boys, self-appointed members of 'Team Stinger' were at the Stud to farewell their hero with a guard of honour when the float sailed through the gate. It was a rowdy departure.

Two hours later, Lorrie and Cassie headed for Brisbane in Lorrie's Subaru, closely followed by Kitty, Cooper and Bill Harris in Cooper's Land Rover.

Earlier, when it was time for Lorrie to pack, she hedged. Breaking her ties with the Stud was something she couldn't bring herself to face. She left most of her things behind, knowing she'd have to come back for them. But by then the caper would be over.

Cassie shed a tear when she loaded her bags into the boot of the Subaru and held tight to Lorrie's hand for a long minute when she got into the car.

"Damn, I hate goodbyes," she said, "I hate it when good things end."

"Everything ends, kiddo, even things that should never have started."

Cassie understood that if she said what she was thinking, it would make everything worse, so she shut up and said nothing.

LILLIAN ST CLARE FLEW in from Hong Kong on Friday morning. Jewel collected her at the airport, checked her in at the Brisbane Marriott, and the two of them went into a huddle over the media coverage. Lillian booked Click Roberts to cover the VIP event at Kings Park for a feature story in *Ultimate Cool*.

COOPER AND KITTY MCCOY, together with Bill Harris, signed in at the Brisbane Hilton, and late on Friday afternoon, Cooper drove to Boondall to check on The Stinger. Jeff had him sponged, brushed and ready to bed down.

The deception was working well. Sting was looking splendid. Lorrie was happy with him. Cooper was happy that Lorrie was happy. All was well.

LOVEBOAT WILLIAMS FLEW IN from Singapore early on Friday night. Frank was at the airport to drive him to his Brisbane apartment where he was staying as a guest for the weekend. In Loveboat's luggage, CK Dexter Beaumont, the Albuquerque high roller, was waiting to be re-born.

MICHAEL J FLYNN FLEW UP from Sydney on Friday afternoon and checked in at the Brisbane Marriott. He dined that evening with Lillian St Clare at Cha-Cha-Char Restaurant on the river. When they entered the trendy steakhouse from the riverside boardwalk, mouths froze on the spot. Lillian and Michael J were a mega-watt eyeful. Hand it to Lillian, at the age of forty-plus she could still deep-freeze a restaurant and upstage the T-bones and French fries.

SAM HUTCHINSON AND JENNY Preston, the television couple from the Flinton race day, invited by Jewel Blanch as guest judges for 'Fashions on the Field,' and to interview Lillian St Clare, flew in from Sydney on Friday afternoon, and checked in at The Heritage Hotel. Jenny was such a blast in one of her wildest nouveau ensembles that hardly anyone noticed that Sam, the famous sports commentator, was with her. When she sashayed through the foyer on her way to the elevators, the carnival rattle of her baubles bangles and beads drew one serious chap's sharp eyes away from the pages of the latest issue of *Fin Review*!

AT FIVE P.M. IN the Boondall Shopping Centre carpark, Lorrie met with Rex Powell, spokesman for the three-person betting team of Rex, Betty and Edna. Lorrie handed him a fat envelope of hard cash. "I'm briefing you early instead of at the track because it will be better to invest tonight or early tomorrow.

"As usual, we do not want to be associated with a plunge before the race."

"Is a plunge likely?" asked Rex.

"There's some out-of-town talk. The Stinger. Horse fourteen. Race Five."

"Where will we meet after the race?"

"I'll let you know. You and the girls are on twenty-five per cent."

"Twenty-five?"

"It's a bonus. Tell the girls I said hello."

AT THE BOONDALL STUD, Eddie held off going to bed but made the move just after nine p.m. because he knew what was coming at him the next day. Lorrie couldn't sleep, she didn't want to. Cassie was bedding down at Boondall that night, and when she saw Lorrie's light on at ten p.m. she knocked on Lorrie's door.

"I can't sleep either," said Cassie, "my head's an earthquake."

Together they walked across to the stables where the Thoroughbred twins, kept well apart, were sleeping peacefully.

It was a beautiful early autumn night, and the stars were splattered across the sky in glittery patterns. The two girls stood together looking up at them.

Lorrie's words were tentative. "After all this time, it's happening, Cass, I never thought it would."

Cassie took her hand and held it. "You and me, both."

A cautious cough came from the shadows. Seconds later Jeff appeared and moved over to them. He said, "You chicks should be asleep, you're taking on the world tomorrow."

Cassie replied, "We're all taking on the world tomorrow, which is why you're not asleep either."

Lorrie took Jeff's hand. "Let's stay close for a while, just the three of us. We've done what we had to do, it hasn't been easy, and right now I need both of you."

Jeff had the last word. "We need each other, kids. Maybe If we talk a while, we'll feel better."

They were not sure how long they stood talking but when they finally parted it was way past midnight. Ring-in Day had drifted in on the early morning breeze, and it wasn't going anywhere.

COOPER MCCOY ARRIVED AT Boondall as scheduled at eight a.m. to check on The Stinger. He'd had his oats and his morning walk, he'd been sponged and brushed. He looked a million.

"Give me five, boy," said Cooper. The Stinger did his trick.

"I'm taking him for another walk soon," said Jeff, "and I'll be with him all day, so until he's ready to do his stuff this afternoon, it's just Lorrie, him, Cassie and me. Lorrie wants to keep his mind on the job."

"Understood," said Cooper.

He had a short meeting with Lorrie. "Last word. Anything I can do?"

Lorrie, a picture of calm, said, "Go back to the hotel, get into your spiffy gear and get ready for a good day."

"Spiffy gear?"

"As you know, jeans are not allowed in any of the members' areas of the track."

"Is a Kenzo suit spiffy enough?

"Kenzo is better than spiffy. You'll look good in it."

Cooper smiled a smile. "You'd look good in anything."

Lorrie allowed a beat or two to pass then added, "Whatever happens today, Cooper, I want you to know I've done my best . . . we all have."

"You didn't have to tell me."

"Have a great time at the track."

Cooper turned to go, then stopped, turned back, and faced Lorrie. "I know I don't have to say this, but what you and Cassie have done for us, for Kitty and me, is something we can never forget. What you've done for my horse is out of this world. For now, you've got other things on your mind and I don't want to muscle in."

Lorrie stood still for a few seconds then closed in to kiss him on the cheek. "Thanks for that, Cooper."

He registered the kiss, smiled, and walked away. Lorrie watched him go, paused a while, then joined Eddie, Jeff and Cassie for a light breakfast.

AT FRANK DAVENPORT'S APARTMENT, Loveboat Williams morphed into CK Dexter Beaumont before Frank's eyes—a startling transformation that would have fooled Loveboat's mother. His hairpiece and face fuzz were works of art. "Little tricks a friend of mine in the movie business whipped up. They cost an arm and a leg, but they do have to pass scrutiny close-up. Subtle but effective."

"Amazing," said Frank.

"You haven't seen the Armani suit I'm wearing today. It's new, so is everything else. I don't know for sure, but I think CK Dexter Beaumont is a bit of a wanker. No wonder Mike Flynn thinks he's cool."

AT ELEVEN-THIRTY A.M. Eddie was beginning to feel tense. "We should get The Stinger to Nudgee, it's getting late."

Despite the tension, everything was going as planned. Eddie and Jeff left for the vineyard while Cassie and Lorrie got busy with the fetlock bandages. The drive to Nudgee along the quiet back road was uneventful. No traffic. When they arrived at the vineyard, the caretaker, a crusty gent of about seventy, opened the gate, showed Jeff where to park, and helped unload the float while Eddie checked to make sure they weren't being observed. There was no one else around.

"Handsome animal," said the caretaker, "know a bit about horses, had one with fetlock powder puffs just like that one. Nice aesthetic touch, those powder puffs. Nature can be creative."

"Very," said Eddie, still tense, but feeling more relieved.

"He'll be okay," said the caretaker, "nobody in the place but me today. I'll look after him. No need to worry about a thing. How long will he be here?"

Jeff had the excuse ready. "We're having the stables fumigated this morning. We'll collect him later this afternoon."

The caretaker nodded. "Yeah, well he can't be there when they're chucking all that stuff around, can he? He can stay until tomorrow if you like."

"Let's leave it at that, then."

The old man gave a little shrug. "Up to you," he said.

"We'd better get back to Boondall," said Eddie.

"Just a second," said the caretaker, "What's your horse's name?"

Jeff answered immediately, "Thunderdome."

"Nice name."

He and Jeff climbed into the Range Rover, the caretaker closed the gate behind them, and Jeff hit the road.

"Do you think you should have told him the name of our horse?'

"No sweat, Eddie, it won't mean anything to him. I couldn't tell him it was The Stinger, could I?"

"Guess not."

"Relax, Boss, we're looking good."

It was a quick trip. Back at Boondall, Eddie threw a nervous glance at the camouflaging fetlock bandages the girls had applied. "You're sure they're right?"

Lorrie gave him a look. "We know how to bandage a horse, Dad."

"Just checking."

Jeff was rearing to go. "I want to leave for the track as soon as possible, and I want to take it nice and slow. I'll be towing a million-dollar cargo and I don't need problems."

"Soon as you can," said Eddie.

Lorrie took his hand. "Get it together, Dad."

"I can't think straight."

Lorrie stayed calm. "Everything is under control, Dad. Cassie can go to the track with Jeff, you can come with me, and it would be nice for you and Frank to join the McCoys in the Committee Room for lunch"

Jeff had loaded the float. "I'm on the way. Ready, Cass?"

Cassie joined Jeff in the front seat, and he drove off.

Lorrie put her arm around Eddie and said, "Let's make this just another Saturday afternoon at the racetrack, Dad."

"Damn it, baby, I don't ever want to go through this again."

Lorrie tightened her grip. "After today, you won't have to."

37

THE BIG DAY AT KINGS PARK:
THE GREATEST SHOW ON EARTH

AT ELEVEN-THIRTY-FIVE, Blue Larner's chartered Volvo, packed to capacity, pulled up at the main gate of Kings Park, and arriving punters got a first-hand look at the adrenalin pump of Roma. On the side of the Volvo was an impressive vinyl scroll emblazoned with the words, 'Team Stinger.' Blue's boys were trailing streams of gold and green ribbons, Eddie's stable colours. Gold and green hats sat on the heads of the young girls, and gold flowers were pinned to their dresses. The Volvo's older passengers were satisfied with gold and green rosettes. The only things missing were the pink breasted Mitchell cockatoos, but the incessant crowd chatter filled in nicely.

One of the more curious of the arriving Brisbane punters asked Blue a question, "Is this some sort of convention?"

"You bet, fella," said Blue, "The Team Stinger convention."

"What's that, mate?

"Ask me after Race Five, if you can pull me out of the sky."

IN THE COMMITTEE ROOM, Kitty and Cooper McCoy lunched quietly with Bill Harris, Frank Davenport and Eddie. Members of the racing fraternity, some of whom were old friends of Charlie McCoy, paid their respects and stopped to chat with Kitty. Cooper was looking anxious. Races One and Two had been run, and The Stinger's turn was no more than two hours away.

Kitty sensed Cooper's restlessness and defined the cause. "You can't be at the horse stalls with your horse, love. Lorrie wants him focused on the race. Trust her."

"I do, Kit, I do."

"So, do I, and so does half the population of Roma."

IN THE VIP SUITE on top of the Members Stand, Michael J Flynn hosted a private soiree for his cluster of special guests. They included heavies from the Magic Millions Yearling Sales plus several Brisbane notables including Colin Clive, Manager of the State Racing Authority. The star turns were Lillian St Clare, CK Dexter Beaumont, Jewel Blanch, Jenny Preston and Sam Hutchinson. The champagne was Veuve Clicquot NV, the catering was spectacular, and the atmosphere was elite. The third race had been run and the 'Fashions on the Field' finalists were due to be judged after the running of the fourth race.

Lillian was an elegant vision in black and white with a white organdie picture hat littered with black ruffles. Jewel wore her signature navy white and red, and Jenny looked like a Latin siren in orange and purple fringes. Michael J cruised in Prada, upstaging every male in sight, except for Sam Hutchinson, who was ten years younger, and smoothly masculine in cream imitation suede.

When the starters for Race Four took to the saddling paddock, Jewel, Jenny and Sam departed to prepare for the judging of 'Fashions on the Field' finals on the main grandstand lawns.

The Ring-in Race was thirty-five minutes away.

Loveboat Williams was having the time of his life. None of his fellow guests had ever met an Albuquerque horse trader, and as few had been to Albuquerque, it was easy for him to prattle on about the wonders of the city's famous Hot Air Balloon Festival, the marvels of its genuine Tex-Mex restaurants, and it wondrous re-invented KiMo Theatre of the performing arts. Nobody really listened too closely to anything. The Veuve was flowing, and the afternoon, as Lillian noted, was 'simply too divine for words.'

THE FOURTH RACE WAS suddenly over; the 'Fashions on the Field' finals had yielded a winner and two runners-up. Sam was signing autographs for wild-eyed fans. Lillian was posing patiently for media photographers, and answering silly questions put to her by twittery young journalists, who were busting to know if the famous Michael J Flynn was her current squeeze.

Click Roberts was darting about doing his kinetic oiled-grasshopper imitation.

One of the female journalists waited for him to stand still, and asked a typical question, "Do you think Lillian St Clare and Michael J Flynn are a squeeze item?"

Quick as a flash, Click responded, "Come on, chick, turn on your upstairs lights. Why would she be squeezing him when she can squeeze me?"

He aimed his camera at her and clicked off a dozen frames. "Taking pictures of hot babes is my second-best talent. Guess what my best one is?"

AT THE HORSE STALLS with Jeff, Lorrie was looking a treat in her favourite shade of mushroom pink. She was the prettiest picture of calm anyone had ever seen. Nobody would have guessed that deep inside a hundred butterflies were doing their best to steal her cool and send her into a flap.

At the given time, Jeff, bridle and horse at the ready, took off from the horse stalls for the saddling enclosure with Lorrie, who knew only too well that his silence meant that he was as jittery as she was.

CASSIE, COMPOSED AS THEY come, was getting into her silks in the jockey's room. Frank and Eddie had already left the Committee Room to take up aisle seats in the Members Stand. They appeared to be breathing.

Kitty, Cooper, and Bill Harris vacated the Committee Room minutes before Frank and Eddie, to place last-minute bets in the bookies' ring, where they were pleasantly surprised to discover that Flasher Doyle had The Stinger posted at forty to one.

JUST OUTSIDE THE TRACK, under the big fig trees near the entrance turnstiles, Russell Mackay, the director of Michael J's deviously planned fifth race demonstration, was briefing his twelve-strong team of actors. His instructions were clear, concise, repeated twice, and understood. There were no questions.

He summed up. "Make the demonstration big and make it loud. It's got to look spontaneous and authentic. When the stewards and race officials look curious, keep it up until I call cut, then we're out of there fast. Put a clamp on it and get lost in the crowd. Our job will be over."

Russell handed each of the twelve a cash envelope along with a final instruction. "We'll move straight to our designated position once we're through the turnstiles and remember, we're just average racegoers enjoying a day at the track."

One of the team discreetly peeped inside his envelope. "Damn easy money for twenty minutes on a racetrack. Do we know what the name of the movie is?"

"Don't know, don't care," said his companion.

ON THE WALKWAY THAT ran in front of the main public grandstand, Blue Larner's eighty-strong battalion of power players from Roma teetered on the brink of the adrenalin explosion that had been building all day. One of the boys dashed up to the group and said, "There's one bookie in the ring betting forties on our horse. He's twenty-fives and thirty-threes everywhere else!"

"We gotta get some of that," said Blue. Paper money came from everywhere and there was a race for the bookies' ring. When Blue and the boys got there, they had to wait a minute or two at Flasher Doyle's stand to get forties on their horse. In front of them, Rex Powell was taking the odds for heavy money.

"Damn good bet, cobber," Blue told him, "you'll be in Dubai for Christmas."

Rex gave him a grin. "No I won't, I'll be in Vegas with my two girlfriends."

"Good on you, mate," said Blue. "Blokes like you give blokes like us a good name."

IN THE BARBECUE COURT at the McCoy Stud in Roma, Alice switched on the giant screen and a murmur of excitement swept over the picnic tables. A mini mountain of bets had hit the Roma TAB. It was The Stinger's day, and Alice was living it.

"I'll turn up the volume as soon as the race gets going," said Alice, "anyone for more strawberry fizz?"

AT KINGS PARK, BART Anderson's pre-race blurb was bubbling over the audio.

His binoculars were trained on Race Five's twenty starters, as they paraded in the saddling paddock before the race. The favourite was Phantom Lover at four to one, and Bart was talking up his chances. Law and Order was the second favourite with Misty Mountain, both at fives, and there was money for Ginger Meggs at eights. According to Bart, he was 'an uneven galloper who had shown ability' and 'he looks to be in top shape.' Bart also noted that there had been some interest in The Stinger.

"Cooper McCoy's gelding comes into the race with nothing on his back, and there has been talk of him being the surprise packet. The Stinger has been trained by Lorrie Edwards at the late Charlie McCoy's Stud in Roma, and if he runs well, he'll make a lot of fans in the west happy. He looks a treat but appears to have the job in front of him. Still, with his light weight and Cassie Morgan in the saddle, he could be something of a rough outside chance if the race is run to suit him."

There were cheers from the Blue Larner boys—"The race is gonna be run to suit us, matey," chortled Blue.

IN THE VIP SUITE, Loveboat Williams gave way to an urge to niggle Michael J.

Commenting on Bart's mention of Lorrie Edwards as The Stinger's trainer he said, "Is Lorrie Edwards any relation to your Mating Game nemesis, Eddie Edwards?"

Michael J's eyes had a wicked gleam when he replied, "She certainly is, and she's in for a big surprise today."

"You mean her horse is going to win?" It was a deliberately mischievous question, but Michael J's reply was a nuclear explosion delivered on a venomous whisper—

"I'll let you into a little secret, old sport. Her horse will win, but it's not the horse she's been training. Her shyster father has a well-performed ring-in entered in his place, and this racetrack is about to witness the upset of upsets."

Loveboat, in an instant state of shock, blurted out, 'Tell me you're joking!"

Mickey Flynn lied like a trooper, *"I've found out about it, and the bastards are going down! It's too late to stop the fucken race now, so let them wear the shit! They messed with me and got away with it, but they're not getting away with this! This is my day! It's payback time!"*

Alarm bells turned into screeching sirens in Loveboat's head. His first thought was Frank! He had to get to Frank to warn him. He grabbed for an excuse to get out of the VIP suite. "This is disastrous! I've got money on The Stinger."

The right reply came from Michael J, "Then scoot down to the ring and cover your bet, old sport, before it's too late. We'll be in the Members Stand for the race. I want to see this extravaganza up close!"

Loveboat rushed out of the suite, ignored the elevator, and hit the steps three at a time to get down to the Members Stand, where he caught sight of Frank standing with Eddie. In a second, he was beside his friend. His whisper was low and urgent, "Get to the saddling paddock right now, old mate. He knows!"

Frank was startled. "Who knows?"

Loveboat pulled his arm. "Flynn knows about the bloody caper, mate, we've got to get to the saddling paddock to warn Lorrie."

They headed for the stairs as Kitty, Cooper and Bill Harris were coming up. Cooper said something to Frank about the odds he took on The Stinger, but Loveboat had Frank's arm in a tight grip and kept pulling him.

"How the hell did Flynn find out?" asked Frank.

"Who the fuck cares now? It's too late for questions. Your horse can't win! You guys are dead if he does, and so are the McCoys! Flynn's out to take the lot of you!"

They hit the ground floor and wheeled into the saddling paddock. Lorrie was standing in front of them at the fence.

When Frank got to her he blurted out what Loveboat had told him. Lorrie's face fell. In the saddling paddock, Jeff was hoisting Cassie into the saddle. Lorrie walked quickly over to speak to her, and Cassie leaned down to hear what she was saying.

Jeff, standing by, in the urgency, didn't hear everything, but he did hear Lorrie's final words. "You know how to play it, Cassie, we're in big trouble!"

"I'm on it, kid," said Cassie, and followed the other runners onto the track.

Lorrie took Jeff's arm and they moved to the paddock rail. Lorrie told him about Michael J's bombshell.

Jeff shook his head, and said, "Bloody hell, we didn't expect that, did we?"

LOVEBOAT WAS COOLING DOWN. "Thank god we got to Lorrie in time. We've done the betting money, but we've saved your futures cobber. At least I hope we have."

"What do you mean?"

"If the horse doesn't win, maybe Flynn won't spill the beans. Maybe I can use my best Albuquerque logic to talk him out of it. Not a big chance, but I'll give it a shot! Cross your fingers! We'd better get back to the stand."

When they got there, Eddie was in conversation with the McCoys. Bill Harris had joined Jewel Blanch, Lillian St Clare, Sam Hutchinson and Jenny Preston.

Michael J Flynn, in company with Racing Authority heavy Colin Clive, saw Loveboat enter the stand behind Frank, and asked, "Get your cover bet on, old sport?"

"Phantom Lover," lied Loveboat, and took a place beside Lillian St Clare.

In an urgent whisper, Frank gave Eddie the bad news and watched the blood drain from his face. He was barely able to speak.

He managed a throaty croak. "What do we do now?"

"Say our prayers," said Frank, "and hope to hell that Cassie can throw the race, without making it look deliberate."

Eddie said the first thing that came into his head, "She's a cunning little rider."

"She'll need to be. Eddie."

What he didn't say was that Cassie would need more than cunning to avert the juggernaut that was heading their way if she couldn't hold the brilliant Thunderdome. Damn! The horse was a killer with a light weight, and the rest of the runners were nowhere near him in class! What could Cassie do to stop him from taking the race without raising questions? Frank was losing it fast.

The grand plan, the greatest sure con in the history of cons, was about to blow up in his face! And how many other faces as well? He didn't want to think! He couldn't think!

He glanced at Eddie and felt the sharp stab of his remorse. His hand closed on Eddie's arm when he said, "God, Eddie, what have I done to you?"

Eddie was a mess. "Cassie will find a way, Frank. Lorrie got to her in time."

"She did, and she'll know what to do."

Frank's head was a pakapoo ticket. Maybe Cassie could pull the race. Maybe, just maybe! They were all depending on her. Could she do it? Could she save them all? Could she?

"Cassie's a spunky kid," said Frank, "she'll find a way, she'll have to."

He watched the field leave the saddling paddock to move around to the starting barrier, and he was hit by a wave of nausea. He closed his eyes and said a silent prayer.

"Throw the race, Cass, throw the damn race, do it. Just do it!"

AT THE BOTTOM OF the main grandstand on the edge of the upward sweep of the lawns, Blue Larner's crew readied for the thrill that was now only moments away. They'd waited patiently, and the big moment was set to arrive.

"Get set for Sting's run to the post, boys," said Blue. "Make it big and loud, he's gotta know we're here!"

"We're all tuned up," said one of Blue's boys. "They'll hear us in Roma."

Below them to the left, and within metres of the winners' circle, Russell Mackay's demonstrators were primed for their Oscar-winning performances.

AT THE STUD IN Roma, all eyes were on the giant television screen, and even the Mitchell cockatoos had shut up. Alice was surprised to discover she was looking at the screen and not blinking.

AT KINGS PARK, THE horses had reached the far side of the track, and Bart Anderson's voice came crystal-clear over the hushed lawns and stands.

"The runners are taking time to get into the barriers, and the handlers are rounding up the stragglers. Ginger Meggs was first in, behaving himself for a change, Phantom Lover, looking a picture, is standing quietly at the barrier.

"In goes, The Stinger, drawn in the middle of the field. He sure looks fit, this horse. He's starting at long odds at his first run in the big city with Cassie Morgan on

board. *He's as cool as they come, and it's hard to dismiss him as a chance. The rest of the field is in, Misty Mountain is standing well near the outside. There's the staring signal, they're set for the run to the judge.*

"And there they go."

FRANK AND EDDIE, ALMOST glued together, didn't want to know. Loveboat crossed his fingers, glanced across at Michael J Flynn and caught the glint of his tiger smile.

Bart's call revved up. *"Phantom Lover jumped well to take the lead, Misty Mountain shot out like a champagne cork, and he's darted up to be second as the field gets into stride. There's Law and Order racing up to be third."*

AT THE FENCE IN the saddling paddock, Lorrie took Jeff's hand and squeezed it tight. She didn't want to hear the race call, but it was coming over loud and clear. Beside her, Jeff was as still as death.

"Around the first turn, Phantom Lover ups the ante two lengths in front of Misty Mountain and Law and Order, with Johnny Diamond and Emma Chisit breathing on their flanks. Tour de Force is going well just behind them with Misty Mountain tucked away on the rails covering no ground at all. It's going to be a hot one folks. The pace is on. Phantom Lover's rider has floored the accelerator and he's increased his lead to three lengths. The rider of Law and Order is not taking that and he's niggling his mount along to run second. In the middle of the field, Ginger Meggs is nicely placed, one out from the fence. Further out Cassie Morgan on The Stinger is forced to cover extra ground. Her mount is running an even race under his light weight, but he'll need to be Bernborough to win from there."

Frank felt an instant wave of relief. "Cassie's on it," he said to Eddie, "she's holding him, she's on it."

"Damn," said Eddie, "you're right, she is."

On the paddock rails, Lorrie wasn't breathing. Jeff stood taller to watch the field as it thundered towards the turn into the straight. His eyes locked on the leaders and he narrowed them to focus on The Stinger, somewhere in the middle of the field.

In the stand, Mickey Flynn's eyes narrowed too. *Is that little bitch gonna throw the fucken race? Is she? That's not supposed to happen!*

Close by, Cooper lifted the binoculars to his eyes just in time to see Cassie lift her weight to stand taller in the saddle. Her mount was eight lengths away on the outside of the field, and Cooper felt the electric charge run up his body when he saw Cassie lean toward the running rail like she'd done at Flinton.

"Yes," he whispered, "yes, Cassie, give him his head."

Beside Cooper in the Members Stand, Kitty held her breath, closed her eyes and said to herself, *"Let him win, Charlie, let him win!"*

AT THE BOTTOM OF the public stand, Blue Larner was watching Cassie's move too. He'd seen it a hundred times, and he knew it was the signal. He raised his arm and yelled, "Get set, lads!"

Bart Anderson's call revved up. *"It's a lottery ticket at the four hundred, and the chances are coming from everywhere. Phantom Lover scoots around the home turn with heaps of gas in the tank. Law and Order and Misty Mountain are out after him, Emma Chisit blew it at the turn letting Ginger Meggs through."*

Then, out of nowhere, Bart's call hit a wild note. *"The Stinger wheeled into the turn on two legs! Damn!*

He's straightened up like a ruler for the run to the money. He's in the centre of the track all on his own, and Cassie Morgan is willing him to win with the ride of her life. Look at this girl go! She's thrown her whip away and she's giving us Wonder Woman! It's Cassie and The Stinger. What are these two? What is this!"

"NOW!" YELLED BLUE LARNER, dropping his arm, "Let him know we're here!"

The mighty eighty-strong roar ripped into the air and startled the punters in the public stand. With Blue Larner setting the decibel levels, it was the chariot race in *Ben-Hur* all over again.

The relentless chant reached Cassie's ears, "Go Sting! Go! Go! Go! Go! Sting, go get 'em, boy! Go!"

Cassie leaned even closer to her mount.

Frank's jaw dropped. "Oh God," he said, "No, Cassie, no!"

Bart Anderson was frantic. "*You better believe it. Cassie Morgan and The Stinger are glued together like Santa Claus and Christmas in the centre of the track. Closer in, Law and Order and Misty Mountain are out after Phantom Lover, and here comes Ginger Meggs on the rails, but The Stinger is set to fire a winning salvo at the short-priced Phantom, who's had the run of the race on the rails. But there'll be no music of the night for him today. The Stinger is taking him to the cleaners. Cooper McCoy's bolter is full of fire as he plunders Phantom Lover's chances and charges past him to the post! It's all over! The Stinger by a good half-length. Phantom Lover in second place, and a close photo for third.*"

MICHAEL J FLYNN SMILED a winner's smile. "And that's one for The Mating Game!"

Blue Larner and his boys had blown a fuse. In a flurry of hugging and tangled ribbons, they had trouble staying on their feet. Frank and Eddie couldn't speak. Loveboat Williams was composing his leniency plea to Michael J Flynn in his head.

Bart's after-race commentary was barely audible over the Roma din. "*The Stinger unleashed a killer run in the straight to steal the race from Phantom Lover in the last fifty metres. Ginger Meggs has got the photo to run third.*"

Cooper and Kitty McCoy were not on the planet. Bill Harris was shaking his head. In Roma, Alice and the CWA Ladies were delirious. On the rails of the saddling paddock, Lorrie and Jeff stood stunned and speechless, holding each other up.

On the track, the three placed horses trotted towards the saddling paddock gate. As they rode through it, Russell Mackay's demonstrators went into action. The first yell puzzled everyone into near silence. "Ring-in! That horse is a ring-in!" It came again. "That horse is a ring-in! It's not The Stinger!"

The chief steward's ear's pricked. "What the hell's that?" The other stewards didn't know. Who did?

The accusation came again, "That horse is a ring-in! It's not The Stinger!" Twenty paid voices picked up the cry and repeated it again and again. Punters on the lawn were dumbfounded. The track was in turmoil. Confusion swamped the Members Stand.

Michael J Flynn, securely snide, spoke to Colin Clive. "This sounds ominous. I don't like it at all. Where there's smoke there has to be fire."

"Let's find out," was Colin Clive's reply.

"WHAT THE HELL ARE you blokes on about?" yelled Blue Larner to the Mackay demonstrators. "That's our horse from Roma! It's The Stinger."

The reply came on loud voices, "It's a ring-in! That race was rigged!"

Blue's boys wanted none of it. The verbal exchanges heated up, and a near-riot was on the agenda. The chief steward knew then that he had a problem. He dismounted and walked over to Cassie, who had also dismounted. The demonstration was beginning to turn nasty, and the television crews were moving in, so was Click Roberts, who immediately sensed a fat paparazzi payout on the way.

AT THE MAIN GATE, one of the security guards answered a call on his handset. After a few seconds, he ended it, telling his companion that the racket had made it difficult to understand what was happening. "Some kind of trouble with a horse called The Stinger," he said.

His mate's ears pricked. "The Stinger? Mate, that's Cooper McCoy's horse."

"Is it? I'm not sure."

"Cooper McCoy. his granddad was Charlie McCoy."

"Charlie McCoy, the big-time trainer?"

"The legend, mate"

"Strewth! Whatever that trouble is, it's getting worse."

"We better look into it!"

"Gung-ho, mate . . . Let's go!"

IN THE SADDLING PADDOCK, Lorrie and Jeff joined Cassie who was answering the question just put to her by the Chief Steward.

"I don't know what they're on about. My horse is The Stinger; I've been riding him in training at the McCoy Stud for four months."

Lorrie gave Jeff a tap on the arm. "Get the bandages off."

She then addressed the Chief Steward, who identified her as The Stinger's trainer.

"I don't know what this is about, but I think I can clear everything up. Cooper McCoy who owns the horse is in the Members Stand with his grandmother, Kitty McCoy."

"Charlie's widow?"

"Before anything gets too out of hand, I'd like to bring them down."

"By all means."

At the saddling paddock entrance Frank, Eddie and Loveboat had come down from the Members Stand, and they were standing together in a state of shock.

After hurrying across the lawn, Lorrie faced them, speaking quickly, "Sorry, Dad, really, it's all right. That's not Thunderdome, he didn't race."

Eddie looked as if he'd been hit. "What?

"Cassie, Jeff and I decided against it, last night. It didn't seem right, Dad."

Eddie was completely bushed. "But I loaded The Stinger into the float this morning. He's at the Nudgee vineyard."

Lorrie shook her head. "He's right over there. Thunderdome's at Nudgee with his fetlocks sprayed with white hair spray."

"White hair spray?"

"A trick, Dad, sorry we had to play it, you wouldn't have understood."

Eddie was still bushed. "Frank said you told Cassie to throw the race."

"I told her to win any way she could because we were in trouble."

Frank Davenport shook his head. "I'm not hearing this."

Loveboat piped up, "I'm hearing it, old mate, and if you don't want to hear the sound of a monster cash payout hitting your bank account, let me know and I'll put a claim on it."

Frank was floored. "Why didn't you say something, Lorrie?"

"I told you right from the start that if I felt uneasy, I'd pull the plug. So, I pulled the plug, but not before I talked it over with Cassie and Jeff late last night when you were asleep. We wouldn't have done it if we weren't convinced that The Stinger could win. Now you tell me, did we make a mistake?"

Frank shrugged. "I guess you didn't."

"Do we have a problem?" asked Lorrie.

Frank shook his head. "I guess we don't."

Lorrie's eyebrows rose. "Any more questions?"

There were exactly none.

Behind them, on the lawns, the demonstration was beginning to resemble a major riot. Russell Mackay tried hard to get his team away from the skirmish, but he reckoned without Blue Larner, who foiled the attempt by having his gangbusters encircle the troublemakers in a ring of Roma muscle. They were trapped.

"You're talking ring-in, well you got a ring-in," Blue told Russell Mackay, "and you're not getting out of it till you tell us what you're on about! That's our horse you're calling a ring-in, and we say that's bullshit! So, what do you say?"

Click Roberts was having a field day; so were the two television camera guys who had moved in on the action.

Russell Mackay had nowhere to go but he tried. "Look, this has been a bit of a mistake."

Blue wasn't buying. "A mighty mistake, fella! We came all the way from Roma to watch our horse piss all over this race, and there is no way we're taking crap from you and your bludger mates! You're trying to put shit on Cooper McCoy and Lorrie Edwards and Cassie Morgan, and I can tell you this, dickhead, you better have a good story, or your arse is grass!"

Blue addressed his gangbusters, "Right, boys?"

The reply came loud and clear, "Right!"

MICHAEL J FLYNN AND Colin Clive had joined the Race Club Chief David Armstrong in the saddling paddock. With them were Cassie, the stewards, and Jeff, who had already removed The Stinger's bandages to reveal his white fetlock markings. Lorrie arrived moments later with Cooper and Kitty. With them was Bill Harris.

As soon as Sam Hutchinson got a handle on the demonstration he fronted and aired his money's worth. "I saw The Stinger run at Flinton and I mentioned it in my show. I've even got images, and I can tell you that horse is The Stinger."

Naturally enough, he was backed up by Cooper and Bill Harris. Kitty McCoy addressed her comments to David Armstrong, whom she'd known for years.

"That's my son's horse, David. I don't know what the fuss is here, but I'm in shock to think that something like this could reflect on Charlie's name and stall the chances of his grandson's future in the racing industry. There is no doubt that this horse is The Stinger, I've seen him in training every day at my property for the past four months. I have watched Lorrie Edwards train him and I have watched Cassie Morgan ride him as she did today, and there is not a thing wrong with my eyes. David, that's Cooper's horse!"

The group heard every word of her statement, despite the racket of the demonstration. Click Roberts, standing with camera at the ready, heard it too, and iced Kitty's cake. "Right on, Mrs McCoy!"

He faced the heavies and spoke up. "I let my peepers slide off some of the hottest chicks in Oz to photograph that piece of horseflesh at a fashion shoot at the McCoy Stud in January. That's The Stinger for sure, and I've got a paparazzi eye for detail, dead set!"

At that point, Cooper walked across to Jeff, who stood confidently holding The Stinger's reins. The horse registered Cooper's approach, his ears pricked, and he took a few steps towards him. Cooper reached up, patted his horse's cheek and said, "Give me five, mate." The Stinger did his trick, bounced his head a few times, and nuzzled into Cooper's face.

Lorrie caught the movement and felt the warmth flow through her body.

"The champ just said hello," Jeff said to Cooper, "and he knows who he's talking to."

In the call booth, Bart Anderson had been keeping the race crowd informed. "*There's been no decision yet on the outcome of Race Five.*"

He filled in the blanks by reporting on the inquiry unfolding in the saddling paddock. The crowd, fascinated by the drama, waited restlessly for news of the outcome. Michael J Flynn was feeling decidedly uncomfortable, but nowhere near as uncomfortable as he was about to feel. One of the track security guards escorted Blue Larner into the saddling paddock and across to the inquisition, excused himself, and addressed David Armstrong.

"I thought you should know that this young man here belongs to a group from Roma, and he has persuaded the spokesman for the demonstrators into admitting that the whole thing was a put-up job."

David Armstrong frowned in disbelief and addressed his question to Blue, "A put-up job? You mean it was planned?"

Blue let fly. "That's what the bloke who organised that ruckus told me."

"You heard him admit it?"

Blue went on: "Damn right I heard him, mister, and so did about fifty other people."

The security guard then addressed Blue, "It might be an idea if you give the full story to Mr Armstrong here, he's the Club President."

Blue took centre stage, quoting Russell Mackay, who had fingered Flasher Doyle and Michael J Flynn as the heavies who had staged the demonstration, and who had briefed Mackay on what to say and when to say it. Mackay had bleated his own innocence and that of his team, claiming they'd done what they'd been paid to do without knowing anything about anything else.

According to Blue, "They shot their lying bludger mouths off for money, and there was no way me and the boys were going to let them trash our horse. What they said was a pack of lies, so we went to bat!"

Blue nodded at Kitty and dropped a wink on Lorrie. "That mob of bludgers didn't know what they were up against when they took us on, Lorrie."

David Armstrong successfully stifled a smile. "Thank you for the information, Mr Larner, we'll take the necessary steps."

He addressed the Chief Steward, "Is there any reason why we need to continue with this inquiry?"

The Chief Steward shook his head. "We've got the correct weight."

"Then let's get on with it. Today's program has been delayed long enough."

Ever so discreetly David Armstrong quietly invited Michael J Flynn and Colin Clive to join him in the Club Boardroom. Bart Anderson got the message that the placings in Race Five were official and announced the decision to the crowd.

In the bookies' ring, Flasher Doyle cast one eye over his payout totals and turned a pale shade of green. "We're in big trouble," said his clerk, "we're in for heavy bets at forty to one on The Stinger, and we've gone down like the bloody Titanic!"

"Shut up," moaned Flasher, "just shut the fuck up!"

In the main grandstand, Rex Powell checked his betting tickets while Betty Coe and Edna Austin checked theirs. "Bloody great day," said Rex. "We're on twenty-five per cent and we're going to have fun in Vegas."

"Everywhere else, too," said Betty.

JEWEL BLANCH WAS PHILOSOPHICAL about the accusations hurled at Michael J. "He played with fire, he got burned. What I'd like to know is why he did it. He doesn't need the money. He doesn't really need to be any bigger than he is, so why did he put himself on the risk list? It doesn't add up."

Lillian saw everything as it was. "Darling, men like Michael J are born narcissists who never stop having love affairs with themselves. And they have to keep reinventing themselves by trying to conquer impossible dreams and taking risks that would frighten lesser men. When you're as much in love with yourself as Michael is, the only man good enough for you is the man you think you'll be, when you've stopped being the man you used to be."

Jewel didn't get it. "That's awfully complex, Lillian."

"So is Michael, darling."

IN THE CLUB BOARDROOM, David Armstrong was a living exercise in diplomacy and restraint, but he made his point, and made it convincingly, as he targeted Michael J Flynn.

"I will not compromise the integrity of this club or the industry in general by giving this unfortunate incident any more attention than it has already had. The less said the better, and I am hoping that in time it will be forgotten and simply disappear. At the same time, Mr Flynn, I cannot fully express my feelings for what you tried to do here today. You went close to involving the name of a legendary racing family in a scandal that cannot be supported by evidence of any kind."

Michael J Flynn spoke in his own defence. "I honestly believed that the Edwards stable had every intention of pulling a ring-in."

David Armstrong wasn't buying. "Then you should have alerted this club and given us the opportunity to investigate. You should have not gone ahead with this cheap carnival spectacle. This club is not a circus, Mr Flynn, and we are not clowns. As it has turned out, your suspicions were incorrect, but you have put our good name in harm's way. For that insult, I am informing you that you are no longer welcome on this racetrack. Further, I will send a detailed report of the incident to every other reputable racing club in the country, including the VRC, which stages the Melbourne Cup Carnival, and I will inform them of my decision to ban you from Kings Park for good. They may make up their own minds about whether they follow suit."

Michael J Flynn winced. "If you don't mind my saying so, I think that's a tad unfair."

"So noted, Mr Flynn, but let me remind you that we have a statement from the demonstrators that incriminates both you and Flasher Doyle. Are you in a position to deny those accusations?"

Michael J was fingered, and he knew it. "No. I'm afraid not."

"That's just as well. It will save us all from further embarrassment, and I can assure you that Mr Doyle's part in this will not be overlooked. He will not come out of it unscathed. Now if my colleague Colin Clive has nothing to add to my comments, I think this matter has been dealt with, and rather leniently under the circumstances."

Colin Clive looked at Michael J Flynn and said, "My sincere thanks for your hospitality today. You have quite a reputation as a wild card in the industry, Mr Flynn, and while I am not totally averse to the colourful and sometimes fascinating nature of wild cards, I don't think they should involve themselves in exercises of a nefarious nature on respectable racetracks. Surely you have better things to do with your time and money, which brings me to ask this one question. With the impressive resources at your disposal, why don't you use them to do something decent for a change?"

Michael J was on the very verge of letting Mickey Flynn loose, but he knew it wouldn't do any good.

There was no proof of any ring-in, and even if he managed to dig something up, it would take weeks of wrangling to pin it down. He'd been outsmarted, he didn't quite know how, and it was entirely possible that he'd never know.

But he realised it was time to retreat, and he decided to do it as graciously as possible.

"Gentlemen," he said, "I am forced to offer you my apologies. I realise that what I am about to say has been said before, and said so much better, but after all, tomorrow is another day!"

Inside Michael J's lonely head, Mickey Flynn whispered, *"Fuck 'em! We'll find another game and another mob of dickheads. It's easy when you're smart and you don't need anybody!"*

THE SIX-P.M. NEWS was all over the demonstration. The television cameras had zeroed in on the ripe exchanges between Blue Larner and Russell Mackay's teamsters, and for once the report didn't have to be tricked up to be entertaining. There were short interviews with Cooper, Lorrie, Kitty and Cassie. There were shots of The Stinger winning the race and wild footage of Blue's boys on the job.

Click Roberts got a look in, too. His take on the incident was a genuine howler. "If they had stuff like this happening every week, old mate, old buddy, more people would go to racetracks."

The coverage totalled a fat twelve minutes on Sky News, and Blue Larner was the new hero of Roma. He looked like a star on television and deftly brushed his newfound fame aside with this—"What else can a bloke do when someone puts dirt on his mates? If you can't stand up and open your mouth, you're a loser. End of story!"

The week before the race, Frank booked a celebration dinner at The Court of the Seven Lamps Restaurant, and although the reason for celebration had changed, he wanted it to go ahead. Cooper, Kitty, Bill Harris and Jewel didn't attend. As soon as Race Five was relegated to the history books, they returned to the Hilton and checked out to avoid any more contact with the media. They were on the road to Roma by 5:45 p.m., and a solid core of Alice's delirious party people decided to hang out until they drove through the gate five hours later.

Loveboat Williams put CK Dexter Beaumont back to sleep in his luggage and morphed back to his familiar self for the evening's dinner. He was yet to do his sums for the successful punt. As he told it to Frank, "I'll know for sure tomorrow, old mate, but it's millions, not including my commission, some independent investments of mine, and a fat slice for the McCoys like you wanted. We've cleaned up, and we'd better lay low for a while."

"What about Mike Flynn?"

"Bad news for sure. His bid to save face by drowning you and Eddie Edwards in a sea of scandal backfired big time, and he'll be way out with the big boys. Adrian Messenger will see to that. I'm not saying he's gone for good. He'll be in limbo for some time and his light has seriously dimmed."

Loveboat went on. "Flasher Doyle, his able assistant, got caught. His payout on The Stinger was huge, and Flynn will have to share the financial burden, but that's their problem. We won, they lost, rules of the game, old mate. Something puzzles me, though."

Lorrie picked up. "What's that?"

Loveboat answered, "Why didn't Flynn question the bandages that covered the tell-tale powder puffs? That could have been awkward."

Lorrie replied, "You mean, were they deliberate camouflage?"

Loveboat looked quizzical. "Wasn't that the original intention?"

"It was," said Lorrie, "I exercised my prerogative and made the change. I explained why at the racetrack."

Jeff piped up, "In any case, I cleared the bandages beforehand with the on-track vet. I said that Sting had sustained minor fetlock injury when he was rocked off balance in the float, and we didn't want to take chances."

"Smart move," said Loveboat.

"I'm full of 'em, mate. Who do you think nailed the hideout?"

Loveboat wasn't finished. "On that subject, I've arranged for Thunderdome to be picked up from there early in the morning. He'll be taken to Sydney and shipped out to a buyer friend of mine in New Zealand." He cast a look at Eddie. "Sorry you have to lose him, but you realise he can't hang round here.

Eddie agreed. "Too bad, but what the heck? Look what I've got in his place."

Fiddling with the olive in his Bombay Sapphire martini, he looked across the table at Cassie to ask her how she'd been so sure she could ride The Stinger to a win.

She answered quietly, "I rode him every day for four months and we bonded. We knew each other and trusted each other. I took him to the outside of the field in today's race to keep him out of trouble, and to give him his head. With his light weight, it was not a big ask. When he felt me transfer my weight from the saddle to the stirrups as we approached the turn, he knew it was time to make his run. He flew around that turn, just as he did at Flinton, and when he heard Blue Larner's boys, that was the cruncher. His ears pricked, and nothing could have stopped him."

Cassie's eyes misted over. "He's a lucky horse, Eddie, he's found love, and love has found him." She eyed Lorrie and Jeff; their eyes were shining. "And I'm not the only one who thinks so."

On that subject, nothing more needed to be said; it had all been said when The Stinger stormed past the post in the last seconds of Race Five at Kings Park on the first Saturday in March.

Raising his martini glass, Eddie said, "Here's to winning."

"Better still," said Loveboat, "here's to winning, when it's bigger than money; and shines bright lights on the future." He toasted the table. "I just love it when the good guys come out on top."

38

THE McCOY STUD IN ROMA:
THE DAY AFTER THE BIG ONE

EARLY ON SUNDAY MORNING, Jeff loaded The Stinger into Cooper's float and took him home to Roma. Just after midday, Lorrie, looking radiant in her Lorrie clothes, very much unlike the jeans and sweatshirt trainer who'd helmed The Stinger's victory campaign, revved her Subaru and headed west to check-out of the five-star country comfort of the McCoy Stud. She got there as the sun was well on its way to the horizon. Kitty and Alice, still afloat on the pride cloud, had managed to dismiss the demonstration as the only irritating happening of a truly wonderful day that had yielded several bonuses.

Cooper's share of The Stinger's prize money was on the way. His on-track wins were impressive. So were those of Kitty and Bill Harris. Alice and the CWA ladies collected a nice haul at the Roma TAB, and Blue Larner and the farmhands were also in the money.

In the glow of a blazing outback sunset, Kitty and Alice were sitting on the terrace under the pepperina trees, while the pink Mitchell cockatoos hopped about in the branches. Lorrie's Subaru drove up and purred to a stop.

"She'll be here to pick up the rest of her things," said Alice, "are we going to let her go?"

"It's not up to us," said Kitty.

Alice looked at her. "Not officially, but I'll tell you now, if I can do anything to stop her from leaving, I'm all geared up"

"Is that crystal-ball talk, Alice?"

"Don't knock it, love."

Lorrie got out of her car and walked to the terrace. The greeting exchanges were warm and sincere.

"Cooper's on the telephone," Kitty told her, "the reporters have been calling all day. The one he's talking to is pushing for him to be on one of those current affair things. He doesn't want to do it, and I've never known anyone to talk Cooper into anything he didn't want to do. He's the real McCoy, just like Charlie."

"I'll get some tea," said Alice.

Lorrie smiled. "I'd really like to check on The Stinger."

Kitty nodded. "Blue has him fed and he's ready for bed, but that horse owes you, Lorrie, and he'll be glad to see you."

Lorrie crossed over to the stables and caught the familiar aroma of blue's pine-scented disinfectant. The Stinger was standing in his stall when she approached, and when he saw her, he moved over to the Dutch doors. She opened the doors and he came to her. Her hand touched his head, and with a little whinny, he pushed affectionately against it.

She closed her eyes and saw him wheeling into the King Park straight with Cassie's earnest face brushing again his mane. She saw his run to the post and heard the love shouts of Blue Larner's cheer squad—mind pictures and sounds that would stay with her for as long as she lived.

The Stinger's run had been a risk, but had it? What if, deep down, it had been something he wanted not only for himself but for those who loved him?

At every workout since the Flinton run, he had shown improvement. Day after day he gave a little more, and the more he gave the more he wanted to give. The best thing now, was that The Stinger's future did not have to include his disappearance. He wasn't going anywhere! When Lorrie, Cassie and Jeff decided to give him his chance, they threw down the gauntlet—and he picked it up.

But despite the positive result, Lorrie was not able to fight her guilt. She carried it heavily, and it prodded her every time she thought of what the ring-in could have done to the McCoy Stud, and to the people whose lives it held together, had it been exposed.

She heard the step on the walkway and knew who it was. When she turned, Cooper was looking at her.

"Sting's going to miss you," he said. "So am I."

She was ready. She'd told herself she could never stay at the McCoy Stud, but she felt she had to tell Cooper why she was going, and why she couldn't come back.

"You have to know the truth, Cooper. Mike Flynn knew it, and that's why he staged that demonstration. He expected Thunderdome to win the race. That's the way it was planned. It was a set-up. Nothing but a cheat from the start."

"So why didn't it happen?"

"It doesn't matter why. It was still a cheat. You have to know it, and Kitty has to know it. It was a cheat!"

Cooper shook his head. "Nobody has to know about something that didn't happen, but what I want to know is, why didn't it happen? Come on, Lorrie, you can answer that."

She didn't speak so Cooper said, "All right then, I'll tell you why.'

Lorrie faced him. "You don't know why."

He let it out: "It didn't happen because you couldn't let it. When it came down to the wire you couldn't buy it, because you had to show our horse he could be a winner if he got the chance. He got to you, didn't he? He reached out, and got to you, and you couldn't let him down. Am I close?"

Lorrie didn't answer.

Cooper went on, "That might sound like wild talk, but it's not wild to you and me, is it?"

"I'm sorry, Cooper. I can't hear this."

He wasn't up for denials. "It might have been a set-up at the start, but I watched you and Cassie with my horse. I watched how you taught him how to be the horse he wanted to be, and I saw how he responded. I don't care about what was planned, it didn't come off."

"That doesn't change anything."

"It changes everything. That it didn't come off makes what happened on that racetrack yesterday even more incredible. You and Cassie, and Jeff too, you put yourselves on the line. You blew the caper because when the chips were down, you knew it wasn't right."

Lorrie took a breath, but she couldn't speak.

"If you walk away," said Cooper, 'you'll be telling me you don't care about Kitty or Sting or me, and I don't think you can do that. You have grown into this place; you can sense it's where you belong. It's all around you, and you can't throw it away because of a cheating game that didn't come off. This place is part of you; it's where you belong. All you have to do is reach out and take it." He paused and stepped closer.

"No more games, Lorrie, they're all over."

Her wall of guilt was crumbling, but she was still unsure. For weeks she'd been plagued by the terrible feeling that she was a cheat, and the only way to wipe the feeling out, was to close it out.

Cooper's words were still coming. "Can't you see what you've done here? You've brought everything back to life. You've given Charlie back to my grandmother and me. And look at what you've done for Blue Larner. He was the town's loser. I gave him a job to keep him off the streets, and you gave him something to believe in. You've made him a hero."

He took another step closer. "All that is wonderful, but here's the miracle. When I saw Sting wheel into the turn yesterday, I didn't know anything about a cheat. I knew who I was watching. I was seeing the horse he wanted to be, and I knew I'd been right about him all along. It was an amazing moment for me. You've shown him who he is, Lorrie, and if you'll give me the chance, I want to show you who you are."

The wall was crumbling for sure now. "How can you do that, Cooper?"

"By trusting my instincts. I saw something in you the day I met you, and as I got to know you, I realised how special you are. Together we can rebuild this Stud, buy more horses, put the place back in business, give full-time work to Blue Larner and his farmhands, and give Kitty her world back. I want you here with me, Lorrie, because without you, I'll be homesick for the rest of my life."

He paused a moment. "You remember the chick at Flinton who wanted my boots under her bed? The only bed I want my boots under is yours. But there's a condition, you've got to agree to a name change. How does Lorrie McCoy sound?"

The wall crumbled big time. "I love it, Cooper."

"So, do I."

'Let's make it happen, then."

"When?"

"Today."

"It's Sunday. The licence office is closed."

"Tomorrow, then."

Stinger, standing beside Lorrie, moved closer, and nudged her.

She turned to pat his forelock. "I'll put his bridle on and we can take him for a walk."

"Forget the bridle, Lorrie. He'll follow you anywhere, so will I."

Sure enough, when they walked toward the training track, he walked with them, close as could be, and when they reached the running rail Cooper took Lorrie in his arms. Wrapped inside, she felt the warmth and firmness of his virile young body, just like she had on the day of the Flinton run. This time she wasn't backing away.

Still holding her, he said, "Stay with me, Lorrie. Don't go home tonight."

"I am home, Cooper."

"You always were. You told me on Christmas Eve, that your dad's dream was the Melbourne Cup, and that Thunderdome was his chance."

"I'd still like that to happen."

"Then you've got the wrong horse. If you want the Melbourne Cup, the horse who can give it to you is right here with us. All you have to do is tell him you want it and he'll get it for you."

SITTING UNDER THE PEPPERINA trees in the fading light of the dying sun, Kitty and Alice watched what was happening at the training track—Lorrie, Cooper and their horse. She gave her best friend a knowing smile.

"I told you, didn't I, Kit?"

"And I told you he wouldn't make a move until he was sure."

"Doesn't matter. I said it first."

Kitty threw her a warm look. "One of these days, Alice, that crystal ball of yours is going to get a crack in it."

Alice sat back in her chair and smiled one of her misty smiles.

"Who told you that, Kit? Not Charlie McCoy."

At that very moment, Kitty realised that one episode of The Stinger was over and that a new one was all set to go.

THE END

AUTHOR BIOGRAPHY

MY EARLY LIFE WAS spent in live theatre: acting, direction, designing, writing. That led to a career in television; writing cop shows, panel games and soaps for Crawford Productions in Melbourne and Reg Grundy Productions in Sydney and Brisbane.

I partnered in one fine dining room and two theatre restaurants (Victorian melodrama and satirical revue . . . The Mark Twain and The Living Room Brisbane).

As a weekly columnist for the *Brisbane Courier-Mail*, *Brisbane Sun,* and *The Brisbane Sunday Mail*, I had a twenty-two-year second career writing lifestyles, food, theatre, fashion, entertainment and mainstream events (London, Paris, California, Hong Kong, Singapore, Kuala Lumpur, Hawaii, Finland, all Australian capitals). I do not write about people or places I haven't experienced. Currently freelancing.

Happily married: two kids, three grandkids, one poodle.

KENN LORD